Keys To Paradise

by

Omar Mahmoud

Bloomington, IN   Milton Keynes, UK

authorHOUSE®

AuthorHouse™
1663 Liberty Drive, Suite 200
Bloomington, IN 47403
www.authorhouse.com
Phone: 1-800-839-8640

AuthorHouse™ UK Ltd.
500 Avebury Boulevard
Central Milton Keynes, MK9 2BE
www.authorhouse.co.uk
Phone: 08001974150

First published by AuthorHouse 4/19/2007

ISBN: 978-1-4259-9056-5 (sc)

Printed in the United States of America
Bloomington, Indiana

This book is printed on acid-free paper.

Library of Congress Control Number: 2007900231

TABLE OF CONTENTS

FORWARD

In the name of God, the Beneficent, the Merciful.

This book is a very important one in the sense that the author wishes to share his personal experiences with other people for one noble goal; that is leading the life of morality, God consciousness, righteousness and finally gaining admission into the paradise in the hereafter.

The author has used the Christian and Muslim scriptures to show that the prophets of God have consistently called on mankind to believe in the oneness of God, obey His commands, seek forgiveness and lead righteous life without ascribing any partner to the Almighty God. Furthermore, only the righteous succeeds in the hereafter; the evil doers are doomed.

The writer has laid emphasis on some key Qur'anic concepts which are essential for moral development, these are repentance and amendment. The Almighty God has called on people to seek His forgiveness and do righteous works by obeying all His commands and those of His prophet Muhammad (peace and blessing of God be upon him). In addition, one is expected to engage in extra good deeds consistently throughout one's life. This does not only lead to moral rectitude but it also raises the rank of a believer in the sight of God so that he or she may become one of the protégé of God.

To achieve this noble objective; the author has also given some formulas for night prayers (tahajjud) which are very useful because one is expected to earn a lot of rewards. He has stressed in many places in this book that this world is a temporary stage where a believer is expected to work for personal salvation in the eternal life to come in the hereafter. People are cautioned not to be deceived by the devil's delusion who is the number one enemy of human kind, for he has vowed to mislead man into ungodly ways. The only way out is to lead righteous life in this world and shun its detractive glitters which more often than not lead to all sorts of immorality in this world and self damnation in the hereafter. To be forewarned is to be forearmed; therefore the reader of this book should do the right thing now by acting positively.

Dr. Jibril H. Yola
Bayero University, Kano

COMMENTS

In the name of Allah, the Beneficent, the All merciful "Glory to your Lord, the lord of Honour and Power! He is (free) from what they ascribe (to Him) and Peace on the messengers, and praise be to Allah, the Lord and cherisher of the worlds" (Al-Saffaat 37: 180-182).

I was privileged to have read the book "Keys To Paradise". This book was written based on inspiration and the author took a lot of effort, time and financial resources to bring out this book, which he worked on for over a decade. This book has a lot to offer to both Muslims and non- Muslims.

The book has contributed in no small measure to correct several miss repetitive, misquotations and indeed misinterpretation by some Muslims and non-Muslims about Islam. It is necessary that every Muslim should read far and wide as Allah said we cannot worship him if we do not know Him. Furthermore, we should do a lot of da'wah among ourselves and among non-Muslims. This book also serves that purpose. So it should not be restricted to Muslim audience. Most non-Muslims know little or nothing about Islam. To understand Islam they must have open hearts and ready to learn about Islam.

May Allah reward the Author for his effort here in this world and the hereafter; May Allah bless his time and days. May Allah strengthen him and keep him to live longer so that he can contribute more to Islam through his writing. May the forgiving Allah forgive him and bless him with Al-jana firdaus.

Aisha A. Akanbi PHD
Islamic Scholar

DEDICATION

This work is dedicated to the Holy Prophet Muhammad (PBH), through whom mankind and the Jinn know that all prophets of the Almighty God taught Islam. From him we know that Islam takes its hue from Allah. Different gifts and different modes of procedure were prescribed to Allah's messengers in different ages, some above others. To some of them Allah spoke, others He raised to degrees (of honour). To Jesus, the son of Mary, He gave clear signs and strengthened him with the Holy Spirit. He was given no weapon to fight like prophet David who over threw the greatest warrior of his time and became king.

Islam means bowing to the will of Allah. The Muslim position is clear – previous prophets and messengers had only a portion of Allah's complete message. The holy Qur'an is the complete Book. The Muslims do not claim to have a religion peculiar to themselves. Islam is not a sect or an ethnic religion. In its view all Religion is one, for the truth is one. It was religion preached by all the earlier prophets. It was the truth taught by all the inspired Books. In essence it amounts to a consciousness of the Will and Plan of Allah and a joyful submission to that Will and Plan.

Through him mankind and the Jinn know that if any one wants a religion other than Islam, such a one is false to his own nature, as he is false to Allah's Will and Plan. Such a one cannot expect guidance from Allah, for he has deliberately renounced Allah's guidance. "On such people rests the curse of Allah, of His angels and of all mankind."[1]

The Holy Qur'an as a complete and final message from Allah requires a belief not only in its own truth but also in the truth of previous scriptures to prophets of different nations of the world.[2] Thus the holy Qur'an accepts the truth of the Sacred Books of the world, and hence it is again and again spoken of as a Book verifying that which is before it.

Therefore the basis of the relation in which the holy Qur'an stands to other scriptures is that they are all members of one indivisible family: They all have a Divine origin. The uniqueness of the holy Qur'an is that it came as a judge to decide the differences between the various religions.[3] The holy Qur'an proclaims as mentioned already, that prophets had been raised in every nation, and therefore every nation had received guidance from the Almighty God. Yet nation differed from nation even in the essentials of faith. The position of the holy Qur'an is therefore essentially that of a Judge deciding between these various claimants.

The holy Qur'an explains all obscurities. It makes clear what is obscure in the earlier scriptures and explains fully what they stated briefly. Revelation according to the holy Qur'an is not only universal but also progressive and it attains perfection in the final Revelation (which is the holy Qur'an). A Revelation was granted to each nation according to its requirements, and in each age in accordance with the capacity of the people of that age. As the human brain became more and more developed more and more light was cast by revelation on matters relating to the unseen, on the existence and attributes of the Divine Being, on the nature of Revelation from Him, on the requital of good and evil, on life after death, and on paradise and hell. Again it is for this reason that the holy Qur'an is again and again called a Book "That makes manifest". It shed complete light on the essentials of "Faith" and makes manifest what had hitherto of necessity remained obscure.

Again, from the holy prophet Muhammad (PBH) we come to know that the fact that our forefathers were righteous cannot help us, unless we are ourselves righteous. The doctrine of personal responsibility is a cardinal feature of Islam. It is through him it became clear that Allah is the kingdom of heavens and earths. Besides Him one has no friend or helper. Allah is the possessor of power over all things. He is the final goal and the end of all journeys. He is the wonderful – originator of the heavens and earths. Whenever He intends an affair, He simply says to it "Be" and it is. He is Allah the One and Only who is the beginning of everything, and nothing existed before Him; He is the present and nothing is possible without Him; He is the end of everything and nothing comes after Him. He is the Beneficent, the Merciful and He is the Lord of the Throne of Power, the glorious.

He made mankind a single nation and raised prophets as bearers of good news and as warners, and He revealed to them the Book with truth to judge between people concerning that in which they differed. He is the one who normally tries the believers with distress and affliction, and gives good news to those who are steadfast in faith in Him. He is the owner of the kingdom of heavens and earths. He gives kingdom to whom He pleases, and takes it away from whom He pleases. He exalts whom He pleases and makes low whom He Pleases. In His hand is the unending good and He is the possessor of power over all things.

He is Allah who makes the night to pass into the day and makes the day to pass into the night. He brings forth the living from the dead; and He brings forth the dead from the living. He gives sustenance to whom He pleases without measure. Whatever He grants of His mercy, there is none to withhold it, and whatever He withholds none can grant it. He is the Mighty, the Wise.

O men, surely the promise of Allah is true, so let not the life of this world deceive you, and let not the arch-deceiver deceive you about Allah. Surely the Devil is your enemy, so take him for an enemy. He only invites his party to be companions of the burning fire[4].

So be patient; surely the promise of Allah is true, and ask for protection from your sin and celebrate His praises in the evening and in the morning. He is the living; there is no God but He. So call on Him with sincerity in obedience. Praise be to Allah, the Lord of the worlds.

He is Allah besides whom there is no God: The knower of the unseen and the seen; He is the Beneficent, the Merciful. He is Allah besides whom there is no God, the king, the Holy, the Author of peace, the Granter of security, Guardian over all, the Mighty, the Supreme, the possessor of greatness. Glory be to Allah from that which they set up with Him. He is Allah the Creator, the Maker, the Fashioner: His are the most beautiful names. What is in the heavens and the earths declare His glory, and He is the Mighty, the Wise.

I pray: O our Lord Allah, make not our hearts to deviate after Thou has guided us and grant us mercy from Thee; surely Thou art the, most Liberal Giver. O our Lord Allah, make us steadfast in Thine command. Grant us perfect recognition on the day the Holy Prophet Muhammad will entertain his followers to dinner party in Paradise and favour us with a seat on the high table with him, and his family, his companions and their families, his fellow prophets and messengers of God and their families and their companions and their families- Amen

ACKNOWLEDGMENT

I would like to extend my profound gratitude to the following people who were very instrumental towards the completion of this book. Their immense contribution cannot be over emphasized.

I would like to give a lot of thanks to Dr. Jibril H. Yola Head of Department of Islamic Studies Bayero University Kano for taking time out of his busy schedule to proof read the manuscript and offered very important advise that helped to fine tune the book.

I would also like to express my gratitude to Miss Maryam Kemi Akanbi for all her time and effort she put into proof reading the manuscripts at the various stages of typing, and for supervising the typing and mailing to the various people who helped to review the manuscript.

I cannot forget to express my appreciation to Miss Kindness O. Ekeh my secretary who spent long hours bent over her computer typing and retyping the manuscripts, corrections and changes.

I also express my thanks to Mrs. Dorothy Amah, for her contribution to the completion of this book from proof reading and supervision of the production team.

Finally, many thanks to my twin daughters Hajiya Aisha who not only encouraged me to conclude the Manuscript, but also handled the manuscript with most effective scholars who reviewed the book such as Dr. Azare of Bayero University and Dr. Jibril H. Yola who not only reviewed the manuscript, but also wrote the foreward for the book; and who also handled the manuscript with publishers overseas.

LIST OF ABBREVIATIONS

1. MS – Sahih Muslem (Hadith)
   KU – Kanaz al-Ummah Fi
   Sunawi – I – Aqwal wa – I – Afal
   (Hadith) by Al – Shaikh Ala
   Al – Din Ali al – Muttaqi

2. Msh – Mishkat al- Masabih (Hadith)
   by Shaikh Wali al – Din
   Muhamuad Abd Allah

3. GB – The Gospel of Barnabas by M.A Yusseff

4. Q – The Holy Quran

5. (INJIL)– The Holy Bible

6. Dhikr – Invoking the holy names of the Almighty God

7. Mohammed – Muhammad

CRITICS AND RESPONSES

Mr Saeed Archer
Ah-Attique Publishers Inc.
Canada 28th Feb. 2006

My very dear Saced Archer,

As Salaamu Alaykum! Your Three (3) Grounds For Rejecting My Manuscript: "Keys To Paradise" For Your Publication

I was out of Nigeria since January 2006 and returned on 21st day of February 2006 to find your Email in which you stated three (3) grounds for rejecting my manuscript for publication as follows:

Ground one for your rejection of Manuscript

On page 49 of the Manuscript, the last paragraph: Is there a Sahih Hadeeth for this? If yes please give us the reference.

Response

1. The manuscript is based on the Holy Qur'an and Hadith. In Surat 2:62, the Holy Quran says: "Those who believe (in the Holy Qur'an); and those who follow the Jewish (scriptures); and the Christians and the Sabians, any who believe in Allah and the last Day; and work righteousness, shall have their reward with their Lord on them shall be no fear, nor shall they grieve".

2. In the scripture one of the twelve disciples and secretary of the holy Jesus Christ was called Barnabas. The holy Jesus Christ (peace be upon him) said the following concerning Barnabas:

   2.01 One day, after teaching his disciples, Peter said: "O teacher, behold we have left all to follow thee, what shall become of us?"

Jesus answered: "Verily ye in the day of Judgement shall sit beside me, giving testimony against the twelve tribes of Israel".

'And having said this Jesus sighed, saying "O Lord, what thing is this? For I have chosen twelve and one of them is a devil".

'The disciples were sore grieved at this word; whereupon Barnabas questioned Jesus with tears, saying: "O master, will Satan deceive me, and shall I then become reprobate?'

'Jesus answered: "Be not sore grieved Barnabas, for those whom God has chosen before the creation of the world shall not perish. Rejoice for thy name is written in the Book of Life' (GB. 19 page 17)

Please refer to the Gospel of that Barnabas at page 46 verse 41 line 4 to 5 of second to the last paragraph, authored by M.A. Yusseff. That is the source of the last paragraph at page 49 of my manuscript thus: "When Adam and Eve were driven from Paradise for hearken to Satan whereupon Adam turning himself round saw it written above the gate: "There is only one God, and Mohammed is messenger of God". Whereupon weeping, he said: "May it be pleasing to God: O my son, that thou come quickly and draw us out of misery".

Ground Two Of Your Rejection Of Manuscript

"On page 68, item (vi): this item and the following paragraph states that Jesus, alayhe Salaam, believed that "God is every where". According to our understanding of the Qur'an and Sunnah, Allah is "fee Samah" by His sight He sees everything, for He is the All-seer, by His hearing he hears everything for He is the All-Hearer, these are just two of His Attributes. We say about Allah what He says about Himself….."

Response

A. About Jesus Christ (peace be upon him), the Holy Quran says: "And Allah will teach him the Book and wisdom, the Torah and the Gospel (Q3:48)

B. Jesus Christ (peace be upon him) said: "Every word of mine is true, because it is not mine but God's, who hath sent me to the house of Israel….. (GB 26 page 26)." "Believe me when God chose me to send me to the house of Israel, He gave a book like unto a clear mirror which came down into my heart in such wise that all that I speak cometh forth from that book. And when that book shall have finished coming forth from my mouth, I shall be taken up from the world".

Peter one of the twelve disciples asked Jesus thus: "O master, is that which thou now speakest written in that book?"

Jesus replied: "All that I say for the knowledge of God and the service of God, for the knowledge of man and for the salvation of mankind all this cometh forth from that book which is my Gospel (Injil)" (GB. 168 page 182) and Holy Qur'an tells us further that Jesus Christ (peace be upon him) said: "I am indeed a servant of Allah: He hath given me Revelation and made me a prophet. And He hath made me Blessed wheresoever I be, and hath enjoined on me prayer and Zakat as long as I live. (He hath made me) kind to my mother, and not over bearing or unblest. So peace is on me the day I was born, the day that I die, and the day that I shall be raised up to life again (Q19:29 – 33)

"Such (was) Jesus the son of Mary (it is) a statement of truth about which they (vainly) dispute (Q19:34)

And in the Gospel of Jesus reproduced by Barnabas, Philip one of the twelve disciples of Jesus asked Jesus Christ (Peace be upon him): "We are content to serve God, but we desire, however, to know God. For Isaiah the prophet said: "Verily thout art a hidden God', and God said to Moses his servant: "I am that which I am". (Exodus 3: 14)

Jesus answered: "Philip, God is a good without which there is naught good: God is a being without which there is naught that is; God is life without which there is naught that liveth; so great that He filleth all and is everywhere...." (GB 17 page 15)

Jesus Christ (peace be upon him) is not the only one who said that "God is everywhere". He merely cited item (vi) on page 68 of my manuscript from scriptures before his time.

Despite that, among the 99 names of Allah published by Prof. Tevfik Topuzoglu of the University of Istanbul at page 69 there is "Ash-Shahid (the witness)."

Meaning: "He who is present everywhere and observes all things". Does Allah not said that of Himself? Why do you conceal it with pretended broad mindedness and virtue?

From the foregoing analysis your ground number two (2) for rejecting my manuscript is most unsound and unIslamic.

Ground Three (3) For Your Rejecting My Manuscript

"On page 85 and 86 of the manuscript, number 21 of a list of items: this talks about the number of times for making saying of thikr and concludes that a person, khalifa Daudu Mahmud Salihun" "In 3 years, he recites "Lailaha Ilallahu" at least 70 million times, "in addition to reciting other Surahs and thikr". Since we were not with Kalifa Daudu, we did some mathematics: 70 millions (of thikr) divided by 3 (years) divided by 365 (days in a year) divided by 24 (hours in a day) divided by 60 minutes in an hour = 44 and change. This says to us that should a person recite "Lailaha Ilallahu" 70 million times in 3 years, he would have to say it at least 44 times each minute for 3years. Given the fact that Khlifa Daudu had to eat, sleep, and do other things (during which time he could not make thikr). Is it possible for him or anyone else to recite "Lailah Ilallahu" 70 million times in 3 years? We don't think so".

"The above are some of the reasons why we rejected the manuscript entitled "Keys to Paradise by Dr M.S. Umoru".

Response

A. I am amazed and ashame that a Muslim of your standing, can due to biases and petty prejudices, reduce serious Islamic matter of faith in Allah, to Mathematical theory of probabilities. My heart bleed! I achieve on a regular basis (unless I am not well) 99,999 counts of "Laillaha Ilallahu Al-hamdillahi" in 2 hours, 45 minutes every night; and some nights I achieve between 121,000 and 134,000 counts in 3 hours 15 minutes. It is a practice one starts gradually and Allah helps you on.

B. Just because you have failed to develop your innate physical and spiritual abilities; you concluded that 70,000 counts "cannot be achieved" in one seating after mid night voluntary prayers. What has become of Muslims – I wonder. When I was 18 years old (in 1953), it used to take me all night to recite "Ina'azalillahu" to the end 1000 counts. By the time I was 45 years old, I could recite it 1000 counts in less than 5 minutes. The same with Kursiyu, Fatiatl Kitab and QULHUWA etc. It is a matter of sincere devotion and constancy.

C. Hazrat Anas Bin Malik (R.A.A) relates that the holy prophet (PBH) said: "Only hard work brings high reward......" (Tirmiz and R.U.S. Vol. 1 page 40). And Ghulam Ahmad says in some of his writings that I read in September 1959 during one of my visits to the Ahmadiya Mission office in Kano – Nigeria, that nearestness to Allah is not an exclusive preserve for prophets and messengers of Allah. It is also for those who strive hardest in the sincere Remembrance of Allah. The holy Qur'an confirms Ghulam Ahmad's claim in Surat Al-Waqia verse 10: "And those foremost (in faith) will be foremost in the Hereafter. There will be those nearest to Allah, In Garden of Bliss. A number of people from those of old, and a few from those of later times".

D. Those of old are definitely prophets and messengers of Allah and their companions. As the holy prophet (PBH) is the seal of prophets of Allah the few from those of later times are definitely those who sincerely strive hardest in the Remembrance of Allah. To dispute this, does not only make the disputer an ignorant person to be turned away from, but also one of those persons Jesus Christ (peace be upon him) described thus: "........ and all this shall be because ye walk not now in His law. And ye have the key and open not: rather do ye block the road for those who would walk in it (GB 67 page 72).

E. Righteousness does not consist of wearing pale faces and heavy beard. Hazrat Sahl Bin Hunaifa (R.A.A) relates that the holy prophet (PBH) said: "One who supplicates Allah sincerely for martyrdom is raised by Him to the status of a martyr although he dies in his bed (Muslim & R.U.S. Vol. 1 page 48). The harder you strive, the higher your status with Allah. There is no limit to striving in the cause of Allah.

Therefore, to subject matter of Faith in Allah and constant devotion to Him to mathematical theory as basis of belief is most irresponsible on the part of any Muslim.

Summary

There is a book that I saw and read a part of it many years ago that contains II, III Attributes of Allah; and what most Muslims know are only 99 Attributes of Allah. Out of the 99 Attributes of Allah, you only quoted two to dispute

Jesus Christ (peace be upon him)'s claim that: "God is every where" and this you disputed with an attitude of arrogant rejection. What boldness! Be warned for Jesus Christ (peace be upon him). Says: "I say unto thee that he who despiseth the prophecy despiseth God". And the Holy Quran says "Those who conceal the clear (signs) we have sent down and the Guidance after we have made it clear for the people in the Book-on them shall be Allah's curse and the curse of those entitled to curse". (Q2: 160)

Again as regard your arrogant rejection of the possibility of a devote Muslim's ability to achieve 70 million counts of recitation of "Laillaha illallahu" in 3 years, is clearly an embarrassment. "To each is a goal Allah turns him". We ought to come together and strive hard as in a race towards all that is good. For Allah has power over all things (Q2: 148)

Please return my manuscript at your early convenience; and be informed that I will make your critical observations and these responses a part of the book entitled: "Keys to paradise". It will be published very soon and by the Grace of the Almighty God you will see it in all book shops in major cities of the world.

Yours faithfully,

Dr. M.S. Umoru
(Executive Chairman)

KEYS TO PARADISE PREFACE

There are bad men and women in every community. But if the leaders connive at the misdeeds of the community, as now prevalent in the world, even worse, if leaders themselves share in the misdeeds as was the case of Pharisees and scribes against whom the holy *Jesus* spoke out, then that community is doomed. It is reported by Abu Sa'id al Khudri that the holy prophet said "whoever sees a forbidden thing done, he must prevent it by the force of his hand; and if he has no power for this action, then he should prevent it with his tongue; and if he cannot do this, he should at least feel it as a vice in his heart; and this is the lowest degree of ones faith. Another Hadith tells us that once the companion of the holy prophet (PBH) asked him: O messenger of Allah! Can we people be destroyed even when there are certain pious and God fearing persons among us? He answered: Yes, for the pious may keep silent, and do not prevent others from forbidden things". Hazrat Aisha said: "Once the Holy Prophet entered the house and I guessed from his face that something had happened to him. He did not talk to any one, and after having ablution he entered the mosque. I tried to hear behind the wall what he said: so he sat at the pulpit, and after praising Allah, he said: "O Muslims, Allah has commanded you to introduce people to good deeds, and prevent them from sins; otherwise a time will come when you will pray to Him, but He will not listen to you; you will ask your needs of Him, but He will not grant them; you will demand His help against your enemies, but He will not help you". After stating this, he came down from the pulpit.

Muslims the world over, must understand that the strength and stability of the Muslim Nation depends upon the propagation of Islam. A Haddith tells us, that Hazrat Abu Darda, who was a distinguished companion of the Holy Prophet (PBH) says: "You must command people to do good, and refrain form evil; otherwise Allah will appoint a ruler over you who will not respect your elders, and will not have mercy on your younger ones.

Then you people will pray to him, but He will not help you; you will ask pardon of Him, but He will not pardon you for Allah himself says in the Holy Quran: "O believers; if you help Allah, only then He will help you and make your feet firm (against your enemies)".

The Holy *Jesus* says: "The only way out is repentance and amendments. Those who fail to repent and make amend cannot escape the damnation of hell[1]. And the Holy Qur'an says: "Justice and Allah's wrath will seize them unexpectedly"[2]. Repent and make amend before it becomes too late[3]. When the Day of Decision comes, the joy and peace will be for those who lived a righteous life. Those who fail to repent and make amend; their own nature and actions will speak against them[4].

Mankind should work in disciplined ranks to repel evil, for Allah is ONE[5]. Ascribe not to Allah things derogatory to Him. It is derogatory to believe that Allah has a Son in biological sense: it is derogatory to believe in "Trinity"[6]. The gospel of 'Unity' of God preached by all the Prophets of the Almighty God including the Holy *Jesus*, Son of Mary, and Islam, is the cure for evil. No power of evil can overcome Allah's servants who are sincere and true[7]. According to the Holy prophet (PBH), Allah says- "O son of man, devote yourself to My Worship, and I will deliver you of the worldly anxieties, and will remove your poverty, otherwise, I will fill your heart with a thousand worries and will not remove your poverty". To Allah alone is devotion due, know that variety in creation points to "Unity" in Allah's plan. Remember that all nature proclaims Allah's Grace and loving kindness[8], and know that Allah's signs are many, but they all point to His Unity; and worship due to Him alone[9].

Again, Mankind must live a righteous life: This means a life of faith, kindness, prayer, charity, probity and patience under suffering[10]. Wickedness cannot screen itself behind a sacred relic, nor can a sacred relic help the enemies of faith. The fact that our fathers were righteous cannot help us, unless we are ourselves righteous. The doctrine of personal responsibility is the cardinal feature of Islam. And this is the message preached by all the Prophets of God, including the Holy *Jesus* Son of Mary.

Allah guides the human spirit in wondrous ways. Therefore, have absolute faith in Allah and put your trust in Him; for mankind is ONE. All things good, beautiful and useful, it is our lord Allah that made them to be so. The life of this world should not blind us to the realities of the hereafter. Remember the sure event[11]. Know that as with a tremendous earth-quake, this world will be dissolved[12]. Instead of seeking ephemeral good, it is better for you to seek the eternal home of peace from Allah[13]. A Hadith tells us that "the heart of a Muslim whose object is the life of hereafter, is made indifferent to the worldly pleasures, yet the world is subdued to him, and on the other hand, whoever adores the world, he is overpowered by miseries and calamities, yet he cannot receive more than his due portion".

Therefore do not shut out the Remembrance of Allah (in the manner detailed in this book) from your soul. Know that Allah chooses prophets among men, blessed them with the insight into the unseen world and learn what it holds for Mankind and the Jinn. So by their noble office, they mediate between the two worlds: they stood on the frontier. Endeavor to accept their message and reject falsehood. Know that Allah works through out His worlds in mercy and justice. Therefore repent and make amend before it becomes too late. Be patient and strive with constancy, for Allah's plan is righteous and for the good of his creatures[14]. Know that it is only Allah's message through his prophets is the light that leads and the mercy that forgives[15].

Give-up pride of worldly goods, Allah is with those who live in self restraint; and a pure and righteous life[16]. Know that pride is the root of evil and must perish[17]. High and low will be leveled at Judgement; only those who repent and make amendments shall be with hope on that Day[18]. Eschew evil, pay not evil back with evil[19]. Know that the Judgement day will be a terrible day. Continue on the path of righteousness, for the virtues which go with faith lead to success and bliss[20]. Mercy and truth are from Allah alone. Not wealth but righteousness that will attain the happy end; for Allah is the only reality[21]. This world's strengths, skills, beauty and powers are like spider's web; flimsy before the eternal verities[22].

Know that life without faith has no stable foundation. True values will come in the end. All powers, wisdom, beauty and truth flow from Allah[23]. It is imperative that this is known and well understood. There are grades in nature. In the next world, the good will reach Bliss, while evil will be doomed[24]. Therefore, avoid self glory, envy and suspicion, for they lead to evil[25]. Solomon and other Men of Power and vision, never forgot Allah. Therefore, strive hard to win the final bliss[26]. Never you despair because of your sins, repent and make amend for Allah's mercy is unbounded[27]. Believe in Allah for He forgives sin again and again, and accept Repentance and Amendment. Know that the Day of requital is ever drawing nearer and nearer[28]. Know that the best of men is the man of faith, whose law of life is the will of Allah[29]. This book is designed to guide you. Know that creation is for just end. Learn the truth and serve Allah as he showed be served. Be kind to parents and evil will be undone. Learn patience, perseverance and be steadfast in prayers[30].

Know that all acts, good or evil have inevitable consequences, therefore remember Allah constantly, praise and serve Him[31]. Evil will not escape justice, nor good it's reward[32]. Follow Allah's Light in humble dedication and sincerity. Seek Him and trust Him and all your sorrows, difficulties, penuries and dammed anguish, and all manners of enemies are undone. Know that Allah is the Lord of the ways of Ascent, mystery of time, and new world after Judgement. Therefore strive hard to be among the honored ones in the Garden of Bliss[33]. Understand that Allah leads on man by stages to the highest[34]. This is why the Holy *Jesus* Son of Mary said to his followers "I have much to tell you, but you cannot bear them now, until the Spirit of Truth comes who will lead you into all Truths[35]. The spirit of Truth is Muhammad (PBH) or Mohammed according to the holy *Jesus*. The message sent through him to mankind and Jinn is Islam. And this book is all about that message (Islam). No matter your dislike for Islam and biases, endeavor to read this book at least with a view to fault it. Learn from Allah's signs and law. The choice is yours[36].

Know that every difficulty is linked with Ease and Joy[37]. You are better advised never to pile up things that are ephemeral.[38] Seek refuge in Allah from all outer ills and from all inner ills. [39]

Consequences Of Rejecting Faith In Allah And His Remembrance

1. Remember how much love Noah had for his people and accordingly taught them and warned them against all manners of evil and rebelliousness. They all rejected him and flouted his message. The consequence was Allah's justice that overtook them in this world and that of the hereafter is even greater. And Noah was saved in the Ark[40]. Therefore understand the issues raised in this book. Dispute not Allah's signs, for nothing avail, if soul is lost and/ or dead[41]. Ah! Woe that Day to the rejecter of the truth[42] Soon Judgement must come. Therefore adore Allah, yea! Adore Allah. There is but ONE ALLAH, who is the beginning of everything, known and unknown and nothing existed before Him, He is the present, and nothing is possible without Him and He is the end of everything and nothing comes after Him. He is ONE and ONLY, without any partner, He is the final goal and the end of all journeys. Every deed has its own fruit! Therefore, know that Judgement must come. Respond to the call and invitation of this book: Repent and make amend while there is time[43].

2. Remember prophet Hud warned the people of Ad against sinful acts, and Thamud people by prophet Salih.[44] These two prophets were rejected by their people and defied Allah and were wiped out of existence. The punishment of the hereafter is even greater. Know that Allah reigns in Heavens and Earths.[45] Know that the life of this would is empty and ephemeral. What matters is the hereafter, for Allah holds the keys of the unseen[46]. Endeavour to pray for the eternal garden of bliss promised by Allah to the righteous. That is the reward as well as final Abode. That is the promise binding up Allah[47] and that is the sort of thing to be prayed for from Allah which he has made binding upon Himself, and not ephemeral things, even though they may be good. That is the sort of thing Allah has promised and undertaken to give.

3. Remember the angels on their mission of justice to the people of Lot, stopped to give good news to Abraham. The people of Lot persisted in their abomination and perished, and so did Madyan people; Prophet Shu'aib preached to them in vain to avoid evil. They too perished for their frauds[48]. Allah forbids evil.[49] if sinners have respite, it is only for a term. Judgement must come, so draw near to Allah in humility and reverence.[50] Remember the lesson taught by the arrogance of Pharoah who misled his people. They were consumed by the red sea.[51]

4. Know that no matter the mockery of men, Allah's truth will always prevail. The world can plot eleven trillion plots and much more, if it can, cannot defeat Allah's plan and will.[52] Therefore obey Allah's call, and hold all else as naught. The evil ones and the wicked will not thrive[53]. The enemies of Islam cannot put out Allah's light. Wealth is for good use, not for hoarding. Strive and struggle for Allah in a straight fight[54]. Hardest striving is needed against evil[55]. The plots of the wicked will always end in shame. The penalty comes in unexpected ways, for nature proclaims the glory of Allah.[56] He provides man with all the means for growth, social, moral and spiritual.[57] Know that Prophets will witness against those who reject Truth. Therefore, be faithful in intent and action.[58] The holy *Jesus*, son of Mary said: "I am not son of God, and I am not God. Wherefore when God shall come to judge, my words like a sword shall pierce such one that believe me to be more than man",[59] [60] The Holy Qur'an says: "The evil consequences of rejecting the truth are inevitable and must soon

come to pass".[61] The gifts of nature, solace of mind and soul come from Allah. Therefore trust Him alone, for Judgement will come.[62] Allah is the only Reality, for He alone knows what is hidden.[63]

5. Terrible will be the Judgement Day. Therefore, repent and make amend before it becomes too late.[64]

TRIAL AND TRIBULATIONS

1. Know that sorrows, difficulties, penuries, sufferings and dammed anguish are trials from Allah. Allah says in the Holy Qur'an thus: "Or do ye think that ye shall enter the garden (i.e. Paradise) without such (trials) as come to those who passed away before you? They encountered suffering and adversity, and were shaken in spirit, that even the messenger and those of faith who were with him cried: "When (will come) the help of Allah". Ah verily, the help of Allah is near.[65] Allah leads on man by stages to the highest.[66] Know that after difficulties Allah promises ease, and Allah never fails in His promise. It is a promise binding on Him. Therefore, be patient, and be not afraid to proclaim the truth of Allah. Keep away from evil, but recognize the sincere and the humble even if not of your flock.[67] And know that in all the miracles of the holy *Jesus* son of Mary, he claimed no divinity.[68]

2. Remember Allah, and He will remember you. Be grateful to Him and never reject Him.[69]

3. Allah's nature is sublime, so far beyond mankind and jinn's limited conceptions. He is a personality and not a mere abstract conception of philosophy. He is near us, He cares for us, and we owe our existence to Him alone. He is the ONE and ONLY God, the ONLY ONE to whom worship is due. All other things or beings that we can think of, are His creatures and in no way comparable to Him. He is eternal without end. He is not limited by time or place or circumstance. He is the Reality. Never think of Him of having a son or a father, for that would be to import animal qualities into our conception of Him. He is not like any other person or thing that we know or can imagine His qualities and nature are unique. So, Remember Him as He should be remembered and fear Him as He should be feared. Yea! Fear Allah for He is very severe in punishment. Do not be deceived that some one died for your sins. No Prophet of God was given that message by

Allah. No where did Allah made that promise. Do not be deterred by set backs and failures. The temporary relationship the fleeting events, our triumphs and defeats, difficulties, sorrows, penuries and damned anguish in this would are the bridges through which we must cross to the higher world. Our temporal experiences are the foundation on which our greater and real life is built up.

4. In order for us to rise above the mere animal part of us and achieve dignity as spiritual being and noble destiny, we must constantly remember Allah in the manner taught in this book, endeavour to realize His presence, acknowledge His goodness and accept His guidance. If a group of people or individual fails to remember Him, by deliberately turning away, He will withdraw His grace and that will be a severe penalty indeed.[70]

INTRODUCTION

I begin this work with the name of the Almighty God, the most Beneficent, and the most Merciful. This work is the product of the two dreams I had during my business trip to Houston, Texas U.S.A in the month of March, 1989. One of the two dreams took place in Amsterdam on the 12th day of March 1989, and the second dream took place in New York, on the 16th day of March 1989.

On our arrival by K.L.M. flight from Kano – Nigeria to Amsterdam, my wife by name Hajiya Halimat Sa'adiya and I, discovered that our personal luggage were misdirected to London, and we had to pass a night in Amsterdam, to collect the luggage the following day. We checked into Mariot Hotel, room 636. While sleeping in the room, I had a dream that I was inside the compound of a very old University. The main gate of the University was massive, dignified and very ancient. While I was in the compound, a personality appeared before me. In his hands, were manuscripts that were well and neatly bounded together. On them, was an inscription – "Prophet Muhammad (PBH) is an evolution of the Almighty God". I was shocked at reading the inscription and looked at the personality with curiosity. He handed to me the manuscripts. He again, handed to me a package, which contained the copies of holy Books of all the prophets, of the Almighty God, among them was a copy of the Holy Qur'an. I was surprised that he knows my name, for he said to me. "Mahmud, here is an assignment for you. Go and find the meaning. "Prophet Muhammad (PBH) is an evolution of the Almighty God" from all these materials which I have handed to you". I was about to ask him few questions, and the dream was interrupted by my wife that returned from where she went to buy fruits for me. So I woke up and the time was 6:00pm.

On our way back from Houston, we arrived too early for our Concord flight to Paris. It was about 6:00 am and our flight was scheduled to depart J.F. Kennedy Airport at 2:00pm. It was for this reason we checked into PLAZA Hotel, room number 700. It was in this room, of this Hotel, that I had the second dream. In the dream, I saw Prophet Ibrahim (Alaihi Salam) in a certain city. People began to gather around him, to pay him homage. In seeing the multitude, he turned himself into a huge ball of light, and moved away from the area, in an unimaginable speed. I followed him to where he went. I discovered that he was a very old man of Arab complexion. He was lying down facing up, recovering from the great speed. I came close to him, and I heard it said: "Let him rest, let him rest. Nobody should disturb him". Then I held back. As the news of where he was spread, ocean of humanity began to surge towards the place from all the corners of the globe to pay homage to him. It was at this stage I became desperate, as I feared that if they arrived at the place with the world dignitaries I might not get the chance to be close to him as I was then. So, I knelt down by his side, and kissed his forehead. I tried to offer prayers to the Almighty God to bless him and the Holy Prophet Muhammad (PBH), but I could not recollect anything as my memory failed.

He sat up and held my two hands, and got up. That was the time I realized that where we were, was not an open field. He placed his right hand over my shoulder and came out from where we were to receive the ocean of mankind and the Jinn that surged from every corner of the globe to pay homage to him. He stood behind my back placed his two hands on my shoulders, and addressed the unimaginable gathering. What he said, reinforced my desire to carry out exhaustive research into the meaning "Muhammad (PBH) is an evolution of the Almighty God". My findings, which can be improved upon by my fellow men, are contained in this book of Thirteen Chapters.

We now live in a world dominated by evil. Mankind and the Jinn have strayed too far from their moral base. In the book of ODES, Conficius says "He who offends against Heaven has none to whom he can pray. Heaven's imperative in the minds of men, serves as the fulerum" Mencius from the Conficius School says even the gaining of power over the whole world, would not justify killing one man or committing a single act of unrighteousness to accomplish it. Worldly rank is not nobility of Heaven, but that of men, which is empty and ephemeral unless grounded in man's inborn moral sense and reflective of a hierarchy of true values. This means, worldly power, glory, wealth, position and all that man scramble for, are but a fleeting show. They will all come to an end one day. R.H. Dufty says that even scientists (who were doubters of life after death) have (now) all agreed, that eventually the whole Universe will collapse on itself one day, and there is no knowing-what the nature of any subsequent existence will be. The pharaoh of Egypt (i.e. the father of Ramses) says: "Death is the vehicle used to cross the bridge between present existence to commence real living". This means that our present existence is like a departure station waiting for the arrival of the vehicle (Death) to take us across the bridge to commence real living that knows no death. Mankind should therefore not be deceived to believe in the beautiful cities with all the attractions and luxuries. History tells us that he who indulges in luxuries, cannot escape ruin, and no one now pays attention to the lessons of history.

Prosperity must never be measured by wealth and worldly gains alone, but also by the health of the mind and the spirit. The down ward course in evil is rapid. The most tragic consequences are that, evil persuades its victims to believe, that they are pursing good. They think evil to be their good. They go deeper and deeper into it and become more and more callous.

This book serves as a road map, a compass and a rudder, to journey successfully and smoothly, from the enclave of the accursed Satan to salvation. And to reinforce the belief of those on the right path, to intensify their constant remembrance of the Almighty God. It is Jihad which is one of the most important duties ordained by the Holy Qur'an. Jihad literally means an effort and or an endeavour in the way of the Almighty God. The word does not mean (as it is erroneously supposed by many among the non-Muslims) a fanatical war analogous to that denoted by the word "crusade". A tradition of the Holy Prophet Muhammad (PBH) says "The greatest Jihad is that which one launches against one's own lusts". Thus, jihad signifies helping your religion, defending the truth, justice and equity, repelling aggression and tyranny, fighting temptations, educating, and training your own spirit and serving humanity.

The signs of the end of the present existence are all over the place and yet majority of mankind and the Jinn pays no heed. Prophecies have been made by the righteous servants of the Almighty God. These include the prophets of the Old Testament, Jesus Christ, the Holy Qur'an and the Hadith. The Holy Bible says "For nation shall rise against nation and kingdom against kingdoms and there shall be famines and pestilences and earthquakes in diverse places. All these are the beginning of sorrows.[71] They have happened and have continued to happen, and yet mankind and the Jinn pay no heed. The holy Qur'an on the other hand tells us that Gog and Magog are two nations that will be let loose, and will sally forth from every point of eminence.[72] This prophecy appears to be taken root in the recent war waged against Iraqi by North America and Great Britain.

A Hadith says: "No one will have the power to fight against them".[73] According to another Hadith, the Almighty God said: "I have created some of my servants whom no one can destroy but myself.[74] This means, that the stage we have reached now in existence is the Almighty God's intervention: and it will be too late to repent, when that intervention happens. There is another Hadith that says "They will drink the waters of the whole world".[75] This is what the World Bank and IMF have done to the world economy. These institutions created by Europe and America rejoice in leaving every country they impose their model of economic reforms on, in worste state than prevail before the introduction of their reform programmes. They rejoice in creating poverty in every nation on the surface of the globe through usury, immorality and all manners of rebelliousness.

If, inspite of Allah's loving care any particular men or group of men or nations, misuse their powers, or willfully disobey Allah's Law, Allah will set them aside and substitute others in their place with like powers. Allah's gifts are free, but let no one think that he can monopolise them without being called to answer for the trust. The man of Allah must not be discouraged by the whole world being at some moment, completely against him. Allah can in a moment make a complete change. Either the same men that fought against him will be his zealous adherents or another generation will spring up, which will carry the flag of righteousness to victory. Allah's will and plan work in their own good time. [76]

CHAPTER ONE
REPENTANCE AND AMENDMENT

The only straight way to the Almighty God, is Repentance and Amendment. Even the accursed Devil, if he repents today and beseech the Almighty God, for forgiveness, he will be forgiven, despite the sordid and absurd degree of his rebelliousness, and uncountable atrocities he has caused on earth. The dialogue between the holy *Jesus* and Satan is a serious case in point. The dialogue is contained in the Scriptures thus: "When he had prayed to the Lord, his disciples came to him and said: 'O Master, two things we would (like to) know, One is how thou talkest with Satan, who nevertheless thou sayest is impenitent; the other is, how God shall come to judge in the day of Judgement?"

"*Jesus* replied: "Verily I say unto you, I had compassion on Satan, knowing his fall, and I had compassion on mankind whom he templeth to sin. Therefore I prayed and fasted to our God who spoke to me by His angel Gabriel: "What seekest thou, O *Jesus*, and what is thy – request?" I answered: "Lord, thou knowest of what evil Satan is the cause and that through his temptations many perish, he is thy creature Lord, whom thou didst create, therefore, Lord have mercy upon him".

'God (Almighty) answered: "*Jesus*, behold, I will pardon him, only cause him to say: 'Lord, my God, I have sinned, have mercy upon me' and I will pardon him and restore him to his first state".

"I rejoiced greatly", said *Jesus*, 'when I heard this, believing that I had made this peace' Therefore I called Satan, who came saying "what must I do for thee, O *Jesus*?"

'I answered: "Thou shalt do it for thyself O Satan, for I love not thy services, but for thy good have I called thee".

'Satan replied: "If thou desirest not my services, neither desire I thine; for I am nobler than thou, therefore thou art not worthy to serve me thou who art clay, while I am spirit".

"Let us leave this," I said, 'and tell me if it were not well thou shouldst return to thy first – beauty and thy first state. Thou must know that the angel Michael must needs on the day of Judgement strike thee with the sword of

God one hundred thousand times, and each blow will give thee the pain of ten hells'.

'Satan replied: "We shall see in that day who can do most, certainly I shall have on my side many angels and most potent idolaters who will trouble God, and He shall know how great a mistake He made to banish me for the sake of a vile (piece of) clay".

'Then I said: "O Satan, thou art infirm in mind, and knowest not what thou sayest "Then Satan, in a derisive manner, wagged his head, saying: "Come now, let us make up this peace between me and God; and what must be done say thou, O *Jesus*, since thou art sound in mind".

"I answered: "Two words only need be spoken". 'Satan replied: "What words?" 'I answered, "These: I have sinned, have mercy on me". Satan replied: "Now willingly will I make this peace if God will say these words to me' Satan departed shrieking and said; it is not so O Jesus, but thou tallest a lie to please God.

"Now depart from me", I said "O cursed one, for thou art the wicked author of all injustice and Sin, but God is just and without any sin".

'Now consider' said *Jesus* to his disciples, 'how he will find mercy'.

'They answered: "Never, Lord, because he is impenitent".[72]

The Satan's anger arose from the fact that the Almighty God created man and breathed something of His own spirit into him, and placed him in his uncorrupted state even above the angels. And in himself, man summed up the Almighty God's great world: man is in himself a microcosm. When the Almighty God asked Satan to bow down for man "And behold, we said to the angels: Bow down to Adam and they bowed: Not so Iblis: he refused and was haughty: he was of those who reject faith".[73] His disobedience angered the Almighty God, and he was cursed and banished. Since then the Satan became the sworn enemy of man and yet man voluntarily follows him and his rebelliousness against the Almighty God. Rebelliousness is now a status symbol. The arrogant sinners now have the impudence to accuse those that speak against unrighteousness as uncivilised and intolerant people. Take the case of pornography for an example: There had been complaints that pornographic materials are evil and the world would be better without them. As these complaints were sinking down into the hearts of mankind, a legal argument orchestrated by Satan, suddenly emerged on the scene that "Pornographic materials should by law be tolerated". Similarly, homosexual practices have been considered immoral, but Wolfenden Committee report in Great Britain recommended a few years ago, that it should be tolerated and should therefore not be made an object of legislation. The Law must only enforce what the society believes to be right, and must not lead public opinion on moral issues. The Committee played into the hands and machinations of Satan. If Wolfenden Committee had known that its report would turn up to 82% of world population into immoral practices, it would have hesitated. Friedrich Schiller[74] Says: "Man acting by himself and without religion, is unable to break the chains that oppresses him without sinking in the process into still deeper slavery".

Every Friday and every Sunday, Muslims and Christians gather to supplicate to God Almighty for His mercy. And we wonder why prayers are no longer answered as of old. Conficius says he who offends against Heaven has none to whom he can pray. This is true, for unless one recognizes the imperatives of Heaven, one cannot be a noble man. Mencius says even the gaining of power over the whole world, would not justify killing one man, or committing a single act of unrighteousness to accomplish it. Mencius went on to say that among the greatest pleasures in the life of a noble man, to rule the world would not be one of them. The three are that his parents are still be alive, and his brothers well, that he feels no shame over his own conduct and that he has able student. This is true, because worldly rank is not nobility of Heaven, but that of men, which is empty and ephemeral, unless grounded in man's inborn moral sense and reflective of a hierarchy of true values.

The holy *Jesus* says: "Verily I say unto you, that it is better to burn a city, than to leave there an evil custom.[75]

The Persian Empire crumbled due to the corruptions of the Zoroastrian religion, which crept in under the Parthian Dynasty of the Arsacids. The Sasanians that overthrew Arsacids failed to purity the Old Persian belief in the dual principles of good and evil. They only adhered to fire worship, as the Chief feature of their cult. In manners and morals, they succumbed to the vices of arrogance, luxury, sensuality and monopoly of power and privilege, which the office of religion was to denounce and root out. In order for mankind to find a way out of the enclave of the accursed Devil, there is the urgent need to begin to constantly remember the Almighty God, realize His presence, acknowledge His goodness and accept his guidance.

Mankind should repent and amend its ways. Otherwise, the Almighty God will withdraw His Grace, and that will be a severe penalty indeed.[76]

If, in spite of the Almighty God's loving care, any particular men, or group of men misuse their powers, or willfully disobey God's law, the Almighty God vowed to set such people aside, and substitute others in their place, with like powers. The Almighty God's gifts are free, but let no one think that he can monopolise them, or misuse them without being called to answer for the trust.

The only straight way, to the Almighty God is repentance and amendment. These are what will enable mankind and jinn to shake off the chains of Satan, and achieve nearness to the Almighty God.[77] How many times did the holy *Jesus* say: "I am not God, and I am not son of God?" Uncountable times the holy *Jesus* said so and yet over 90% of Christian population believe in "Trinity". The incident that took place after 40 days of prayers on Mount Sinai by the holy *Jesus* and his disciples explain the truth of the Gospel of *Jesus* (*INJIL*): "*Jesus* drew nigh to the river Jordan, to go to Jerusalem, and he was seen by one of them who believed *Jesus* to be God. Whereupon, with greatest gladness crying ever! "Our God cometh O Jerusalem prepare thee to receive him" And he testified that he had seen *Jesus* near Jordan… *Jesus* marveled greatly seeing the multitude, which covered the ground with people, and said to his disciples: "Perchance Satan hath raised sedition in Judea. May it please God to take away from Satan the dominion which he hath over sinners"

'And when he had said this, the crowed drew nigh, and when they knew him, they began to do him reverence as unto God. Whereupon *Jesus* gave a great groan and said. "Get ye from before me, O mad men, for I fear lest the earth should open and devour me with you for your abominable words!" Whereupon the people were filled with terror and began to weep. Then *Jesus*, having lifted his hand in token of silence, said! "Verily ye have erred greatly, O Israelites, in calling me, a man, your God. And I fear that God may for this give heavy plague upon the holy city, handing it over in servitude to strangers, O! A thousand times accursed Satan that hath moved you to this!"

'And having said this, *Jesus* smote his face with both his hands, whereupon arose such noise of weeping that none could hear what *Jesus* was saying. Whereupon, once more, he lifted up his hands in taken of silence, and the people being quieted from their weeping, he spoke once more: "I confess before heaven, and I call to witness everything that dwelleth upon the earth, that I am a stranger to all that ye have said: seeing that I am a man born of mortal woman, subject to the Judgement of God, suffering the miseries of eating and sleeping, or cold and heat, like other men. Wherefore when God shall come to judge, my words like a sword shall pierce each one (of them) that believe me to be more than man."

'And having said this, *Jesus* saw a great multitude of horsemen, whereby he perceived that there were coming with the Governor, Herod and the high Priest. Then *Jesus* said: "Perchance they also have become mad".

'When the Governor arrived there with King Herod and the high Priest every one dismounted and they made a circle round about *Jesus*, in so much that the soldiery could not keep back the people that were desirous to hear *Jesus* speaking with the high Priest.

'*Jesus* drew near to the high Priest with reverence but he was wishful to bow himself down and worship *Jesus*, when *Jesus* cried out! "Beware of that which thou doest, Priest of the living God, Sin not against our God!"

The high Priest answered: "Now is Judea so greatly moved over thy signs and thy teaching that they cry out that thou art God; wherefore constrained by the people, I came hither with the Roman Governor and King Herod. We pray thee therefore from our heart, that thou wilt be content to remove the sedition which is arisen on thy account. For some say thou art God, some say thou art son of God, some say thou art a prophet".

'*Jesus* answered: "And thou, O high Priest of God, wherefore hast thou not quieted this sedition? Art thou also perchance, gone out of thy mind? Have the prophecies with the Law of God so passed into oblivion, O wretched Judea, deceived of Satan"

'And having said this, *Jesus* said again: "I confess before heaven, and call to witness everything that dwelleth upon the earth, that I am a stranger to all that men have said of me, to wit, that I am more than man. For I am a man born of a woman, subject to the Judgement of God, that live here like as other men, subject to common miseries. As God liveth, in whose presence my soul standeth, thou has greatly sinned, O Priest, in saying what thou hast said. May it please God that there come not upon the holy city great vengeance for this sin".

'Then said the Priest: "May God pardon us, and do thou pray for us".

'Then said the Governor and Herod: "Sir, it is impossible that man should do that which thou doest, wherefore we understand not that which thou sayest".

'*Jesus* replied: "That which ye say is true, for God worketh good in man, even as Satan worketh evil... But tell me O Governor and thou O king, ye say this because ye are strangers to our law, for if ye read the Testament and Covenant of our God, you would see that Moses with a rod made the water turn into blood, the dust into fleas, the dew into tempest and the light into darkness. He made the frogs and mice to come into Egypt, which covered the ground; he slew the first-born, and opened the sea, wherein he drowned Pharaoh. Of these things I have wrought none. And of Moses, every one confesseth that he is a dead man at this present. Joshua made the sun to stand still, and opened the Jordan, which I have not yet done. And of Joshua every one confesseth that he is a dead man at this present. Elijah made fire to come visibly down from heaven, and rain, which I have not done. And of Elijah, every one confesseth that he is dead man. And (in like manner) very many other prophets, holy men, friends of God, who in the power of God have wrought things which cannot be grasped by the mind of those who know not our God Almighty and merciful, who is blessed for ever".

'Accordingly, the Governor, the Priest and the king prayed, *Jesus* that in order to quiet the people he should mount up into a lofty place, and speak to the people.'

'*Jesus* went up on to one of the twelve stones which Joshua made, the twelve tribes take up from the midst of Jordan, when all Israel passed over their dry shod, and he said with a loud voice: "Let our Priest go up into a high place where he may confirm my words". Thereupon the high Priest went up thither to whom *Jesus* said distinctly, so that every one might hear.

1. Question: Jesus said: "It is written in the Testament and Covenant of the living God that our God hath no beginning, neither shall he ever have an end?"

   1.01 The high Priest answered: "Even so is it written therein"

2. Question: Jesus said: "It is written there that our God by His word alone hath created all things?'

   2.01 The high Priest answered: "Even so it is"

3. Question: *Jesus* said: "It is written there that God is invisible and hidden from the mind of man seeing, He is incorporeal and uncomposed without variableness?"

    3.01 The high Priest answered: "So it is truly".

4. Question: *Jesus* said: "It is written there how that the heaven of heavens cannot contain Him?

    4.01 The high Priest answered: "So said Solomon the Prophet, O *Jesus*"

5. Question: *Jesus* said: "It is written there that God hath no need, for as much as He eateth not, sleepeth not, and suffereth not from any deficiency?"

    5.01 The high Priest answered: "So is it".

6. Question: *Jesus* said: "It is written there that our God is every where, and that there is not any other God but He, who striketh down and maketh whole and doeth all that pleaseth Him?"

    6.01 The high Priest answered: "So is it written".

'Then *Jesus*, having lifted up his hands said: "Lord, our God, this is my faith wherewith I shall come to thy Judgement; in testimony against every one that shall believe the contrary. And turning himself towards the people, he said: "Repent for from all that of which the high Priest hath said that it is written in the book of Moses, the Covenant of God forever, ye may perceive your sin, for that I am a visible man, and a morsel of clay that walketh upon the earth, mortal as are other men. And I have had a beginning, and shall have an end; and (am) such that I cannot create a fly over again"

'Thereupon the people raised their voices weeping, and said: "We have sinned, Lord, our God against Thee, have mercy upon us and they prayed *Jesus*, every one, that he would pray for the safety of the holy city, that our God in His anger should not give it over to be trodden down of the nations".

'Thereupon, *Jesus* having lifted up his hands, prayed for the holy city and for the people of God, every one crying" so be it" Amen.

'When the prayer was ended, the Priest said with a loud voice: "Stay *Jesus*, for we need to know who thou art, for the quieting of our nation".

'*Jesus* answered: "I am *Jesus* son of Mary, of the seed of David, a man that is mortal and feareth God, and seek that to God be given honour and glory".

'The Priest asked *Jesus*: "In the book of Moses it is written that our God must send us the Messiah, who shall come to announce to us that which God willeth, and shall bring to the world the mercy of God. Therefore I pray thee, tell us the truth, art thou the Messiah of God whom we expect?"

'*Jesus* answered: "it is true that God hath so promised, but indeed I am not he, for he is made before me and shall come after me".

'The Priest questioned *Jesus* further: "By thy words and signs at any rate we believe thee to be a prophet and an holy one of God, wherefore I pray thee in the name of all Judea and Israel that thou for love of God shouldst tell us what wise the Messiah will come?"

'*Jesus* answered: "As God liveth, in whose presence my soul standeth, I am not the Messiah whom all the tribes of the earth expect; even as God promised to our father Abraham saying: "In thy seed will I bless all the tribes of the earth. But when God shall take me away from the world, Satan will raise again this accursed sedition by making the impious believe that I am God and son of God, whence my words and my doctrine shall be contaminated insomuch that scarcely shall there remain thirty (30) faithful ones, whereupon God will have mercy upon the world, and will send His messenger for whom He hath made all things; who shall take away the dominion from Satan which he hath over men. He shall bring with him the mercy of God for salvation of them that shall believe in Him, and blessed is he who shall believe his words. Unworthy though I am to untie his hosen, I have received grace and mercy of God to see him".

'Then answered the Priest with the Governor and the King saying: "Distress not thy self O *Jesus*, holy one of God, because; in our time shall this sedition be any more seeing that we will write to the sacred Roman senate in such wise that by imperial decree none shall any more call thee God or son of God".

'*Jesus* replied: "with your words, I am not consoled, because where ye hope for light darkness shall come"...but my consolation is in the coming of the messenger, who shall destroy every false opinion of me, and his faith shall spread and shall take hold of the whole world, for so hath God promised to Abraham, our father. And that which giveth me consolation is that his faith shall have no end, but shall be kept inviolate by God".

'The Priest questioned *Jesus* further: "After the coming of the messenger of God, shall other prophets come?"

'*Jesus* replied: "There shall not come after him true prophets sent by God but there shall come a great number of false prophets whereat I sorrow. For Satan shall raise them up by the just Judgement of God and they shall hide themselves under the pretext of my gospel"

'King Herod question *Jesus* thus: "How is it a just Judgement of God that such impious men would come?"

'*Jesus* replied: "It is just that he, who will not believe in the truth to his salvation, should believe in a lie to his damnation. Wherefore I say unto you, that the world hath ever despised the true prophets and loved the false, as can be seen in the time of Micchaiah and Jeremiah. For every like loveth his like".

'The high Priest asked *Jesus* a final question: "How shall the messiah be called and what sign shall reveal his coming?"

'*Jesus* replied: "The name of the Messiah is admirable, for God himself gave him the name when he had created his soul, and placed it in a celestial splendour. God said: "Wait Mohammed; for thy sake I will create Paradise, the world and a great multitude of creatures, whereof I make thee a present in so much that whosoever shall curse thee, shall be accursed. When I shall send thee into the world I shall send thee as my messenger of salvation, and thy word shall be true, insomuch that heaven and earth shall fail, but thy faith shall never fail". 'Mohammed' is his blessed name".

Then the crowed lifted up their voices saying: "O God send us thy messenger: O Mohammed, come quickly for the salvation of the world".

"And having said this, the multitude departed with the Priest, the Governor and King Herod, having great dispute concerning *Jesus* and concerning his doctrine. Whereupon the Priest prayed the Governor to write unto Rome to the Senate the whole matter; which thing the Governor did, wherefore the senate had compassion on Israel and Decreed that on pain of death none should call *Jesus* the Nazarene Prophet of the Jews, either God or son of God. Which Decree was posted up in the temple, engraved upon copper".

Despite these glaring facts from the Gospel of *Jesus*, Christians raise Churches all over the world upholding the absurd doctrine of "Trinity". When shall mankind ever learn? On account of mankind the Satan was accursed, and as a result Satan swore to destroy mankind by turning them against the Almighty God. *What an irony*!

The greatest among the major sins according to the Hadith of the holy messenger of God, Prophet Mohammed (PBH) is shirk,[78] that is associating any one or anything with the Almighty God: that is to believe that the Almighty God has an equal, or to worship something or some one other than Him, such as a stone, a tree, a star, the sun, the moon, or a prophet, a saint, or an angel. The Almighty God says: "Indeed God does not forgive associating anything with Him, and He forgives whatever is other than that to whomever He wills".

The Almighty God's messenger – the Holy Prophet Mohammed (PBH) once asked his companions: "Shall I not inform you about three great sins?" They said: "Yes, messenger of Allah". He then continued; 'Associating other objects of worship with Allah, Disobedience to parents, lying under oath and bearing false witness".[79]

Mankind has indeed voluntarily strayed too far from its moral base and Satan now holds man captive: what moral lessons can you teach a child of single parent in the guise of human right? Mankind is gradually developing a world to be populated by bastards. What moral lessons that can be taught to people that believe that a man can marry a man, and womon can marry a woman, all in the guise of satan orchestrated "human right'. What moral lessons that can be taught to a people that believe in killing infant babies to worship the accused satan for money, and in exhuming the bodies of dead people from their grave, cut off their heads for sale to ready buyers, in their worship of the accursed Satan for worldly power.

This book intends to serve as a compass and beckoning light for those struggling to escape from the fortified enclave and chains of Satan, not only to journey back to moral base, but to the salvation of God Almighty. This brief life span is not the sum total of man's existence. Man takes off this body of flesh, as he did to his placenta at the time of his birth, and is alive still in another guise, though its nature is beyond our ken. No one knows what awaits him in the life that is fast approaching, and the state mankind will find itself after the desolation of this mortal life; and mankind cannot read the hand, which holds that destiny in its determination. These are among the reasons the Almighty God chooses prophets among men, blesses them with insight into the unseen world to learn what it holds for man. So by their noble office, they mediate between the two worlds: They stand on the frontier, they taught us a verifiable fact of history, that he who indulges in luxuries cannot escape ruin, because where there is unregulated growth, there is decay.

The way out of this quagmire is repentance and amendment, this is the lesson taught by all the Prophets of God, as the only straight way to the Almighty God, as it is the only escape rout from the enclave of the accursed Satan and the only means of shaking off his chains. *Therefore repent and amend your ways as from now; Yesterday is a cancelled cheque, forget it; Today is a cash cheque use it: Repent and amend your ways, because Tomorrow is a promissory note, and may never mature.* This means that you may never see tomorrow. Therefore avoid delaying your repentance and amendment: say right now "Lord my God I have sinned, I have been deceived by the accursed Satan, pardon me and I promise Thee never to return to the path of Satan as long as Thou sufferest me to live" Amen. Since repentance is what is required, do it today and now.

Jesus once addressed his people in Jerusalem thus: "As God liveth, your own tongues condemn your pride, inasmuch as our God is loved more by the sinner that repenteth, knowing the great mercy of God upon him… wherefore there is most rejoicing in the presence of the angels of God over one sinner that repenteth than over 99 righteous persons. O Jerusalem, O Israel, I weep over thee, for thou knowest not thy visitation, because I would fain have gathered thee for love of God thy creator, as a hen gathereth her chickens under her wings and thou wouldst not, wherefore God saith thus unto thee: "O city, hard hearted and perverse of mind, I have sent to thee my servant to the end that he may convert thee to thine heart and mayest repent; but thou, O city of confusion, hast forgotten all that I did upon Egypt and upon Pharaoh for love of thee, O Israel, many times weepest thou that my servant may heal thy body of sickness; and thou seekest to slay my servant because he seeketh to heal thy soul of sin".[80]

"Shalt thou, then alone remain unpunished by Me? Shalt thou, then, live eternally? And shall thy pride deliver thee from my Hands? Assuredly not, for 1 will bring princes with an army against thee, and they shall surround thee with might and in such wise will I give thee over into their hands that thy pride shall fall down into hell".[81]

"I will not pardon the old men or the widows, I will not pardon the children but I will give you all to famine, the sword, and derision and the temple whereon I have looked with mercy, I will make desolate with the city, insomuch that ye shall be for a fable, a derision and a proverb among the nations. So is my wrath abiding upon thee and mine indignation sleepeth not". But "if Jerusalem shall weep for her sins and do penance, walking in my ways, I will not remember her iniquities any more, and I will not do unto her any of the evil which I have said. But Jerusalem weepeth for ruin and not for dishonouring of Me, wherewith she hath blasphemed my name among the nations. Therefore is my fury kindled much more! As I live eternally, if Job, Abraham, Samuel, David, and Daniel my servants, with Moses, should pray for this people, my wrath upon Jerusalem will not be appeased". [82]

Jesus said: "Our God promiseth His mercy to the sinner saying! "In that hour that the sinner shall lament his sin, by myself, I will not remember his iniquities for ever".[83] *Jesus* said: "God sendeth his prophets and servants into the world in order that sinner may repent, and He sendeth not for the sake of the righteous, because they have no need for repentance, even as he that is clean hath no need of the bath".[84] Barnabas once asked *Jesus*: "How long ought penitence to last?" *Jesus* replied: "As long as a man is in a state of sin he ought always to repent and do penance for it. Wherefore as human life always sinneth, so ought it always to do penance, unless ye would make more account of your shoes than of your soul, since every time that your shoes burst ye mend them".

Once a person repent and makes penance, the Satan is defeated. The accursed Devil has a way of deceiving people often by way of carnal desire. This is the state where a person assigns the status of truth to untruth and attached religiously to all its whimsicalities. It is a very dangerous situation, because the person considers himself on the right path in his own manner and feels no necessity of Istighfar (Repentance). As a result of it he is completely lost. This weapon of Satan is highly sophisticated as it is the stage that evil persuades its victims to believe that they are pursuing good. They think evil to be their good. They go deeper and deeper into it and become more and more callous.[85] Remember that the Almighty God is the final goal and the end of all journeys. Who ever expects to meet Him, let him repent and make penance, and be constant in His worship and admit no one as partner, for He is ONE and ONLY, who is Himself, of Himself and for Himself. He is always very pleased with the person who is repentant and seeks His forgiveness, provided it is in right earnest and with the sincerity of heart and intentions, with the resolve that the same would not be repeated in the future. Such a resolution totally nullifies the previous act.

Be warned, for *Jesus* once said: “Believe me, Barnabas, that every sin, however small it be, God punisheth with great punishment, seeing that God is offended at sin. Wherefore, since my mother and my faithful disciples that were with me loved me a little with earthly love, the righteous God hath willed to punish this love with the present grief, in order that it may not be punished in the flames of hell. And though I have been innocent in the world, since men have called me “God”, and “son of God”, God in order that I be not mocked of the demons on the day of Judgement, hath willed that I be mocked of men in this world by the death of Judas, making all men to believe that I died upon the cross. And this mocking will continue until the advent of Mohammed the messenger of God, who, when he shall come, shall reveal this deception to those who believe in God’s law”.[86]

I therefore repeat that the only straight way to the Almighty Allah is Repentance and Amendment: Do it today and you are on the right path to happiness and salvation of Allah.

CHAPTER TWO
FALSE PROPHESTS IDENTIFIED

All the false prophets, wicked doctrines and the contamination of the Gospels are the Satan's efforts to destroy man. When he was banished from Paradise by the Almighty God, on account of man; the accursed Satan swore to lie in wait for man in every stratagem of war, and ambush him in every path to the salvation of the Almighty God, and turn him instead against the Almighty God his creator. The accursed Devil does this by tempting man with worldly power, glory, wealth, and positions etc, which are empty and ephemeral, so that man can fall headlong together with him into oblivion. The Satan is aware that man is always thirsty of his creator *Allah Subhanahu Wata'ala.* To make man lose the straight path to Him, the accursed Satan raises false prophets to mislead man.

Jesus said that the Almighty God is unchangeable "and therefore that which God ordained as man's way of salvation, this hath he caused all the prophets to say. As God liveth, in whose presence my soul standeth, if the book of Moses with the book of our father David had not been corrupted by the human traditions of false Pharisees and doctors, God would not have given his word to me. And why speak I of the book of Moses and the book of David? Every prophecy have they corrupted, in so much that they do a thing not because God hath commanded it, but men look whether the doctors say it, and the Pharisees observe it, as though God were in error, and man could not err".

"Woe, therefore, to this faithless generation, for upon them shall come the blood of every prophet and righteous man, with the blood of Zechariah son of Berachiah, whom they slew between the temple and the altar"

"What prophet has not been persecuted? What righteous man have they suffered to die natural death? Scarcely one! And they seek now to slay me. They boast themselves to be children of Satan, and therefore they do his will: Therefore the temple with the holy city shall go to ruin, insomuch that thou shall not remain of the temple one stone upon another".

The quickest way to identify a false prophet is his contradiction of the Gospel. *Jesus* once said: "As God liveth in whose presence I stand, though I now weep for pity of mankind, on that Day, (i.e. the day of Judgement) I shall demand justice without mercy against those who despise my words and most of all against those who defile my gospel"[87] … as for me, I am now come to the world to prepare the way for the messenger of God, whom ye call Messiah; who shall bring salvation to the world. But beware that ye be not deceived, for many false prophets shall come, who shall take my words and contaminate my gospel" [88]

The following are two examples of false prophets: One from Christian world and one from Muslim world: Paul of Tarsus is one of such prophets in Christianity. In his epistle to the Galatians, he says: "But I make known to you brethren, that the gospel which was preached by me is not after man, neither was I taught it, but by the revelation of *Jesus* Christ".[89] Paul's assertion is that the gospel he preached was not derived from any human service, but rather that it had been communicated to him by God Almighty through *Jesus* Christ, who was no longer upon the earth. In other words, he had received divine revelation. But in his alleged case, it is *Jesus* Christ instead of Angel Gabriel, who supposedly brought to him this message from God, to take unto men. And as the power of God (The Holy Spirit) enabled prophets to carry out their ministry so Paul makes the claim that he too possessed it: "And they (the Apostles) glorified God in me".[90]

These two claims combined, imply an implied claim to Prophethood, whereas if he had only made the latter claim, one might simply say that he was making a claim to be equal to the Apostles as the 'New Testament' portrays them. Further evidence of that implied claim to prophethood is provided in the following claim: "In the day when God shall judge the secrets of men by *Jesus* Christ according to my gospel".[91] Not the gospel of *Jesus*, but a different message that he claims to have received from God. Indeed, in Paul, *Jesus*' prophecy regarding false prophets was partially fulfilled.

A second example of false prophets was Ghulam Ahmad, the founder of Ahamadiyya Muslim Mission. He claimed thus: [92] "It should be noticed that the gospels contain two kinds of prophecies about the coming of *Jesus*:

(1) The promise of his coming in the latter days; his coming is a spiritual character and resembles the second coming of the prophet Elijah, in the time of *Jesus*. So like Elijah, he has already appeared in this age, and it is I (Ghulam Ahmad) a servant of humanity, who has come as the promised Messiah, in the name of *Jesus* (on whom be peace). And *Jesus* has given the news of my coming in the gospels. Blessed is he who out of respect for *Jesus* ponders with honesty and truth over my

coming, and thus save himself from thumbling". Now let us examine Ghulam Ahmad's claim:

(2) The name of the promised Messiah was given by *Jesus* thus: 'the high Priest asked *Jesus*: "How shall the Messiah be called and what sign shall reveal his coming?"[93]

'*Jesus* answered: "The name of the Messiah is admirable, for God Himself gave him the name when he had created his soul, and placed it in a celestial splendour. God said: 'Wait Mohammed, for thy sake I will to create paradise, the world, and a great multitude of creatures, whereof I make thee a present, insomuch that whoso shall bless thee; shall be blessed and whoso shall curse; thee shall be accursed. When I shall send thee into the world, I shall send thee as my messenger of salvation and thy word shall be true, insomuch that heaven and earth shall fail, but thy faith shall never fail". "Mohammed" is his blessed name. 'Then the crowd lifted up their voices saying: "O God, send us thy messenger: O Mohammed, come quickly for the salvation of the world".[94] The name of the promised Messiah is 'Mohammed' and not Ghulam or Ghulam Ahmad. Here Ghulam Ahmad has failed the first test of a claim to prophethood; because he has contradicted the gospel of *Jesus*.

(3) The high Priest asked *Jesus*: "... wherefore I pray thee in the name of all Judea and Israel that thou for love of God shouldst tell us in what wise the Messiah will come?" *Jesus* answered: "As God liveth, in whose presence my soul standeth, I am not the Messiah whom all the tribes of the earth expect, even as God promised to our father Abraham, saying: "In thy seed will I bless all the tribes of the earth. But when God shall take me away from the world, Satan will raise again this accursed sedition, by making the impious believe that I am God and son of God, whence my words and my doctrine shall be contaminated, insomuch that scarcely shall there remain thirty faithful ones, whereupon God will have mercy upon the world, and will send his messenger for whom he hath made all things, who shall come from the South (of Jerusalem) with power, and shall destroy the idols with the idolaters; who shall take away the dominion from Satan which he hath over men. He shall bring with him mercy of God for salvation of them that shall believe in him, and blessed is he who shall believe his words".[95]

Ghulam Ahmad said: "… And it is I (Ghulam Ahmad), a servant of humanity (not a servant of God) who has come as the promised Messiah in the name of *Jesus*..." No prophet of God ever claimed to be a 'servant of humanity", but a servant of God Almighty. Again, *Jesus* prophecised that the promised Messiah would come from the south, (of Jerusalem) and India or Pakistan are not located in the south of Jerusalem.

(4) The family lineage of the promised Messiah was given by *Jesus* thus: "The scribe said to *Jesus*: I have seen an old book written by the hand of Moses and Joshua, servants and prophets of God, which book is the true book of Moses … And thus saith the book that Moses said: "Lord God of Israel, mighty and merciful, manifest to thy servant the splendour of thy glory. Whereupon God showed him His messenger (i.e. the Messiah) in the arms of Ishmael, and Ishmael in the arms of Abraham. Nigh to Ishmael stood Isaac, in whose arms was a child, who with finger pointed to the messenger of God, saying: "This is he for whom God hath created all things".

'Whereupon Moses cried out with Joy: "O Ishmael, thou hast in their arms all the world, and paradise! Be mindful of me, God's servant, that I may find grace in God's sight by means of thy Son, for whom God hath made all".

Ghulam Ahmad was not a descendant of Ishmael, his claim therefore; that he was the promised Messiah is false, more so that his claim contradicts the gospel of *Jesus*.

(5) Andrew, one of the disciples of *Jesus*, once asked *Jesus* thus: "Thou have told us many things of the Messiah therefore of thy kindness tell us clearly all". And in the like manner the other disciples besought him!

Accordingly *Jesus* said: "… Verily I say unto you, that every prophet when he is come hath borne to one nation only the mark of the mercy of God. And so their words were not extended save to that people to which they were sent. But the messenger of God, when he shall come, God shall give to him as it were the Seal of His hand, insomuch that he shall carry salvation and mercy to all the nations of the world that shall receive his doctrine. He shall come with power upon the ungodly and shall destroy idolatry insomuch that he shall make Satan confounded; for so promised God to Abraham, saying: "Behold, in thy seed I will bless all the tribes of the earth; and as thou hast broken into pieces the idols, O Abraham, even so shall thy seed do"' James asked *Jesus*: "O Master tell us in whom this promise was made, for the Jews say – "In Isaac", and the Ishmaelite say – "In Ishmael"

'*Jesus* replied: "David whose son was he and of what lineage?"

'James answered: "Of Isaac, for Isaac was father of Jacob and Jacob was father of Judah of whose lineage is David".

'Then *Jesus* said: "And the messenger of God (i.e. the Messiah) when he shall come of what lineage will he be?"

'The disciples answered: "Of David" whereupon *Jesus* said: "Ye deceive yourselves for David, in spirit calleth him Lord [96] saying thus: "God said to my Lord, sit thou on my right hand until I make thine enemies thy footstool. God shall send forth thy rod which shall have lordship in the midst of thine enemies". If the messenger of God, whom ye call Messiah, were son of David, how should David call him Lord? Believe me, for verily I say unto you, that the promise was made in Ishmael; not in Isaac".[97]

'The disciples said to *Jesus*: "O Master, it is thus written in the book of Moses that in Isaac was the promise made".

'*Jesus* answered with a groan: "It is so written, but Moses wrote it not, nor Joshua, but rather our rabbis, who fear not God. Verily, I say unto you that if ye consider the words of the Angel Gabriel, ye shall discover the malice of our scribes and doctors. For the angel said: "Abraham, all the world shall know how God loveth thee; but how shall the world know the love that thou bearest to God? Assuredly, it is necessary that thou do something for love of God". 'Abraham answered: "Behold the servant of God, ready to do all that which God shall will". 'Then spake God, saying to Abraham: "Take thy son, thy first born Ishmael, and come up the mountain to sacrifice him". 'How is Isaac first born, if when Isaac was born Ishmael was seven years old"?

'Then answered *Jesus*: "Verily I say unto you, that Satan ever seeketh to annul the laws of God, and therefore he with his followers, hypocrites and evil-doers, the former with false doctrine, the latter with lewd living, today have contaminated almost all things, so that scarcely is the truth found. Woe to the hypocrites! For the praises of this world shall turn for them into insults and torments in hell".

"I therefore say unto you that the messenger of God is a splendour that shall give gladness to nearly all that God hath made, for He is adorned with the spirit of understanding and of counsel, the spirit of wisdom and might, the spirit of fear and love, the spirit of prudence and temperance, he is adorned with the spirit of charity, and mercy, the spirit of justice and piety, the spirit of gentleness and patience, which he hath given to all His creatures. O blessed time, when he shall come to the world! Believe me that I have seen him and have done him reverence, even as every prophet hath seen him: seeing that of his spirit God giveth to them prophecy. And when I saw him, my soul was filled with consolation, saying: "O Mohammed, God be with thee, and may he make me worthy to untie thy shoe latchet, for obtaining this, I shall be a great prophet, and holy one of God".[98]

Here again, Ghulam Ahmad failed to fit into *Jesus* description of the "promised – Messiah".

(6) *Jesus* said: "Everything that conformeth to the book of Moses, that receive ye for true, seeing that God is one, the truth is one, whence it followeth that the doctrine is one and the meaning of the doctrine is one; and therefore, the faith is one. Verily I say unto you that if the truth had not been erased from the book of Moses, God would not have given to David our father, the second: And if the book of David had not been contaminated, God would not have committed the gospel to me; seeing that the Lord our God is unchangeable and hath spoken but one message to all men. Wherefore when the messenger of God shall come, he shall come to cleanse away all wherewith the ungodly have contaminated my book".

There is no greater contamination than the claim by Ghulam Ahmad thus: "I shall try to prove in this book that *Jesus* (Peace be on him) did not die on the cross; he did not go up to the heavens nor should it ever be supposed that he will ever again come from the heavens to the earth; that, rather, he died at the age of 120 years at Strinagar in Kashmir, and that his tomb is to be found in the Khan Yar Street of that town". [99]

Here, Ghulam Ahmad not only contradicted the gospel of *Jesus*, he also had the audacity to contradict the Holy Qur'an; the following are the proofs:

1. After spending a lot of time educating his disciples on the imperatives of constant remembrance of God as the main key to paradise, *Jesus* said: "Ye needs must seek of the fruits of the field the wherewithal

> to sustain our life, for it is now eight days that we have eaten no bread. Wherefore I will pray to our God, and will wait you with Barnabas".

'So all the disciples and apostles – departed by fours and by sixes and went their way according to the word of *Jesus*. There remained with *Jesus* his secretary by name Barnabas); whereupon *Jesus*, weeping said: "O Barnabas, it is necessary that I should reveal to thee great secrets which, after that I shall be departed from the world, thou shalt reveal to it".

'Then answered Barnabas, weeping and said: "Suffer me to weep, O Master and other men also, for that we are sinners. And thou art a holy one and prophet of God, it is not fitting for thee to weep so much".

'*Jesus* answered: "Believe me Barnabas that I cannot weep as much as I ought. For if men had not called me God, I should have seen God here as He will be seen in paradise and should have been safe, not to fear the day of Judgement. But God knoweth that I am innocent, because never have I harboured thought to be held more than a poor slave (of God) Nay, I tell thee that if I had not been called God, I should have been carried into paradise when I shall depart from the world, whereas now, I shall not go thither until the Judgement. Now, thou seest if I have cause to weep. Know, O Barnabas, that for this, I must have great persecution, and shall be sold by one of my disciples for thirty pieces of money, whereupon I am sure that he who shall sell me, shall be slain in my name, for that God shall take me up from the earth and shall change the appearance of the traitor, so that every one shall believe him to be me; nevertherless, when he dieth an evil dieth, I shall abide in that dishonour for a long time in the world. But when Mohammed shall come, the sacred Messenger of God (i.e. the promised Messiah) that infamy shall be taken away. And this shall God do, because I have confessed the truth of the Messiah; who shall give me this reward, that I shall be known to be alive and to be a stranger to that death of infamy".

'Then answered Barnabas: "O Master, tell me who is that wretch, for fain would choke him to death".

'Hold thy peace" answered *Jesus*, "for so God willeth and he cannot do otherwise, but see then, that when my mother is afflicted at such an event, thou shalth tell her the truth in order that she may be comforted".

'Then answered Barnabas: "All this will I do, O Master, if God please".[100] This prophecy of *Jesus* was fulfilled as follows: "Having gone forth from the house *Jesus* retired into the garden to pray, according as his custom was to pray, bowing his knees a hundred times and prostrating himself upon his face. Judas, accordingly, knowing the place where *Jesus* was with his disciples went to the high Priest, and said: "If ye will give me what was promised, this night will I give into your hand *Jesus*, whom ye seek; for he is alone with eleven companions"

'The high Priest answered: "How much seekest thou?"

'Said Judas: "Thirty pieces of gold" Then straightway, the high Priest counted unto him the money and sent a Pharisee to the Governor to fetch soldiers, and to Herod, and they gave a legion of them, because they feared the people; wherefore they took their arms and with torches and lanterns upon staves went out of Jerusalem.[101]

'When the soldiers with Judas drew near to the place where *Jesus* was, *Jesus* heard the approach of many people, wherefore in fear he withdrew into the house. And the eleven were sleeping.

'Then God, seeing the danger of his servant, commanded Gabriel, Michael, Rafael and Uriel, His Ministers, to take *Jesus* out of the world!

'The holy angels came and took *Jesus* out by the window that looketh toward the South. They bare him and placed him in the third heaven in the company of angels, blessing God for ever more'[102]

'Judas entered impetuously before all into the chamber whence *Jesus* had been taken up. And the disciples were sleeping. Whereupon the wonderful God acted wonderfully, insomuch that Judas was so change in speech and in face to be like *Jesus*, that we believed him to be *Jesus*. And he, having awakened us, was seeking where the Master was. Whereupon we marveled, and answered: "Thou, Lord, art our Master; hast thou now forgotten us?"

'And he, smiling said: "Now are ye foolish that know not me to be Judas Iscariot"

'And as he was saying this, the soldiery entered, and laid their hands upon Judas, because he was in every way like to *Jesus*'

'We having heard Judas saying, and seeing the multitude of soldiers; fled as beside ourselves!

'And John, who was wrapped in a linen cloth, awoke and fled, and when a soldier seized him by the linen cloth, he left the linen cloth and fled naked. For God heard the prayer of *Jesus*, and saved the eleven from evil![103]

'The soldiers took Judas and bound him, not without derision. For he truthfully denied that he was *Jesus* and the soldiers mocking him, said: "Sir, fear not, for we are come to make thee king of Israel, and we have bound thee because we know that thou dost refuse the kingdom".

'Judas answered: "Now have ye lost your senses! Ye are come to take *Jesus* of Nazareth, with arms and lanterns as (against) a robber; and ye have bound me that have guided you, to make me King!"

'Then the soldiers lost their patience, and with blows and kicks they began to flout Judas, and they led him with fury into Jerusalem!

'John and Peter followed the soldiers a far off; and they affirmed to Barnabas that they saw all the examination that was made of Judas by the high Priest, and by the council of the Pharisees, who were assembled to put *Jesus* to death. Whereupon Judas spoke many words of madness, insomuch that every one was filled with laughter, believing that he was really *Jesus* and that for fear of death, he was feigning madness. Whereupon the scribes bound his eyes with a bandage, and mocking him said: "*Jesus* prophet of the Nazarenes; (for so they called them who believed in *Jesus*), tell us, who was it that smote thee)?" And they buffeted him and spat in his face:

'When it was morning time, assembled the great council of scribes and elders of the people, and the high Priest with the Pharisees sought false witness against Judas, believing him to be *Jesus*: and they found not that which they sought. And why say that the Chief Priests believed Judas to be *Jesus*? Nay, all the disciples with Barnabas believed it and more, the poor virgin mother of *Jesus*, with her kinsfolk and friends, believed it, insomuch that the sorrow of every one was incredible. As God liveth Barnabas forgot all that *Jesus* had said (i.e. has prophecised): how that he should be taken up from the world and that he should suffer in a third person, and that he should not die until near the end of the world, Wherefore Barnabas went with the mother of *Jesus* and with John to the cross".

'The high Priest caused Judas to be brought before him bound and asked him of his disciples and his doctrine'.

"Whereupon Judas, as though beside himself, answered nothing to the point, the high Priest adjured him by the living God of Israel that he should tell him the truth".

'Judas answered: "I have told you that I am Judas Iscariot, who promised to give into your hands *Jesus* the Nazarene; and ye, by what art I know not, are beside yourselves, for ye will have it by every means that I am *Jesus*!

'The high Priest answered: "O perverse seducer, thou hast deceived all Israel, beginning from Galile even unto Jerusalem here, with thy doctrine and false miracles; and now thinkest thou to flee the merited punishment that befiteth thee by feigning to be mad? As God liveth, thou shall not escape it! And having said this he commanded his servants to smite him with buffetings and kicks, so that his understanding might come back into his head. The derision which he then suffered at the hands of the high Priests' servants is past belief for they zealously devised new inventions to give pleasure to the council ... afterwards they led him bound to the Governor, who secretly loved *Jesus*. Whereupon he thinking that Judas was *Jesus* made him enter into his chamber and spoke to him, asking him for what cause the chief Priest and the people had given him into his hands.

'Judas answered: "If I tell thee the truth, thou wilt not believe me, for perchance thou art deceived as the (Chief) Priests and the Pharisees are deceived".

'The Governor answered (thinking that he wished to speak concerning the law): "Now knowest thou not that I am not a Jew? But the (Chief) Priests and the elders of thy people have given thee into my hand; wherefore tell the truth, that I may do what is just, For I have power to set thee free and to put thee to death".

'Judas answered: "Sir, believe me, if thou put me to death, thou shalt do a great wrong for thou shall slay an innocent person; seeing that I am Judas Iscariot, and not *Jesus* who is a magician, and by his art hath so transformed me".

'When he heard this, the Governor marveled greatly, so that he sought to set him at liberty. The Governor therefore went out, and smiling said "In the one case, at least, this man is not worthy of death, but rather of compassion. This man saith ... That he is not *Jesus*, but a certain Judas who guided the soldiery to take *Jesus*, and saith that *Jesus* the Galilean hath by his magic art so transformed him, wherefore, if this be true, it were a great wrong to kill him, seeing that he were innocent. But if he is *Jesus* and denieth that he is, assuredly he hath lost his understanding and it were impious to slay a mad man".

'Then the chief Priest and elders of the people with the scribes and Pharisees, cried out with shouts, saying: "He is *Jesus* of Nazareth, for we know him; for if he were not the malefactor we would not have given him into thy hands. Nor is he mad, but rather malignant, for with this devise he seeketh to escape from our hands and the sedition that he would stir up if he should escape would be worse than the former".

'Pilate (for such was the Governor's name) in order to rid himself of such a case, said: "He is a Galilean, and Herod is king of Galilee: wherefore it pertaineth not to me to judge such a case, so take him ye to Herod".

'Accordingly they led Judas to Herod, who of a long time had desired that *Jesus* should go to his house. But *Jesus* had never been willing to go to his house, because Herod was a Gentile, and adored the false and lying Gods, living after the manner of unclean Gentiles. Now when Judas had been led thither, Herod asked him of many things, to which Judas gave answers not to the purpose, denying that he was *Jesus*.

'Then Herod mocked him, with all his court, and caused him to be clad in white as the fools are clad, and sent him back to Pilate saying to him, "Do not fail in justice to the people of Israel!"

'And this Herod wrote, because the chief Priests and scribes and the Pharisees had given him a good quantity of money. The Governor having heard that this was from a servant of Herod, in order that he also might gain some money, feigned that he desired to set Judas at liberty. Whereupon he caused him to be scourged by his slaves who were paid by the scribes to slay him under the scourges. But God who had decreed the issue, reserved Judas for the cross in order that he might suffer that horrible death to which he had sold another. He did not suffer Judas to die under the scourges, not withstanding that the soldiers scourged him so grievously that his body rained blood. Thereupon, in mockery they clad him in an old purple garment, saying: "It is fitting to our new king to cloth him and crown him! So they gathered thorns and made a crown, like those of gold and precious stones which kings wear on their heads. And this crown of thorns they placed upon Judas' head, putting in his hand a reed of scepter, and they made him sit in a high place. And the soldiers came before him, bowing down in mockery saluting him as king of the Jews. And they held out their hands to receive gifts, such as new kings are accustomed to give, and receiving nothing they smote Judas, saying: "Now how art thou crowned, foolish king, if thou wilt not pay the soldiers and servants?"

'The Chief Priests with the scribes and Pharisees, seeing that Judas died not by the scourges, and fearing lest, Pilate should set him at liberty, made a gift of money to the Governor, who having received it, gave Judas to the scribes and Pharisees as guilty unto death, Whereupon they condemned two robbers with him to the death of the cross.

'So they led him to mount Calvary, where they used to hang malefactors, and there they crucified him naked, for the greater ignominy!

'Judas truly did nothing else but cry out: "God, why hast thou forsaken me, seeing the malefactor hath escaped and I die unjustly?"

'Verily I say that the voice, the face and the person of Judas were so like to *Jesus*, that his disciples and believers entirely believed that he was *Jesus*; wherefore some departed from the doctrine of *Jesus*, believing that *Jesus* had been a false prophet and that by magic art he had done the miracles which he did: For *Jesus* had said that he should not die till near the end of the world; for that at that time he should be taken away from the world!

'But we that stood firm in the doctrine of *Jesus* were so encompassed with sorrow, seeing him die who was entirely like to *Jesus*, that we remembered not what *Jesus* had said. And so in company with the mother of *Jesus*, we went to Mount Calvary, and were not only present at the death of Judas, weeping continually, but by means of Nicodemus and Joseph of Abarimathia, we obtained from the Governor the body of Judas to bury it. Whereupon we took him down from the cross with such weeping as assuredly no one would believe, and buried him in the new sepulcher of Joseph; having wrapped him up in an hundred pounds of precious ointments.[104]

'Then returned each man to his house, Barnabas with John and James, his brother, went with the mother of *Jesus* to Nazareth.

'Those disciples who did not fear God, went by night and, stole the body of Judas and hid it, spreading a report that *Jesus* was raised again, whence great confusion arose. The high Priest then commanded, under pain of Anathema, that no one should talk of *Jesus* of Nazareth. And so there arose great persecution, and many were stoned and many beaten, and many banished from the land, because they could not hold their peace on such a matter'.

'The news reached Nazareth how that *Jesus*, their fellow citizen, having died on the cross was risen again whereupon, Barnabas prayed the mother of *Jesus* that she would be pleased to leave off weeping, because her son was risen again. Hearing this, the Virgin Mary, weeping said: "Let us go to Jerusalem to find my son. I shall die content when I have seen him".[105]

'The virgin returned to Jerusalem with Barnabas, James and John, on that day on which the decree of the high Priest went forth'.

'Whereupon, the virgin, who feared God, albeit she knew the decree of the high Priest to be unjust, commanded those who dwelt with her to forget her son... God who discerneth the heart of men knoweth that between grief at the death of Judas whom we believed to be *Jesus*, our Master, and the desire to see him raised again, we with the mother of *Jesus*, were consumed.

'So the angels that were guardians of Mary ascended to the third heaven, where *Jesus* was in the company of angels and recounted all to him'.

'Wherefore *Jesus* prayed God that He would give him power to see his mother and his disciples. Then the merciful God commanded his four favorite angels, who were Gabriel, Michael, Rafael, and Uriel, to bear *Jesus* into his mother's house and there keep watch over him for three days continually, suffering him only to be seen by them that believe in his doctrine'.

'*Jesus* came, surrounded with splendour, to the room where abode Mary, the virgin, with her two sisters and Martha and Mary Magdalene and Lazarus, and Barnabas, John, James and Peter, Whereupon, we fell down as dead. *Jesus* lifted up his mother and others from the ground saying: "Fear not, for I am *Jesus*; and weep not, for I am alive and not dead". We remained every one for a long time beside himself at the presence of *Jesus*, for we altogether believed that *Jesus* was dead. Then the virgin, weeping said: "Tell me, my son, wherefore God, having given thee power to raise the dead, suffered thee to die, to the shame of thy kinsfolk and friends, and to the shame of thy doctrine? For every one that loveth thee hath been as dead.[106]

'*Jesus* replied, embracing his mother: "Believe me mother, for verily I say to thee that I have not been dead at all; for God hath reserved me till near the end of the world". And having said this he prayed the four angels that they would manifest themselves, and give testimony how the matter had passed!

'Thereupon the angels manifested themselves like four shining suns; insomuch that through fear every one again fell down as dead!

'Then *Jesus* gave four linen cloths to the angels that they might cover themselves, In order that they might be seen and heard to speak by his mother and her companions. And having lifted up each one, he comforted us, saying: "These are the Ministers of God: Gabriel, who announceth God's secrets; Michael, who fighteth against God's enemies; Rafael, who receiveth the souls of those that die; and Uriel, who will call every one to the Judgement of God at the last day.

'Then the four angels narrated to the virgin how God had sent for *Jesus*, and had transformed Judas, that he might suffer the punishment to which he had sold another'.

'Then said Barnabas: "O Master is it lawful for me to question thee now, as it was lawful for me when thou dwelledst with us?"

'*Jesus* answered: "Ask what thou pleaseth, Barnabas, and I will answer thee"

'Then said Barnabas: "O Master, seeing that God is merciful, wherefore hath he so tormented us, making us believe that thou wert dead? And thy mother had so wept for thee that she had been nigh to death: and thou who art holy one of God, on thee hath God suffered to fall the calumny that thou wert slain amongst robbers on the mount Calvary?"

'*Jesus* answered: "Believe me Barnabas, that every sin, however small it be, God punisheth with great punishment, seeing that God is offended of sin. Wherefore, since my mother and my faithful disciples that were with me loved me a little with earthly love, the righteous God hath willed to punish this love with the present grief, in order that it may not be punished in the flames of Hell. And though I have been innocent in the world, since men have called me "God" and "son of God", God, in order that I be not mocked of the demons on the day of Judgement, hath willed that I be mocked of men in this world by the death of Judas, making all men to believe that I died upon the cross. And this mocking shall continue until the advent of Mohammed, the messenger of God who, when he shall come shall reveal this deception to those who believe in God's law".

'Having thus spoken, *Jesus* said: "Thou art just, O Lord our God, because to thee only belongeth honour and glory without end"[107]

'And *Jesus* turned himself to Barnabas and said: "See, Barnabas that by all means thou write my Gospel concerning all that hath happened through (out) my dwelling in the world. And write in like manner that which hath befallen Judas, in order that the faithful may be undeceived, and every one may believe the truth".

'Then answered Barnabas: "All will I do, if God will, O Master; but how it happened unto Judas, I know not, for I saw not all".

'*Jesus* answered: "Here are John and Peter who have seen all, and they will tell you all that has happened".

'And then *Jesus* commanded us to call his faithful disciples that they might see him. Then did James and John call together the seven disciples with Nicodemus and Joseph, and many other of the seventy-two and they ate with *Jesus*'.

'The third day, *Jesus* said: "Go to the mount Olives with my mother, for there will I ascend again unto heaven, and ye will see who shall bear me up"

'So there went all, saving twenty-five of the seventy-two disciples, who for fear had fled to Damascus And as we all stood in prayer, at mid-day came *Jesus* with a great multitude of angels who were praying to God: and the splendour of his face made us sore afraid, and we fell with our faces to the ground. But *Jesus* lifted us up, comforting us and saying: "Be not afraid, I am your Master".

'And he reproved many, who believed him to have died and risen again, "saying: Do ye then hold me and God for liars? For God hath granted to me to live almost unto the end of the world, even as I said unto you. Verily I say unto you, I died not, but Judas the traitor. Beware, for Satan will make every effort to deceive you, but be ye my witness in all Israel, and through out the world, of all things that ye have heard and seen.

'And having thus spoken, he prayed God for the salvation of the faithful, and the conversion of sinners. And his prayer ended, he embraced his mother, saying: "Peace be unto thee, my mother, rest thou in God who created thee and me". And having thus spoken, he turned to his disciples, saying: "May God's grace and mercy be with you".

'Then before our eyes the four angels carried him up into heaven.[108]

And yet, Ghulam Ahmad, founder of the Ahmadiyya Muslim Mission claimed on page 19 of the missions book that "... He (*Jesus*) did not go up to the heavens nor should it ever be supposed that he will ever again come from the heavens to the earth..."

There is a Hadith of the holy prophet Mohammed (PBH) that confirmed the return of *Jesus* from heavens toward the end of the world thus: "It is narrated on the authority of Huthaifa Bin Ousaid Al-Ghafari that the holy prophet (PBH) said: "The last hour will not be established until you see before it ten (events):

(1) The smoke,

(2) Ad-Dajjal,

(3) The beast

(4) The rising of the sun from the west,

(5) The descend of *Jesus*, son of Mary (May peace be upon him)

(6) The Gog and Magog,

(7) The three collapses: One in the east,

(8) One in the west

(9) One in Arabia, and

(10) At the end of fire which comes out of Al- Yemen, and a gale (of wind) throwing the people into the sea".

Again, the Holy Qur'an says: "And for their saying we have killed the Messiah, *Jesus*, son of Mary, the messenger of Allah, and they killed him not, nor did they cause his death on the cross, but he was made to them as such.

And certainly those who differ therein are in doubt about it. They have no knowledge about it, but only follow a conjecture, and they killed him not for certain"[109]. The holy Qur'an went on to say: "Nay, Allah exalted him in His presence. And Allah is ever mighty, wise".[110] The Holy Qur'an further says: "And *Jesus*, son of Mary shall be a sign for the coming of the hour (the day of Judgement): Therefore have no doubt about the (Hour) but follow ye me: this is the straightway.[111]

Despite the position of the Gospel of *Jesus*, the Hadith of the holy prophet Mohammed (PBH), and the Holy Qur'an, Ghulam Ahmad disagreed and held tenaciously to a wicked doctrine that "...he (*Jesus*) did not go up to the heavens nor should it ever be supposed that he will ever again come from the heavens to the earth ..."

Ironically, all the authorities he cited as the basis for his claims, none of them originated from the book of Moses (i.e. Torah), the Gospel of *Jesus* (i.e. the *INJIL*), the Hadith of the holy prophet Mohammed (PBH) and none originated from the Buddhist scriptures and the Holy Qur'an: The authorities he cited were all from uninspired sources as follows:

1. **P.W Rhys Davids,** *M.A. PhD. Buddhism. The Society for promoting Christian Knowledge, Northum Borland Avenue, Charring Cross W.C. 43, Queen Victoria Street, London E.C 1887.*

2. **By T. W Rhys Davids**, *1831* ***Indian Buddhism, The Hibbert Lectures –2nd Edition*** *Published by Williams and Norgate, 14, Henrietta St. Covent Garden, London 1891.*

3. **Sir M. M. Williams page 135 *"Buddhist Decaloque"***

4. **H. T. Principe** "***Tibet, Tartary and Mongolia"***

5. Ting A. ***"Record of the Buddhist Religion Practiced in India and the Malaya Archipelago (AD. 671 – 695)"*** Translated **by J. Takakusu** B.A, PhD. Page 223 – 224.

6. **Oldenberg, Dr. Herman *"Buddha: His life, His Doctrine, His order"***

7. **Francois Bernier London 1891 *"Travels in the Moghul Empire"***

8. **George Forster** "***Letters on a journey from Bengal to England***" R Fauldor London, 1808

9. **H.W. Bellews, C.S.I** "***Races of Afghanistan***" Thacker spink & co… 1884

10. **Balfour, Edward. Surgeon General** "***The Encyclopedia of India and of Eastern and Southern Asia* – 1885"**

11. **Rev. Joseph Wdf, D.D, LL.D** ***"Narration of a Mission to Bokhara in the years 1843 – 1845"*** John W. Parker, West Stand, London 1845

12. **George Moore, M.D** *"The lost Tribes"*

13. **Josephus Flavius** "***Antiquities***" *Translated by: Jewish W.M. Whiteson* London, Hurst Rees, Orme & Brown

14. **G.T. Vigne** Esg. "***A personal narrative of a visit to Chuzin, Cabul, in Afghanistan***" F.R.G.S London, EC 1840

15. **James Bryce, M.A. IL.D, F.R.S.E and Keith Johnson "*Encyclopedia of Geography*"** F.RG.S London 1880.

16. **Colonel G. Malleson, C.S.I** ***"History of Afghanistan"*** Published at the India Office 1878

17. ***L. P Ferrier, 1858 "History of the Afghans"*** *Translated by: W.M. Jesse Published John Murray, London.*

These were the authorities upon which all the claims by Ghulam Ahmad to Messiahhood, and that *Jesus* never went "up to the heaven, nor should it ever be supposed that he will ever again come from the heaven to the earth, that rather, he died at the age of 120 years at Srinagar, in Kashmir, and that his tomb is to be found in the khan Yar Street of that town.[112] Ghulam Ahmad also contradicted the Gospel of *Jesus*, the Hadith of the holy prophet Mohammed (PBH) and the Holy Qur'an thus: "... I might say again that *Jesus* (peace be on him) meeting the disciples after his crucifixion. His traveling up to Galilee, eating bread and meat; his display of wounds on his body: staying a night with the disciples at Emmaus; fleeing secretly ... there is no evidence in the Gospels that any one saw *Jesus* ascend to the heavens,..." [113]

All these academic theatrical arguments are a condemnation of oneself to hell punishment. *Jesus* said: "Believe me, mother for verily I say to thee that I have not been dead at all, for God hath reserved me till near the end of the world..." In an answer to Barnabas question when he came down from heaven when he was taken up by the Almighty God at the time of the betrayal of Judas, *Jesus* said: "Believe me, Barnabas, that every sin, however small it be, God punisheth with great punishment seeing that God is offended at sin. Wherefore, since my mother and my faithful disciples that were with me loved me a little with earthly love the righteous God hath willed to punish this love with the present grief, in order that it may not be punished in the flames of Hell. And though I have been innocent in the world, since men have called me "God" and "Son of God", God in order that I be not mocked of the demons on the day of Judgement, hath willed that I be mocked of men in this world by the death of Judas, making all men to believe that I died upon the cross. And this mocking shall continue until the advent of Mohammed, the messenger of God, who when he shall come shall reveal this deception to those who believe in God's law"[114] Again Barnabas reports: "And having thus spoken (on mount Olives), he prayed for the salvation of the faithful and the conversion of sinners. And his prayers ended, he embraced his mother, saying: "Peace be unto thee, my mother, rest-thou in God who created thee and me". And having thus spoken, he turned to his disciples saying: "May God's grace and mercy be with you". "Then before our eyes the four angels carried him up into heavens". And Ghulam Ahmad said: "There is no evidence in the gospels that anyone saw *Jesus* ascend to the heavens..."[115]

The Ahmadiyya Mission also published "100 Hadiths titled "The Riyadh as Salihi of Imam Nawawi, Translated from Arabic by Mohammed ZAFRULAKHAN". The forward by C.E Bosworth Professor of Arabic studies in the University of Manchester"

The 100 collections were designed to back up Ghulam Ahmad's claim against the Gospel of *Jesus* (the *INJIL*) the Hadith of the holy prophet (PBH) and the Holy Qur'an. His collections No 67, he said: "The Angel Gabriel told me that *Jesus*, son of Mary lived up to the age of one hundred and twenty years". This statement is purported to have been made by the holy prophet (PBH), and the Sahabi" that rendered it was not mentioned. And the authority was not disclosed, contrary to the tradition of Hadith of the holy prophet Mohammed

(PBH). This reinforces the belief that Ghulam Ahmad wanted to use it to support his theory that *Jesus* lived up to 120 years and died and buried in India. If Ghulam Ahmad was infact inspired, he should have been able to tell the world the year, month and day, *Jesus* died and buried in India; because the holy prophet Mohammed said in a Hadith, "that event is one of the major signs of the end of the world". *Jesus* said that in his second coming he would come with Elijah and Enoch. Ghulam Ahmad failed to tell the world where these two elect of God died and were buried.

"Jihad" is what is required just now to ward off the accursed Satan. As mentioned already, Jihad literally means an effort and/or an endeavour in the way of the Almighty Allah. The word does not mean, as it is erroneously supposed by many among non-Muslims, a fanatical war analogous to that denoted by the word "Crusade". A tradition of the Holy Prophet Mohammed (PBH) says: "The greatest Jihad is that which one launches against ones lusts" Thus Jihad signifies helping your religion, defending the truth, justice and equity, repelling aggression and tyranny, fighting temptations, educating and training your own spirit, and serving humanity.

The new call to respect only the beliefs of society in the guise of human right, and to regard any act against such beliefs as treason is a dangerous trend that must be resisted by Muslims the world over. The so-called civilized societies of the world, have accepted "single parent" as one of the human right principles, thus moving their societies and/or the world to an era to be dominated by bastards. Their societies and/or the world is now glutted by homosexual, lesbians, ritual killers etc. Immorality is now a status symbol. And *Jesus* once said "It were better to burn a city than to leave there an evil custom". Conficius says he who offends against Heaven has none to whom he can pray, and Mencius from the Conficius school says even the gaining of power over the whole world would not justify killing one man or committing a single act of unrighteousness to accomplish it.

Therefore, human life in this world of worries and woes; beset with difficulties dangers, pains and sorrows; it is repentance and amendment, and constant remembrance of Allah that can make them bearable: you will, never feel – abandoned as the unbelievers feels. You will feel that the Divine Friend (Allah) is ever with you to help you in your trials and tribulations, solve your difficulties, guide you in your plans and schemes and bestow upon you His grace and Mercy.

The so-called civilized societies are now making efforts to force it on others that law can only enforce what society believes to be right or wrong: That law must not lead public opinion on moral issues. This means evil in the world has reached a certain stage of rebellion and defiance. The laws instituted by Allah are to leave rebelliousness and defiance of God's law to gather momentum and then rush with fury to its own destruction. History has it, that mankind is often given a certain amount of respite, as a last chance; but failing repentance and amendment, its days are numbered. The believers, therefore, should not worry over the apparent worldly success of evil, but should get on with their own duties in spirit of trust in Allah.[116]

Prophet Noah's mission for example was to a wicked world, plunged in sin. The mission had a double character, as in the mission of all the prophet of Allah: it had to warn men against evil and call them to repentance and amendment and constant remembrance of Allah, it had to give them the glad tidings of Allah's grace and mercy in case they turned back to Allah: It was a guidance and mercy:

And yet, the unbelievers were even bold enough and prayed Noah thus: "O Noah thou hast disputed with us and (much) hast thou prolonged the dispute with us: Now bring upon us what thou threatenest us with, if thou speakest the truth.[117]

Noah's reply was "Truly, Allah will bring it on you if He wills, and then ye will not be able to frustrate it".[118] They were eventually destroyed. The same thing happened to the people of Rass, the Thamud, the Ad, the Pharaoh, the brethren of Lut, the companions of the Wood, and the people of Tubba etc.

Therefore abandon wicked doctrines devised by the accursed Satan, to destroy mankind, repent and amend, and be constant in remembrance of Allah. These are the keys to progress and prosperity in this life and the keys to paradise. Prosperity in life is not to be measured by wealth and worldly gains alone, but also by the health of the mind and the spirit. Worldly rank is not nobility of Heaven, but that of men, which is empty and ephemeral, unless grounded on man's inborn moral sense, and reflective of a hierarchy of true values.

CHAPTER THREE
WHO IS GOD ALMIGHTY

When I was a small boy I asked my father Salihun Bin Umar (Rahamatu LLahi Alaihi): "Who is God, and where is He?" He replied: "Mahmud, Mahmud, who taught you this?" I replied: "It is you Daddy". He replied: "God forbid! I do not remember saying anything like this to you". I was shocked at his reaction, so I was nervous and kept quiet. He called my mother Halimat Sa'adiya with a very angry voice. She rushed to meet me with my Dad. She asked: "I hope nothing is wrong?" My father replied – "Seat down, and listen to the amazing questions of your son about the Almighty God". She looked at me and asked: "About what?" My father replied: "About God". My mother cried: "O God I pray, the wicked in the community did not give him witchcraft. Did you eat food in anybody's house when you went out to play with your mates? She held my two ears and squeezed them. I felt the pain. This was the first time my father and mother joined in anger with me. As the last born I was always loved by them, and cared for tenderly. My shock increased; and I was shaking. My father held my hand and carried me on his laps to calm me down. I became genuinely afraid that the Almighty God must be something of intense fear.

In a calm tone, my father insisted to know where I got the idea of these questions: "Who is God, and where is He? I replied: "Every time you are in prayers, you always say: "O Lord, our God, I beseech Thee to bless me and my family and the end of my life". Again, before you leave for palace meeting with His Royal Highness, the OBA of Agbede, you always say to us "I will join you in farm later God willing: may God guide you on your way to the farm and in the farm". My mother opened her mouth and her two hands to her chest in total surprise at what I said. I concluded by saying: "I have since been expecting to see this Almighty God my father always mentions in his prayers and hardly any discussion, without him mentioning "God willing". On the way to the farm, inside the farm, and each time we were sent to fetch water from the stream, I was always with the hope of seeing this 'Almighty God' of my father to no avail. This is the reason; I summoned the courage to rush in to meet you immediately you concluded the 4pm prayers to see if I could find this God with you in this room".

My mother asked my father: "What do we do?" My father replied: "Halima, do you remember what that old Ilorin Mallam by name Jakpe and Mallam Mama Farin from Sokoto told me concerning this boy, the day his naming ceremony was performed?" My mother appeared not to remember anything; my father directed that I should be sent to one of the local Quranic schools in Agbede town. Consequently, he handed me over to one Mallam Bello, son of the Chief Imam of Agbede. The Mallam handed me over to live with his mother by name Halimat Sa'adiya. This means that my mother and my Mallam's mother had the same name.

My teacher, Mallam Bello, apart from teaching Qur'an to children was also buying and selling scents. Whenever his fellow Mallams came to him to buy scents from him, he used to say: "This one in this bottle is very good to use in prayers. God Almighty often accepts prayers of a supplicant when it is used". After about 7 months of staying with him and of hearing him mentioning God, I asked his mother who was looking after me: "Mother, who is God, and where can He be found?' She was a very gentle and kind woman (May the Rahamah of God be upon her) She showed me a lot of affection as a mother and was always teaching me Islam privately, quite different from the Quranic studies, her son was teaching us. She said to me in a very kind and solemn voice: "Mahmud, where do you hear this?" I could not reply fearing the trouble I had with my parent not to re-surface. I opened my eyes like a fool looking at her. She said to me: "Ok, Ok, come with me, your teacher will explain it to you. That is why your father brought you to him, so that he can teach you Islam". This calmed me down and was full of happiness within me. So we went to my teacher Mallam Bello. The mother explained the matter to him. He became very furious, and looked at me with anger and said: "Is that the reason why you do not pay attention to your Quranic studies. Let me warn you, I know you are a spoiled child talking nonsense". His Mother that tried to explain to him the need to use it as an opportunity to lead me into Islamic knowledge, was not listened to by him. So she took my hand and walked back to her room. The hostility of my teacher Mallam Bello, increased and I told my father, who promptly withdrew me from his school to another school headed by Mallam Muhammadu Odalumhe of Iyoko quarters, Agbede and finally to Mallam Ibrahim Jibril Emokpere of Uwazimoroh quarters, Agbede. I could not find any answer to my enquiry: "Who is God, and where can He be found?"

When I finished my primary school at Agbede in 1952 at the age of 18 years, my father directed that I should leave home for Kano by saying: "Go to Kano and begin your life with WALIYI Shaibu bin Mohammed (RahamatuLLahi Alaihi) that had been requesting that you come to him in Kano to complete both your Quranic studies and western education. Perchance you will find from him what you want in life". He offered prayers and blessed me and advised me as follows:

1. "The tongue is the enemy of the head from which it came. Therefore reason before you say anything and never you say anything before reasoning what to say" He held his tongue out of his mouth and repeated to me: "This is the enemy of the head" and

2. He said: "Mahmud before you take any decision in your life, evaluate all options available and then make a decision. Immediately you have decided on what to do never you turn back. Burn all the bridges behind you".

On 26th December 1952, I began my 5 days journey to Kano, and arrived in Kano in the morning of 1st January 1953, in the company of my late friend Alhaji A.M Ibrahim, I was well received by Waliyi Shaibu. After 3 months of my living with him, i.e. 14th April 1953, I went and greeted him. It was on a Wednesday after 4p.m. prayers, he touched my head and my nose, and asked me: "What is troubling your mind?" I answered by narrating to him how it all happened, and my consequent desire to have a convincing answer to my enquiry: "I want to know who is God, and where can He be found?' He kept quiet for a while and sat erect and said: "This is one of the reasons I asked your mother to convince your father to allow you come to me in Kano when you were much younger for your primary school and Quranic studies". He asked me "are you familiar with Dhikr" I replied: "Anything you ask me to do, I will try" He took a very deep breath and said: "Mahmud I am going to give you a Dhikr to perform for 26 Thursday nights, and what ever you dream about do not let anybody know except myself. In the night of Thursday recite after *Ishai* prayer:

1. Inna, anzalnahu to the end (i.e. Ch. 97 of the Holy Quran) 1000 times.

2. Sharabazu, kharabazu, rabazu bin Abdullahi. 510 times.

I kept on performing it as he instructed me. On the 17th Thursday night, I had a dream: A voice repeated the call: "Mahmud, God is Himself, of Himself and for Himself". I woke up, and quickly noted it down to report to my guardian - Waliyi Shaibu bin Mohammed (Rahamatu Lhahi Alaihi) the following day.

In the morning, I rushed to report to him what I was told in a dream. He smiled at me a very brilliant smile. The smile awoke in me a very strange feeling – a burning desire to study the Holy Qur'an, which I neglected up to that age of 18 years. Before this time, my interest was first and foremost to know "who God is, and where I can find Him" My increased respect for Shaikh Shaibu grew instantly in my heart. It was a very strange and unique feeling that ran through my mind within few seconds of my sitting on the floor, right in front of him.

He said to me, with his right hand on my head: "Come back to me after the 8pm prayers so that I call tell you the meaning of your dream. Come with a pen and paper". After the 8pm prayers I went back to him, and he got up from where he was sitting in the frontage of his house, and held my hand and I followed him to his secluded room. He said to me: "The following are the explanations of your dream:

1. "God is Himself" means, He is the beginning of every thing and nothing existed before Him. Anything, therefore, that has a beginning is not God, and can never be God. He is a spiritual Being, and it is Him alone that must be worshipped.

2. "God is of Himself", means nothing is possible without Him. This demand constant – remembrance of Him and

3. "God is for Himself," means He is the end of everything and nothing comes after Him. That is why the Holy Qur'an says 'God is the final goal and end of all journeys'. Everything comes from Him, exist by Him and end with Him". He recited chapter 112 of the Holy Qur'an thus:

    a. Say: He is Allah, the ONE (AND ONLY)

    b. Allah, the Eternal, Absolute,

    c. He begetteth not, nor is he begothen

    d. And there is none like unto Him.

When I decided to write this book, following the dream I had in room no 636, Marriot Hotel, Amsterdam, on 12th of March 1989 I discovered that it was not only myself that ever wanted to know who God is, and where He could be found. I discovered, through intensive research, that Philip, one of the disciples of the holy *Jesus*, once asked him: "Master, we are content to serve God, but we desire, however to know God. For Isaiah, the prophet said: "Verily thou art a hidden God". And God said to the holy Moses, His servant: "I am that which I am".

'*Jesus* (Peace be upon him)answered: Philip, "God is good without which there is naught that is good: God is a being without which there is naught that is; God is life without which there is naught that liveth; so great that he filleth all and is everywhere. He alone hath no equal. He hath had no beginning, nor will He ever have an end, but to everything hath He given a beginning and to everything shall He give an end. He hath neither father nor mother, He hath neither sons (in biological sense) nor brethren, nor companions. And because God hath no body, therefore He eateth not, sleepeth not, dieth not, walketh not, moveth not, but abideth eternally - without human similitude, for that He is incorporeal, uncompounded, immaterial, of the most simple substance. He is so good that He loveth goodness only: He is so just that when He punisheth or pardoneth, it cannot be gain said: In short, I say unto you, Philip, that here on earth thou cannot see Him nor know Him perfectly; but in His Kingdom thou shalt see Him for ever: Wherein consisteth all our happiness and glory"

'Philip enquired further: "Master what sayest thou? It is surely written in Isaiah that God is our father, how, then, hath He no sons?"

'*Jesus* (Peace be upon him) answered: "Thus are written in the prophets many parables, where thou oughtest not to attend to the letter, but to the sense. For all the prophets that are one hundred and forty-four thousand, whom God hath sent into the world, have spoken darkly. But after me shall come the splendour of all the prophets and holy ones, and shall shed light upon the darkness of all the prophets have said, because he is the messenger of God".

'But for now "I tell you verily that He is God, our Lord; father of all things, for that He created all things. But He is not a father after the manner of nature, for that He is capable of motion, without which generation is impossible. It is then, our God, whose in this world and the field where He soweth is mankind, and the seed is the word of God. So when the teachers are negligent in preaching the word of God, through being occupied in the business of the world, Satan soweth error in the heart of men, whence are come countless sects of wicked doctrine." Have mercy on Israel, O lord, our God, and look with pity, upon Abraham and upon his seed in order that they may serve thee with truth of heart. The disciples answered: "So be it, O Lord, our God!"[119]

As mentioned already, the nature of the Almighty God is taught by the Holy Qur'an. We must therefore avoid the pitfalls into which men and nations have fallen at various times in trying to understand the Almighty God. The first thing we must note is that His nature is so sublime, so far beyond our limited conceptions, that the best way in which we can realise Him is to feel that He is a personality, He in not a mere abstract conception of philosophy. He is near us; He cares for us and we owe our existence to Him. Secondly, He is the ONE and ONLY God, the ONLY ONE to whom worship is due, all other things or beings that we can think of are His creatures and are in no way comparable to Him. Thirdly, He is eternal, without beginning or end, Absolute, not limited by time or place or circumstance, the only Reality. Fourthly, we must never think of Him as having a son or a father and mother, for that would be to import animal qualities in our conception of Him. Fifthly, He is not like any other person or thing that we know or can be imagined. His qualities and nature are unique. We must therefore never conceive of God Almighty after our own pattern, an insidious tendency that creeps in at all times and among all people.

It is a grievous sin to associate anything with the Almighty God. A belief, therefore, that the Almighty God has an equal, or to worship something or some one other than Him, such as a stone, a tree, fire, a star, the sun. This is the greatest sin (Shirk) in the sight of the Almighty God. The holy Quran says: "Indeed Allah does not forgive associating anything with Him, and He forgives whatever is other than that to whomever He wills.[120] Indeed associating (anything with Allah) is a great wrong.[121] Indeed, the one who associate anything with Allah, Allah will forbid him the Garden, and his abode is fire.[122] Who ever ascribes partners to Allah (Shirk) and dies a polytheist (Mushrik) is definitely an inhabitant of the fire, just as any one who believes in Allah and dies a believer is an inhabitant of the Garden.

Jesus said: "As for the faithful, who are in seventy two grades, those of the two last grades, who shall have had the (Islamic) faith without good works... shall abide in hell seventy thousand years. After those years shall have passed the angel Gabriel shall come into hell, and shall hear them say: "O Mohammed, where are thy promise made to us, saying that those who have thy faith shall not abide in hell forevermore?"

"Then the angel of God shall return to paradise, and having approached with reverence the messenger of God, shall narrate to him what he hath heard. Then shall the messenger speak to God and say: "Lord, my God, remember the promise made to me thy servant, concerning them that have received my faith that they shall not abide for evermore in hell".

'God shall answer: "Ask what thou wilt, O my friend, for I will give thee all that thou askest".[123]

'Then shall the messenger of God say: "O Lord, there are of the faithful who have been in hell seventy thousand years. Where, O Lord is thy mercy? I pray thee, Lord, to free them from those bitter punishments".

'Then shall God command the four favorites angels of God that they go to hell and take out every one that hath the faith of His messenger, and lead them into paradise. And this they shall do'. "And such shall be the advantage of the faith of God's messenger, that those that shall have believed in him, even though they have not done any good works, seeing they died in this faith, shall go into paradise after the punishment of which I have spoken"[124]

God is ONE God. There is no God save Him, the Beneficent, the Merciful. God! Save Him there is no other God, the living, the Eternal. Thy glory we extol. *Jesus* (peace be upon him) says: "Verily I say unto you that God is spirit and truth, and so in spirit and in truth must He be worshipped.[125]

CHAPTER FOUR
MUHAMMAD (PBH) AN EVOLUTION OF THE ALMIGHTY GOD

As narrated in the introduction to this work, on the 12th March 1989, I had a dream in room 636, Marriott Hotel Amsterdam. In the dream, I was inside the compound of an old university, and a personality appeared before me, and handed to me ancient manuscripts, well bounded together. On them was an inscription "Muhammad (PBH) is an evolution of the Almighty God". He also handed to me a package which contained copies of holy books of all the prophets of the Almighty God; among them was a copy of the Holy Qur'an. The personality that handed them to me said "Mahmud, go and find the meaning of *Muhammad (PBH) is an evolution of the Almighty God* from these materials which I have handed to you".

I have since my return from Houston, Texas U.S.A to Nigeria on the 18th March 1989 been researching into the meaning "Muhammad (PBH) is an evolution of the Almighty God," on a part time basis. Consequently, I spent 14 years of intensive research work to find the meaning "Muhammad (PBH) is an evolution of the Almighty God". I used British library, Egyptian library, Bayero University, Kano Library, Christian Mission Library, Wusasa Zaria etc. The following are my findings from the scriptures and the Holy Qur'an:

Findings From The Scriptures

1. One day after preaching to his followers, John asked *Jesus*: "O Master, well hast thou spoken, but we like to know how man sinned through pride".

Jesus answered: "When God had expelled Satan, and the angel Gabriel had purified that mass of earth where on Satan spat, God created everything that liveth, both of the animals that fly and those that swim and he adorned the world with all that it hath. One day Satan approached unto the gates of Paradise, and seeing the horses eating grass, he announced to them that if that mass of earth should receive a soul there would be for them grievous labour; and that therefore it would be to their advantage to trample that piece of earth in such wise that it should be no more good for anything. The horses aroused themselves and impetuously set themselves to run over that piece of earth which lay among lilies and roses. Whereupon God gave spirit to that unclean portion of earth upon which lay the spittle of Satan, which Gabriel had taken up from the mass: and raised up the dog, who, barking, filled the horses with fear, and they fled! Then God gave His soul to man, while all the holy angels sang: "Blessed be thy holy name, O God our Lord."

'Adam, having sprung up upon his feet, saw in the air a writing that shone like the sun, which said: "There is only one God and Mohammed is the messenger of God". Whereupon Adam opened his mouth and said: "I thank thee, O Lord my God, that thou hast deigned to create me; but tell me, I pray Thee, what meaneth the message of these words: "Mohammed is messenger of God". Have there been other men before me?

Then said God: "Be thou welcome, O my servant Adam, I tell thee that thou art the first man whom I have created. And he whom thou hast seen (mentioned) is thy son, who shall come into the world many years hence, and shall be my messenger, for whom I have created all things; who shall give light to the world when he shall come, whose soul was set in a celestial splendour sixty thousand years before I made anything".

'Adam besought God, saying: "Lord, grant me this writing upon the nails of the fingers of my hands". Then God gave to the first man upon his thumbs that writing..."[126]

When Adam and Eve were driven from paradise for hearken to Satan whereupon Adam turning himself round saw it written above the gate, "There is only one God, and Mohammed is messenger of God". Whereupon, weeping, he said: "May it be pleasing to God: O my son, that thou come quickly and draw us out of misery"[132A].

'And thus', said *Jesus*, "sinned Satan and Adam through pride, firstly by despising man, and the other by wishing to make himself equal with God." Because in deceiving Adam and Eve Satan said to Eve; presenting himself like a beautiful angel, "wherefore eat ye not of those apples and of corn?"

'Eve answered: "Our God hath said that eating thereof we shall be unclean, and therefore he will drive us from paradise".

'Satan answered: "He saith not the truth" Thou must know that God is wicked and envious, and therefore he brooketh no equals but keepeth every one for a slave. But if thou and thy companion do according to my counsel, ye shall eat of those fruits even as of the others, but like God ye shall know good and evil, and ye shall do that which ye please, because ye shall be equal to God".[127]

This "equality" that is hateful to God, the accursed Satan has devised in "Trinity". The Satan knows that God hates setting up rivals with Him, and in ensuring that the scriptures are contaminated, introduced the doctrine of "Trinity" in the Bible to perfect his plans to destroy mankind.

Jesus (Peace be upon him) said: "Think ye perchance that God hath creased his messengers to be rival; who should be fain to make himself equal with God! Assuredly not, but rather as his good slave, who should not will that which his Lord willeth not.Ye are not able to understand this because ye know not what a thing is sin. Wherefore hearken unto my words, verily, verily, I say unto you, sin cannot arise in man save as a contradiction of God, seeing that only is sin which God willeth not: insomuch that all that God willeth is most alien from sin. Accordingly if our high Priests and Priests, with the Pharisees, persecuted me because the people of Israel hath called me God they would be doing a thing pleasing to God, and God would reward them; but because they persecute me for a contrary reason, since they will not have me say the truth, how they have contaminated the book of Moses and that of David, prophets and friends of God, by their traditions and therefore hate me and desire my death, therefore God hath them in abomination.[128]

2. *Jesus* said: "I therefore say unto you that the messenger of God is a splendour that shall give gladness to nearly all that God hath made, for he is adorned with the spirit of understanding, and of counsel, the spirit of wisdom and might, the spirit of fear and love, the spirit of prudence and temperance, he is adorned with the spirit of charity and mercy, which he hath received from God three times more than He hath given to all His creatures. O blessed time, when He shall come to the world! Believe me that I have seen him and have done him reverence, even as every prophet hath seen him: seeing that of his spirit God giveth to them prophecy. And when I saw him my soul was filled with consolation, saying: "O Mohammed, God be with thee, and may he make me worthy to untie your shoelatchet, for obtaining this I shall be a great prophet and holy one of God."[129]

3. Andrew one of the disciples of *Jesus* said to *Jesus*: "Thou have told us many things of the Messiah, therefore of thy kindness tell us clearly all". And in like manner the other disciples besought him".

'Accordingly *Jesus* said: "Every one that worketh, worketh for an end in which he findeth satisfaction. Wherefore I say unto you that God, verily because He is perfect, hath not need of satisfaction, seeing that He hath satisfaction Himself. And so, willing to work, He created before all things the soul of his messenger, for whom He determined to create the whole, in order that the creatures should find joy and blessedness in God, whence His messenger should take delight in all His creatures which He hath appointed to be His slaves... Verily I say unto you, that every prophet when he is come hath borne to one nation only the mark of the mercy of God. And so their words were not extended save to that people to which they were sent. But the messenger of God, when he shall come, God shall give to him as it were the seal of His Hand, insomuch that he shall carry salvation and mercy to all the nations of the world that shall receive his doctrine. He shall come with power upon the ungodly , and shall destroy idolatry, insomuch that he shall make Satan confounded for so promised God to Abraham, saying: "Be hold in thy seed I will bless all the tribes of the earth and as thou hast broken in pieces the idols, O Abraham, even so shall thy seed do".[130]

4. 'Andrew said: "Master, tell us some sign, that we may know him".

'*Jesus* answered: "He will not come in your time, but will come some years after you, when my gospel shall be annulled, insomuch that there shall be scarcely thirty faithful. At that time God will have mercy on the world, and so He will send His messenger, over whose head will rest a white cloud, whereby he shall be known of one elect of God, and shall be by Him manifested to the world. He shall come with great power against the ungodly , and shall destroy idolatry upon the earth. And it rejoiceth me because that through him our God shall be known and glorified and I shall be known to be true, and he will execute vengeance against those who shall say that I am more than man. Verily I say unto you that the moon shall minister sleep to him in his boyhood and when he shall be grown up, he shall take her in his hands. Let the world beware of casting him out because he shall slay the idolaters, far many more than were slain by Moses, the servant of God, and Joshua who spared not the cities which they burnt, and slew the children; for to an old wound one applieth fire.

"He shall come with truth more clear than that of all the prophets, and shall reprove him who useth the world amiss. The towers of the city of our father shall greet one another for joy: and so when idolatry shall be seen to fall to the ground and confess me a man like other men, verily I say unto you the messenger of God shall be come".[131]

5. "When the prayer was done, his disciples again drew near to *Jesus*, and he opened his mouth and said: "Draw near, John, for today will I speak unto thee of all that thou hast asked. Faith is a seal, whereby God sealeth his elect: which seal He gave to His Messenger (Mohammed) at whose hands every one that is elect hath received faith. For even as God is one, so is the faith one. Wherefore God, having created before all things His messenger, gave to him before aught else the faith which is as it were a likeness of God and of all that God hath done and said. And so the faithful by faith seeth all things, better than one seeth with his eyes; because the eyes can err, nay they do almost always err; but faith erreth never, for it hath for foundation God and His word. Believe me that by faith are saved all the elect of God. And it is certain that without faith it is impossible for any one to please God. Wherefore Satan seeketh not to bring to naught fasting; and prayer, alms and pilgrimages, nay rather he inciteth unbelievers thereto, for he taketh pleasure in seeing man work without receiving pay. But he taketh pains with all diligence to bring faith to naught, wherefore faith ought especially to be guarded with diligence, and the safest course will be to abandon the "wherefore", seeing that the 'wherefore" drove men out of paradise and changed Satan from a most beautiful angel into a horrible devil."[132]

6. The high Priest said to *Jesus*: "In the book of Moses it is written that our God must send us the Messiah, who shall come to announce to us that which God willeth and shall bring to the world the mercy of God. Therefore I pray thee tell us the truth, arth thou the Messiah of God whom we expect?"

Jesus answered: "It is true that God hath so promised, but indeed I am not he, for he is made before me, and shall come after me".

The high Priest said to *Jesus*: "By thy words and signs at any rate we believe thee to be a prophet and an holy one of God, wherefore I pray to thee in the name of all Judea and Israel that thou for love of God shouldst tell us in what wise the Messiah will come".

Jesus answered: "As God liveth, in whose presence my soul standeth, I am not the Messiah whom all the tribes of the earth expect, even as God promised to our father Abraham, saying: "In thy seed will I bless all the tribes of the earth". But when God shall take me away from the world, Satan will raise again this accursed sedition, by making the impious believe that I am God and son of God, whence my words and my doctrine shall be contaminated, insomuch that scarcely shall there remain thirty faithful ones; whereupon God will have mercy and will send His messenger for whom He hath made all things; who shall come from the South (of Jerusalem) with power, and shall destroy the idols with the idolaters, who shall take away the dominion from satan which he hath over men. He shall bring with him the mercy of God for salvation of them that shall believe in him, and blessed is he who shall believe his words".[133]

7. The high Priest asked *Jesus* thus: "How shall the Messiah be called, and what sign shall reveal his coming?

Jesus answered: "The name of the Messiah is admirable, for God Himself gave him the name when he had created his soul, and placed it in a celestial splendour. God said: 'Wait Mohammed; for thy sake I will to create paradise, the world and a great multitude of creatures, whereof I make thee a present, insomuch that whoso shall curse thee shall be accursed. When I shall send thee into the world I shall send thee as my messenger of salvation, and thy word shall be true, insomuch that heaven and earth shall fail, but thy faith shall never fail". 'Mohammed in his blessed name'.[134]

8. Andrew one of the disciples of *Jesus* once asked him: "now how shall the truth be known?"

Jesus answered: "Everything that conformeth to the book of Moses, that receive ye for true; seeing that God is one the truth is one; whence it followeth that doctrine is one and the meaning of the doctrine is one; and therefore the faith is one. Verily I say unto you that if the truth had not been erased from the book of Moses, God would not have given to David our father; the second. And if the book of David had not been contaminated, God would not have committed the Gospel to me; seeing that the Lord our God is unchangeable, and hath spoken but one message to all men. Wherefore, when the messenger of God shall come, he shall come to cleanse away all wherewith the ungodly that have contaminated my book".[135]

9. "*Jesus* went into the wilderness beyond Jordan with his disciples, and when the midday prayer was done he sat down near to a palm-tree, and under the shadow of the palm-tree his disciples sat down"

'Then said *Jesus*: "So secret is predestination, O brethren, that I say unto you, verily, only to one man shall it be clearly known. He it is whom the nations look for, to whom the secrets of God is so clear that, when he cometh into the world, blessed shall they be that shall listen to his words, because God shall overshadow them with His mercy even as this palm-tree overshadow us. Yea, even as this tree protecteth us from the burning heat of the sun even so the mercy of God will protect from the Satan them that believe in that man".

The disciples asked *Jesus*: "O master, who shall that man be of whom thou – speakest, who shall come into the world?"

'*Jesus* answered with joy of hearth: "He is Mohammed, messenger of God and when he cometh into the world, even as the rain maketh the earth to bear fruit when for a long time it hath not rained, even so shall he be occasion of good works among men, through the abundant mercy which he shall bring. For he is a white cloud full of the mercy of God, which mercy God shall sprinkle upon the faithful like rain".[136]

10. Barnabas one of the disciple and secretary of *Jesus* once asked *Jesus*: "O master, hath paradise light from the sun as this world hath?"

Jesus answered: "Thus hath God said to me, O Barnabas: "The world wherewith ye men that are sinners dwell hath the sun and the moon and the stars that adorn it for your benefit and your gladness; for this have I created them"

"Think O ye, then, that the house where my faithful dwell shall not be better? Assuredly, ye err, so thinking: For I, your God, am the sun of paradise, and my messenger (Mohammed) is the moon who from me receiveth all and the stars are my prophets which have preached to you my will; wherefore my faithful, even as they received my word from my prophets here, shall in like manner obtain delight and gladness through them in the paradise of my delights".[137]

The Finding from the Holy Qur'an and Hadith

1. The Holy Qur'an says: "Islam takes its hue from Allah, and who can give a better hue than Allah. It is He whom we worship".[138]

2. Allah's revelation being continuous, all people are invited to accept its completion in Islam, and controversies wiped out.[139] Muhammad (PBH) is the living exponent of the message of Allah as a whole.

3. Muhammad (PBH) says: under the command of the Almighty God: "Say: If ye do love Allah, follow me, Allah will love you and forgive you your sins: For Allah is oft forgiving, most merciful.[140] Islam means, bowing only, to the Will of Allah.

4. If any one desires a religion other than Islam, (i.e. Total Submission to the Will only of Allah), Never will it be accepted of him; and in the hereafter he will be in the ranks of those who have lost[141] Islam is not a sect or an ethnic religion. It was the religion preached by all the earlier prophets. It was the truth taught by all the inspired books. In essence, it amounts to a consciousness of the Will and Plan of Allah and a Joyful submission to that Will and Plan. If any one wants a religion other that that, he is false to his own nature, as he is false to Allah's Will and Plan. Such person cannot expect guidance for he has deliberately renounced guidance.[142] On such people rests the curse of Allah, of His angels and of all mankind.

5. The Holy Qur'an says: "O ye who believe fear Allah as He should be feared, and die not except in a state of Islam.[143]

6. He who obeys the messenger, obeys Allah but if any turn away, we have not sent thee to watch over them.[144] The messenger (Muhammad (PBH) was sent to preach, guide, instruct and show the right/divine way, not to drive people to good. That is not Allah's plan which trains the human will. The messenger's duty is therefore to convey the message of Allah, in all the ways of persuasion that are open to him. If men perversely disobey that message, they are not disobeying him, but they are disobeying Allah. In the same way, those who obey the messenger are obeying Allah. They are not obliging the messenger: they are seriously doing their duty.

7. The Holy Qur'an requires a belief not only in its own truth, but also in the uncontaminated truth of previous scriptures to the prophets of different nations of the world.[145] The Holy Qur'an says "Every nation had a messenger". Again[146] Says "And certainly we sent messengers before thee: There are some we have mentioned to thee and there are some we have not mentioned to thee".

Thus the Holy Qur'an accepts the uncontaminated truth of the sacred Books of the world and hence it is again and again spoken of as a book verifying that which is before it.

Therefore the basis of the relation in which the Holy Qur'an stands to other uncontaminated scriptures is that they are all members of one indivisible family; they all have a Divine origin.

8. The Holy Qur'an comes as a judge to decide the differences between the various religions[147] "Certainly we sent messenger to nations before thee… and We have not revealed to thee, (the) book except that thou mayest make clear to them that about which they differ"

The Holy Qur'an proclaims that prophets had been raised in every nation and therefore every nation had received guidance from God, yet nation differed from nation even in the essentials of faith. The position of the Holy Qur'an was therefore, essentially that of a judge deciding between these various claimants.

The Holy Qur'an explains all obscurities. It makes clear what is obscure in the earlier scriptures and explains fully what they stated briefly, according to the prophecy of *Jesus* (peace be upon him).

9. Revelation according to the Holy Qur'an is not only universal, but also progressive and it attains perfection in the final revelation (which is the holy Qur'an).

10. A revelation was granted to each nation according to requirement and to each age in accordance with the capacity of the people of that age. As the human brain became more and more developed, more and more light was cast by revelation on matters relating to the unseen, on the existence and attributes of the Divine Being, on the nature of revelation from Him, on the requital of good and evil, on life after death, and on paradise and Hell. It is for this reason that the Holy Qur'an is again and again called a Book "that makes manifest". It shed complete light on the essentials of faith and makes manifest what had hitherto of necessity remained obscure. This was why Jesus said[148] "I have yet many things to say unto you, but ye cannot bear them now. How beit when he the spirit of truth is come, he shall guide you into all truth; for he shall not speak of himself, but

whatsoever he shall hear that shall he speak; and he will show you things to come".

11. Finally it is for all these reason that the Glorious Qur'an declares... "This day have I perfected for you (Mankind and Jinn) your religion, and completed my favour to you, and chose for you Islam as a religion".[149]

CHAPTER FIVE
EVILS OF THE WORLD AND THE STRAIGHT PATH TO SALVATION

Rebelliousness is now a status symbol. The arrogant sinners now have the impudence to accuse righteous people of intolerance and morality as an uncivilized behaviors. Take the case of pornography for example: There had been complaints that pornographic materials are evil and the world would be better without them. A legal argument orchestrated by the accursed Devil suddenly emerged on the scene that "Pornographic materials should by law be tolerated". Similarly homosexual practices have been considered immoral, but Wolfenden Committee report in Great Britain recommended that it be tolerated and should therefore not be made an object of legislation. What an irony! In the United States of America, "Single parents" children i.e. bastards, are now populating the country in the guise of human right: The same with sodomy as men now have right to marry fellow men and women now marry follow women, all in the name of western values and human right. Homosexual practices are now predominate in Morocco and indeed Arab world according to BBC interview with a movie Director on 31/04/03.

In Nigeria, "blood money" is now in vogue: Infant babies are stolen from their mothers and slaughtered to worship the accursed satan for money; dead and buried people are exhumed and their head cut off for sale to ready buyers to worship the accursed Devil for power and money. Insecurity of life and property has become a way of life. *Jesus* (peace be upon him) said: "verily I say unto you that it were better to burn a city than to leave there an evil custom"[150]. And the holy prophet Mohammed (PBH) said: "under the law instituted by Allah, when evil reaches a certain stage of rebellion and defiance, it is left to gather momentum and to rush with fury to its own destruction: It is given a certain amount of respite, as a last chance: but failing repentance, its days are numbered"[151]. The God fearing therefore should not worry themselves over the apparent worldly success of evil. Worldly power, glory, wealth, position and all that men scramble for, are but a fleeting show. He who offends against God, has none to whom he can pray. Even the gaining of power over the whole world, would not justify killing one man or committing a single act of unrighteousness to accomplish it.

A Hadith tells us: "When Sodomy becomes popular among a certain people, God forsakes those people and God cares not if these people are killed in a forest"[152] Another Hadith tells us: "A Sodomist is a cursed person: God's curses be on him who commits Sodomy" the prophet (PBH) repeated this three times[153].

Hadrat Abu Hurairah (may Allah be pleased with him) relates that the Holy prophet of God (PBH) observed: "The faith of these three persons is never acceptable to Allah:

1. The Sodomist and the catamite;

2. Two women who maintain unnatural relationship with one another; and

3. A tyranical King (Tabrani)

Remember *Jesus* (peace be upon him) said: "As for the faithful, who are in seventy-two grades, those of the two last grades, who shall have the faith (i.e. Islamic faith) without good works: the one being sad at good works, and the other delighting in evil they shall abide in hell seventy thousand years. After those years shall the angel Gabriel come into hell, and shall hear them say: "O Mohammed, where are the promises made to us that those who have thy faith shall not abide in hell for evermore?" '... then shall God command the four favorite angels of God that they go to hell and take out every one that hath the faith of His messenger and lead them into paradise'. This is the faith that is not acceptable to God Almighty if one is a Sodomist and/or a catamite, i.e. one that has sexual relation with animals. The only way out is Repentance and Amendment. Hadrat Abu Hurairah (may Allah be pleased with him) concludes that the holy prophet (PBH) observed that "He who performs an act of sodomy with a woman (or man) is an infidel, and Bin Amir relates that the prophet (PBH) observed that – "He who uses the anus of a woman for sexual act is a cursed one[154] Ibn Abass (may Allah be pleased with him) reports that the holy prophet (PBH)observed: "The Almighty Allah would not even look at a person who commits sodomy with a male person or performs a sodomist act with a woman"[155]

Allah gives every race and every individual a chance and when the race or individual fails to Repent and Amend, he or it must fall and give place to others. [156]"History has shown that man acting by himself and without religion, is unable to break the chains that oppress him, without sinking in the process into deeper slavery". This negates the foolish argument in the

Western World, that "If the people in a particular community governed by law very strongly want something to be legitimized, and if those who want it criminalized will not actually suffer from the practice, this is a Prima Facia reason for legitimizing the practice"[157] This is the basis of western values: legitimizing illegitimate which should be resisted by the people of God Almighty. Conduct that is repellent to morality must be treated as a criminal act if such is not enforced by law, society itself will disintegrate. Therefore to act against such a setting is a kind of treason. The consensus morality theory advanced by Devlin is sheer nonsense: That is "The people who hold with passion the belief that homosexual practices between consenting males are immoral are suffering from prejudices, and should learn the moral lesson of toleration"[158]. This is sheer nonsense and a sign of one that has strayed far away from moral base.

What God hates, must be hated by every God fearing person, and similarly, what God likes, must be liked by every God fearing person. The holy *Jesus* (peace be upon him) emphasized this point in his Gospel[159]. The messenger of God (the promised messiah) the holy Prophet Muhammad (PBH) once observed "That Hadrat Musa (Moses) was asked by the Almighty God thus: "O Musa (Moses), you have been privileged to talk with me, a favour not granted to any one before you. Now Musa, tell me what have you ever done for me?" Hadrat Musa (peace be upon him) replied: "I perform regular prayers, fasting, payment of *Zakat*, kindness to others, fulfillment of promises etc. The Almighty God replied: "All are for your own good, O Musa; Then Hadrat Musa (Moses) prayed the Almighty God to teach him how to do something exclusively for Him". The Almighty God replied: "Well said, O Musa. There are only two ways to do something exclusively for me:

(i) Hate him that hates Me, and

(ii) Love him that loves Me"

The consensus morality theory that advocates the maxim 'that law can only enforce what society believes to be right, and therefore law must only follow, and not lead public opinion on moral issues, suggest to mankind to tolerate what is hateful to the Almighty God. Conficius tells us, that he who offends against Heaven has none to whom he can pray. And unless one recognizes the imperatives of Heaven, one cannot be a noble man. Therefore Heaven's imperatives in the minds of men serve as the fulcrum. It is for this reason Locke's claim in his letter on Toleration in the case of religious belief, can be considered as the hand work of Satan to lead mankind against their creator Allah. It is the view of Locke that "intolerance in the case of religious belief is fundamentally irrational, since people cannot be compelled to hold religious beliefs other than those, they infact hold"[160]. For Locke, religious belief is crucially a matter of individual conscience which cannot be subjected to the will (of God) that "any attempt to force people to hold orthodox religious beliefs are doomed to failure". What this means is that Godliness is now "Orthodox religious beliefs", which Locke says should be ignored in favour of societal beliefs grounded on immorality.

Neither man nor Jinn was called by the Almighty God to witness the creation of the heavens and earth. And heavens and earth were not created by God for mankind to behave as he will. The holy *Jesus* said that God sent at different times a total of 144,000 prophets to teach mankind "righteousness" as the key to paradise. Locke tells us that societal beliefs now out-weigh that teaching, and calls it "Western Values". This is a case of obstinate rebellion and ingratitude to the Almighty God. The Almighty God is the final goal and the end of all journeys. Who ever expects to meet Him let him begin to work righteousness and be consistent in His worship, and admit no one as partner to Him. He is God, the ONE and ONLY; who is Himself, of Himself and for Himself.

The accursed Satan says: "God brooketh no equals"[161] and he used "equality with God" to deceive Adam and Eve out of Paradise. To destroy mankind completely, the Satan initiated "Trinity". *Jesus* (peace be upon him) says: "Who should be fain to make himself equal with God? "Assuredly not, but rather as His good slave who should not, will that which his Lord willeth not". *Jesus* (peace be upon him) said: "I am not God and I am not son of God. God our creator is God alone and I am God's servant". The following are cited from the Gospel of *Jesus*:

1. "Having finished his devotions, *Jesus* came down from the mountain with his disciples and met ten lepers, who from afar off cried out: *Jesus* son of David, have mercy on us! *Jesus* (peace be upon him) called them near him, and said unto them: 'what will ye of me, O brethren'. They all cried out: 'Give us health". *Jesus* (peace be upon him) answered: 'Ah, wretched that ye are, have ye so lost your reason for that ye say: "Give us health!" See ye not me to be a man like yourselves. Call unto our God that hat created you and He that is Almighty and merciful will heal you. With tears the lepers answered: "We know that thou art man like us, but yet an holy one of God and

a prophet of the Lord: wherefore pray thou to God, and he will heal us".[162]

2. *Jesus* went down, in the second year of his prophetic ministry, from Jerusalem, and went to Naim. Whereupon, as he drew nigh to the gate of the city, the citizens were bearing to the sepulcher the only son of his mother, a widow, over whom every one was weeping. Whereupon, when *Jesus* had arrived the men understood how that *Jesus*, a prophet of Galilee, was coming: and so they set themselves to beseech him for the dead man that he being a prophet should raise him up; which also his disciples did. Then *Jesus* feared greatly, and turning himself to God, said: "Take me from the world, O Lord, for the world is mad, and they will call me God!" and having said this, he wept".[163]

3. Quote: *Jesus* departed from Jerusalem after the Passover and entered into the borders of Caesarea Philippi. Whereupon, the angel Gabriel having told him of the sedition which was beginning among the common people, he asked his disciples, saying: "What do men say of me?"

   They said; 'some say that thou art Elijah, others Jeremiah and others one of the old prophet!

   Jesus asked: 'and ye; what say ye that I am?

   Peter answered: 'Thou art Christ Son of God'

   Then was *Jesus* angry, and with anger rebuked him saying: "Begone and depart from me, because thou art the devil and seekest to cause me offence!

   'And he threatened the eleven, saying: "Woe to you if ye believe this, for I have won from God a great curse against those who believe this":

'And he was fain to cast away Peter; whereupon the eleven besought *Jesus* for him, who cast him not away, but again rebuked him saying: "Beware that never again thou say such words, because God would reprobate thee!"

> Peter wept and said: "Lord, I have spoken foolishly: beseech God that He pardon me.
>
> Then said *Jesus*: "if our God willed not to show Himself to Moses his servant, or Elijah whom he so loved, nor to any prophet, will ye think that God should show Himself to this faithless generation? But know ye not that God hath created all things of nothing with one single word, and all men have had their origin out of a piece of clay? How, shall God have likeness to man? Woe to those who suffer themselves to be deceived of Satan!
>
> And having said this, *Jesus* besought God for Peter, the eleven and Peter weeping and saying: 'So be it, O blessed Lord our God"[164].

4. "At this time we with *Jesus*, by the word of the holy angel were gone to Mount Sinai, and there *Jesus* with his disciples kept the forty days, when this was past, *Jesus* drew nigh to the river Jordan, to go to Jerusalem. And he was seen by one of them who believed *Jesus* to be God. Whereupon, with greatest gladness crying ever 'Our God cometh! Having reached the city he moved the whole city saying: 'Our God cometh, O Jerusalem; prepare thee to receive him! And he testified that he had seen *Jesus* near to Jordan.

> Then went out from the city every one small and great, to see *Jesus*, insomuch that the city was left empty, for the women bare their children in their arms, and insomuch that they forgot to take food to eat.
>
> When they perceived this, the Governor and the high Priest rode forth and sent a messenger to Herod, who in like manner rode forth to find *Jesus*, in order that the sedition of the people might be quieted. Whereupon for two days they sought him in the wilderness near Jordan and the third day they found him, near the hour of midday, when he with his disciples were purifying themselves for prayer according to the book of Moses.

Jesus marveled greatly, seeing the multitude which covered the ground with people, and said to his disciples: 'perchance Satan hath raised sedition in

Judea. May it please God to take away from Satan the dominion which he hath over Sinners!

And when he had said this, the crowd drew nigh, and when they knew him they began to cry out: Welcome to thee O our God! And they began to do him reverence, as unto God. Whereupon *Jesus* gave a great groan and said: 'Get ye from before me, O madmen, for I fear lest the earth should open and devour me with you for your abominable words!' whereupon the people were filled with tenor and began to weep.[165] Then *Jesus* having lifted his hand in token of silence said: 'verily ye have erred greatly, O Israelites, in calling me a man, your God. And I fear that God may for this give heavy plague upon the holy city, handing it over in servitude to strangers. O a thousand times accursed Satan that hath moved you to this!

And having said this, *Jesus* smote his face with both his hands, whereupon arose such a noise of weeping that none could hear what *Jesus* was saying: Whereupon once more he lifted up his hand in token of silence, and the people being quieted from their weeping, he spoke once more: "I confess before heaven, and I call to witness everything that dwelleth upon the earth, that I am a stranger to all that ye have said: seeing that I am a man born of mortal woman, subject to the Judgement of God, suffering the miseries of eating and sleeping, of cold and heat, like other men, wherefore when God shall come to judge, my words like a sword shall pierce each one (of them) that believe me to be more than man.

And having said this, *Jesus* saw a great multitude of horsemen, whereby he perceived that there were coming the Governor with Herod and the high Priest.

Then said *Jesus*: 'Perchance they also are become mad'. When the Governor arrived there, with Herod and the high Priest, every one dismounted and they made a circle round about *Jesus*, insomuch that the soldiery could not keep back the people that were desirous to hear *Jesus* speaking with the Priest.

Jesus drew near to the Priest with reverence, but he was wishful to bow himself down and worship *Jesus*, when *Jesus* cried out: "Beware of that which thou doest Priest of the living God: Sin not against our God".

The high Priest answered: 'Now is Judea so greatly moved over thy signs and thy teaching that they cried out that thou art God, wherefore, constrained by the people, I am come hither with the Roman Governor and King Herod.

We pray thee therefore from our heart, that thou wilt be content to remove the sedition which is arisen on thy account. For some say thou art God, some say thou art son of God, and some say thou art a prophet.

Jesus answered: 'And thou, O high Priest of God, wherefore hast thou not quieted this sedition? Art thou also, perchance, gone out of thy mind? Have the prophecies, with the law of God, so passed into oblivion, O wretched Judea, deceived of Satan![166]

And having said this, *Jesus* said again: I confess before heaven and call to witness every thing that dwelleth upon the earth, that I am a stranger to all that men have said of me, to wit, that I am more than man. For I am man born of a woman, subject to the Judgement of God; that live here like as other men, subject to the common miseries. As God liveth, in whose presence my soul standeth, thou hast greatly sinned, O Priest, in saying what thou hast said. May it please God that there come not upon the holy city great vengeance for this sin!

Then said the Priest: 'May God pardon us, and do thou pray for us'

Then said the Governor and Herod: "Sir, it is impossible that man should do that which thou doest; wherefore we understand not that which thou sayest"

Jesus answered: "That which ye say is true, for God worketh good in man, even as Satan worketh evil. For man is like a shop, wherein whoso entereth with his consent worketh and selleth therein. But tell me, O Governor, and thou O king, ye say this because ye are strangers to our law; for if ye read the Testament and Covenant of our God ye would see that Moses with a rod made the water turn into blood, the dust into fleas, the dew into tempest and the light into darkness. He made the frogs and mice to come into Egypt, which covered the ground; he slew the first born, and opened the sea, wherein he drowned pharaoh. Of these things I have wrought none. And of Moses every one confesseth that he is a dead man at this present. Joshua made the sun to stand still, and opened the Jordan which I have not yet done. And of Joshua every one confesseth that he is a dead man at this present. Elijah made fire to come visibly down from heaven, and rain, which I have not done. And of Elijah every one confeseth that he is a man. And (in like manner) very many other prophets, holy men, friends of God, who in the power of God have wrought things which cannot be grasped by the minds of those who know not our God Almighty and merciful, who is blessed for evermore.[167]

Accordingly the Governor and the high Priest and the king prayed *Jesus* that in order to quiet the people he should mount up into a lofty place and speak to the people. Then went up *Jesus* on to one of the twelve stones which Joshua made the twelve tribes take up from the midst of Jordan, when all Israel passed over their dry shod and he said with a loud voice: 'Let our Priest go up into a high place whence he may confirm my words; thereupon the high Priest went up thither; to whom *Jesus* said distinctly, so that every one might hear:

(i) It is written in the Testament and Covenants of the living God that our God hath no beginning, neither shall He ever have and end.

The Priest answered: 'Even so is it written therein.

(ii) It is written there that our God by His word alone hath created all things.

'Even so it is, said the high Priest.

(iii) *Jesus* said: It is written there that God is invisible and hidden from the mind of men, seeing He is incorporeal and uncomposed without variableness"

'So it is, truly' said the high Priest

(iv) *Jesus* said: 'It is written there how that the heaven of heavens cannot contain Him, seeing that our God is infinite!

'So said Solomon the prophet', said the Priest. 'O *Jesus*'

(v) It is written there that God hath no need, forasmuch as He eateth not, sleepeth not, and suffereth not from any deficiency "So is it" said the Priest.

(vi) *Jesus* said: 'It is written there that our God is every where and that there is not any other God but He, who striketh down and maketh whole and doeth all that pleaseth him'. "So is it written" replied the Priest.

Then *Jesus* having lifted up his hands said: 'Lord' our God; this is my faith where with I shall come to thy Judgement; in testimony against every one that shall believe the contrary. And turning himself towards the people, he said: "Repent for from all that of which the Priest hath said that it is written in the book of Moses, the Covenant of God forever, ye may perceive your sin:; for that I am a visible man and a morsel of clay that walketh upon the earth, mortal as are other men. And I have had a beginning and shall have an end, and (am) such that I cannot create a fly over again!

Thereupon the people raised their voices weeping and said: "We have sinned, Lord our God, against thee; have mercy upon us". And they prayed *Jesus* every one that he would pray for the safety of the holy city, that our God in His anger should not give it over to be trodden down of he nations. Thereupon *Jesus*, having lifted up his hands, prayed for the holy city and for the people of God, every one crying: "So be it". "Amen"[168]

When the prayer was ended the Priest said with a loud voice: "Stay *Jesus*, for we need to know who thou art, for the quieting of our nation".

Jesus answered: "I am *Jesus*, son of Mary, of the seed of David, a man that is mortal and feareth God, and I seek that to God be given honour and glory".

The Priest said: "In the book of Moses it is written that our God must send us the Messiah, who shall come to announce to us that which God willeth, and shall bring to the world the mercy of God. Therefore I pray thee tell us the truth, art thou the Messiah of God whom we expect?"

Jesus answered: "It is true that God hath so promised, but indeed I am not he, for he is made before me, and shall come after me".

The Priest said: "By thy words and signs at any rate we believe thee to be a prophet and a holy one of God, wherefore I pray thee in the name of all Judea and Israel that thou for love of God shouldst tell us in what wise the Messiah will come".

Jesus answered: "As God liveth, in whose presence my soul standeth, I am not the messiah whom all the tribes of the earth expect, even as God promised to our father Abraham, saying: "in thy seed will I bless all the tribes of the earth. But when God shall take me away from the world Satan will raise again this accursed sedition, by making the impious believe that I am God and son of God, whence my words and my doctrine shall be contaminated, insomuch that scarcely shall there remain thirty faithful ones, whereupon God will have mercy upon the world and will send his messenger for whom He hath made all things; who shall come from the south with power and shall destroy the idols with the idolaters; who shall take away the dominion from Satan which he hath over men. He shall bring with him the mercy of God for salvation of them that shall believe in him and blessed is he who shall believe his words".[169] "Unworthy though I am to untie his hosen, I have received grace and mercy from God to see him".

Then answered the Priest, with the Governor, and the king saying: "Distress not thyself, O *Jesus* holy one of God, because in our time shall not this sedition be anymore seeing that we will write to the sacred Roman Senate in such wise that by imperial decree none shall any more call thee God or son of God"

Then *Jesus* said: "With your words I am not consoled, because where ye hope for light darkness shall come, but my consolation is in the coming of the messenger, who shall destroy every false opinion of me, and his faith shall spread and shall take hold of the whole world, for so hath God promised to Abraham our father. And that which giveth me, consolation is that his faith shall have no end, but shall be kept inviolate by God"

The Priest asked *Jesus*: "After the coming of the Messenger of God shall other prophet come?"

Jesus answered: "There shall not come after him true prophets sent by God, but there shall come a great number of false prophets, where at I sorrow. For Satan shall raise them up by the just Judgement of God, and they shall hide themselves under the pretext of my Gospel".

Herod asked: "How is it a just Judgement of God that such impious men should come?

Jesus answered: "It is just that he, who will not believe in the truth to his salvation, should believe in a lie to his damnation. Wherefore I say unto you, that the world hath ever despised the true prophets and loved the false, as can be seen in the time of Michaiah and Jeremiah. For every like loveth his like"

Then said the Priest: "How shall the Messiah be called, and what sign shall reveal his coming?"

Jesus answered: "The name of the Messiah is admirable, for God Himself gave him the name when He created his soul, and placed it in a celestial splendour.

God said: "Wait Mohammed, for thy sake I will to create paradise, the world, and a great multitude of creatures, whereof I make thee a present, insomuch that whoso shall curse thee shall be accursed. When I shall send thee into the world I shall send thee as my messenger of salvation, and thy word shall be true, in so much that heaven and earth shall fail, but thy faith shall never fail" "Mohammed is his blessed name"

Then the crowd lifted up their voices saying "O God send us the messenger O Mohammed, come quickly for the salvation of the world". [170]

5. *Jesus* said to his disciples after teaching them how constant remembrance of God is the key to paradise: "Ye needs must seek of the fruits of the field the wherewithal to sustain our life, for it is now eight days that we have eaten no bread. Wherefore I will pray to our God, and will await you with Barnabas (his secretary)".

So all the disciples and apostles departed by fours and by sixes and went their way according to the word of *Jesus*. There remained with *Jesus*, Barnabas, whereupon *Jesus* weeping said: "O Barnabas, it is necessary that I should reveal to thee great secrets, which after that I shall depart from the world, thou shalt reveal to it".

Then Barnabas weeping said: "Suffer me to weep, O master, and other men also, for that we are sinners. And thou that art a holy one and prophet of God it is not fitting for thee to weep so much".

Jesus answered: "Believe me, Barnabas that I cannot weep as much as I ought, for if men had not called me God, I should have seen God here as He will be seen in paradise, and should have been safe not to fear the day of Judgement. But God knoweth that I am innocent, because never have I harboured thought to be held more than a poor slave. Nay, I tell thee that if I had not been called God, I should have been carried into paradise when I shall depart from the world, whereas now I shall not go thither until the Judgement.

Now thou seest if I have cause to weep, O Barnabas, for this I must have great persecution, and shall be sold by one of my disciples for thirty pieces of money. Whereupon I am sure that he who shall sell me shall be slain in my name, for that God shall take me up from the earth, and shall change the appearance of the traitor so that every one shall believe him to be me; nevertheless, when he dieth an evil death, I shall abide in that dishonour for a long time in the world. But when Mohammed shall come, the sacred messenger of God, that infamy shall be taken away. And this shall God do because I have confessed the truth of the Messiah, who shall give me this reward, that I shall be known to be alive and to be a stranger to that death of infamy:

Barnabas said: "O master tell me who is that wretch for I fain would choke him to death. "Hold thy peace for so God willeth, and I cannot do otherwise, but see thou that when my mother is afflicted at such an event thou tell her the truth in order that she may be comforted."

Barnabas answered: "All this will I do O Master if God please"[171].

6. Then said *Jesus*: "ye speak the truth for now was Israel desirous to establish the idolatry that they have in their hearts, in holding me for God; many of whom have now despised my teaching saying that I could make myself lord of all Judea, if I confessed myself to be God, and that I am mad to wish to live in poverty among desert places, and not abide continually among princes in delicate living. Oh hapless man, that prizest the light that is common to flies and ants and despisest the light that is common only to angels and prophets and holy friends of God"... Even so then let man do for with the outward sight of his eyes and the inward sight of his mind he should seek to know God his creator and the good pleasure of His will, and should not make the creature his end which causeth him to lose the creator. For verily every time that a man beholdeth a thing, and forgeth God, who hath made it for man he hath sinned"[172].

7. Quote: *Jesus* having called together his disciples, sent forth by two and two through the region of Israel, saying: "Go and preach even as ye have heard"

Then they bowed themselves and he laid his hand upon their heads, saying: "In the name of God, give health to the sick cast out the demons, and undeceive Israel concerning me, telling them that which I said before the high Priest".

They departed therefore, all of them save Barnabas, with James and John; and they went through all Judea, preaching penitence even as *Jesus* had told them, healing every sort of sickness, insomuch that in Israel were confirmed the words of *Jesus* that God is one and *Jesus* is prophet of God, when they saw such a multitude do that which *Jesus* did concerning the healing of the sick.

Having passed through Judea the disciples returned to *Jesus*, who received them as a father receiveth his sons, saying: "Tell me how hath wrought the Lord our God? Surely I have seen Satan fall under your feet and ye trample upon him even as the vine dresser treadeth the grapes!"

The disciples answered: "O master, we have healed numberless sick persons, and cast out many demons which tormented men".

Jesus said: "God forgive you O brethren because ye have sinned in saying". We have healed; seeing it is God that hath done all.

Then said they: "We have talked foolishly; wherefore teach us how to speak". *Jesus* answered: "In every good work say: "God hath wrought" and in every bad one say: "I have sinned". "So will we do" said the disciples to him.

Then said *Jesus*: "Now what faith Israel, having seen God do by the hands of so many men that which God hath done by my hands?"

The disciples answered: "They say that there is one God alone and that thou art God's prophet".

Jesus answered with joyful countenance: "Blessed be the holy name of God, who hath not despised the desire of me His servant!"[173]

8. As God liveth in whose presence my soul standeth, God whould pardon Satan if Satan should know his own misery, and ask mercy of his creator, who is blessed for evermore.[174] Accordingly, brethren, I, a man, dust and clay that walk upon the earth say unto you: Do penance and know your sins. I say unto you brethren that Satan, by means of the Roman soldiery, deceived you when ye said that I was God. Wherefore, beware that ye believe them not, seeing they all fallen under the curse of God, serving the false and lying Gods; even as our father David invoketh a curse upon them saying: "The Gods of the nations are silver and gold, the work of their hands, that have eyes and see not, have ears and hear not, have noses and smell not, have mouth and eat not, have a tongue and speak not, have hands and touch not, have feet and walk not". Wherefore said David our father praying our living God, "like unto them be they that make them and trust in them"... To this did Satan desire to reduce you, O brethren, in making you believe me to be God; because I not being

asked to create a fly and being passable and mortal, I can give you nothing of use, seeing that I myself have need to everything. How, then could I help you in all things as it is proper for God to do?"[175]

9. "I tell you that He is God our Lord, father of all things, for that He hath created all things. But He is not a father after the manner of nature…" [176]

10. Then said *Jesus*: "See that for these twenty days we give ourselves to fasting and prayer, for God will have mercy upon you. Verily I say unto you God hath caused this dearth because here began the madness of men and the sin of Israel when they said that I was God, or son of God".[177]

11. "Then the Pharisees drew near to *Jesus* and said: "O master since thou alone in Israel knowest the truth, teach thou us". *Jesus* replied: "I say not that I alone in Israel know the truth, for this word "alone" appertaineth to God alone and not to others. For He is the truth, who alone knoweth the truth. Wherefore, if I should say so I should be greater robber, for I should be stealing the honour of God. And in saying that I alone knew God I should be falling into greater ignorance than all. Ye, therefore, committed a grievous sin in saying that I alone know the truth. And I tell you that, if ye said this to tempt me, your sin is greater still."[178]

12. "Then there drew nigh to *Jesus* a doctor, and said to him: "Good master tell me wherefore God did not grant corn and fruit to our fathers? Knowing that they must need fall, surely He should have allowed them corn, or not have suffered men to see it".

Jesus answered: "Man thou callest me good, but thou errest, for God alone is good"…[179]

13. "The disciples said: "O Master, exceedingly great are thy words, therefore have mercy upon us, for we understand them not".

Jesus said: "Then ye perchance that God hath created His messenger to be a rival, who should be fain to make himself equal with God? Assuredly not, but rather as his good slave, who should not will that which his lord willeth not. Ye are not able to understand this because ye know not what a thing is sin...[180]

14. "*Jesus* said: "Ought man then, because he, cannot find out the mode to deny the fact? Assuredly, I have never yet seen any one refuse health, though the manner of it be not understood for I know not even now how God by my torch healeth the sick. [181]

15. "Then said the disciple: "Verily God speaketh in thee, for never hath man spoken as thou speakest".

Jesus replied: "Believe me when God chose me to send me to the house of Israel; He gave me a book like unto a clear mirror which came down into my heart in such wise that all that I speak cometh forth from that book. And when that book shall have finished coming forth from my mouth; I shall be taken up from the world"

Peter asked *Jesus*: "O master is that which thou, now speakest written in that book?

Jesus replied: "All that I say for the knowledge of God and the service of God, for the knowledge of man and for the salvation of mankind all this cometh forth from that book, which is my gospel".

16. ...then the scribe gave thanks to *Jesus*, and said to him: "Lord, let us go to the house of thy servant, for thy servant will give meat to thee and to thy disciples.

Jesus replied: "I will come thither when thou wilt promise to call me "Brother" and not "Lord" and shalt say thou art my brother and not my servant".

The man promised, and *Jesus* went to his house. [182]

17. Lazarus said: "O master, I thank thee that thou makest the truth to be prized; therefore will God give thee great merit".

Then said Barnabas: "O master how speaketh Lazarus the truth in saying to thee: "thou shalt have merit" whereas thou sadist to Nicodemus that man meriteth naught but punishment? Shalt thou accordingly be punished of God?"

Jesus answered: "May it please God that I receive punishment of God in this world, because I have not served Him as faithfully as I was bound to do.

But God hath so loved me, by His mercy that every punishment is withdrawn from me, in so much that I shall only be tormented in another person. For punishment was fitting for me, for that men have called me God; but since I have confessed, not only that I am not God, as is the truth, but I have confessed also that I am not the Messiah, therefore God hath taken away the punishment from me, and will cause a wicked one to suffer it in my name so that the shame alone shall be mine. Wherefore I say to thee my Barnabas... God is pleased to grant His mercy to His servants when they confess that they merit hell for their sins".[183]

18. Barnabas asked *Jesus*: "O master is it lawful for me to question thee now as it was lawful for me when thou dwellest with us?"

Jesus answered: "Ask what thou pleasest Barnabas, and I will answer thee".

Barnabas said: O master, seeing that God is merciful, wherefore hath he so tormented us, making us to believe that thou wert dead? And thy mother hath so wept for thee that she hath been nigh to death: and thou, who art an holy one of God, on thee hath God suffered to fall the Calvary that thou wert slain amongest robbers on the mount Calvary".

Jesus answered: "Believe me, Barnabas that every sin however small it be, God punisheth with great punishment, seeing that God is offended at sin. Wherefore, since my mother and my faithful disciples that were with me loved me a little with earthly love, the righteous God hath willed to punish this love with the present grief in order that it may not be punished in the flames of Hell. And though I have been innocent in the world since men have called me "God" and "Son of God", God in order that I be not mocked of the demons on the day of Judgement, hath willed that I be mocked of men in this world by the death of Judas, making all men to believe that I died upon the cross. And this mocking shall continue until the advent of Mohammed, the messenger of God, who when he shall come, shall reveal this deception to those who believe in God's law".

Having thus spoken, *Jesus* said: "Thou art just O Lord our God, because to Thee only belongeth honour and glory without end.[184]

Despite these abundant evidences from the Gospel of *Jesus*, Christians the world over have continued with the impunity to uphold the wicked and absurd doctrine of "Trinity".

The holy Quran says:

a. The likeness of *Jesus* with Allah is surely as the likeness of Adam. He created him from dust, then said to him "Be" and he was[185].

b. And the Jews say: Ezra is the son of Allah, and the Christians say: The Messiah is the son of Allah. These are the words of their mouths. They imitate the saying of those who disbelieved before Allah's curse be on them! How they are turned away![186]

The Christian doctrine that *Jesus* Christ was the son of God was borrowed from earlier pagan people. Recent research has established the fact beyond all doubt. Infact, when St. Paul saw that the Jews would on no account, accept *Jesus* Christ as a messenger of God, he reintroduced the abolished sedition by Roman Senate during the reign of King Herod, and Pilate, in Jerusalem, so that it might become more acceptable to the pagans. This means that "Trinity" is a pagan doctrine, and not the Gospel of *Jesus.*

The Christians have taken their doctors of law and their monks for Lords besides Allah, and also the Messiah, son of Mary. And *Jesus* (peace be upon him) enjoined all and sundry to uphold his gospel: There is only one God, worship Him alone, there is no God but He. Be glorified from what they set up with Him.[187]

It is related in a Hadith that when this verse was revealed, Adi ibn Hatim, a convert from Christianity asked the Holy prophet Mohammed (PBH) as to the significance of this verse, for he said: "We did not worship our doctors of law and monks". The holy prophet (PBH) replied: "was it not that the people considered lawful what their priest declared to be lawful, though it was forbidden by God?"

Hatim replied "Yes, that is true."

The holy prophet (PBH) replied: "That is what the verse means".[188] Muslims who accord a similar position to their pirs or saints are guilty of the same error. What is required is Repentance and Amendment.

CHAPTER SIX
HOW IS ALLAH REMEMBERED

It has been stressed right from the beginning of this book, that the key to paradise is the much Remembrance of Allah. The reader has been deliberately kept in suspense, as to how best to remember Allah. The Torah (the book of Moses) stressed it, the *INJIL* (the Gospel of *Jesus)* emphasized it, the Hadith of the holy prophet Muhammad (PBH) stressed it, and the Holy Qur'an also stressed it. This chapter is to give you the secret on how is Allah remembered i.e. the easiest, the most effective and acceptable way to remember Allah.

Remember what *Jesus* (peace be upon him) said, "Verily I say unto you, that every prophet when he is come hath borne to one nation only the mark of the mercy of God. And so their words were not extended save to that people to which they were sent. But the messenger of God (i.e. the holy prophet Mohammed PBH), when he shall come God shall give him as it were the Seal of His Hand, insomuch that he shall carry salvation and Mercy to all the nations of the world that shall receive his doctrine (i.e. Islam) ..."[189] Therefore pay attention to what that Holy Prophet Mohammed (PBH) said regarding the way and manners to obtain the *Keys to Paradise*: Get the *Keys* in your pocket today and with them journey happily to the grave at your death which is inevitable.

REMEMBRANCE OF ALLAH IN THE HADITH

1. The Holy prophet Muhammad (PBH) has said that 'La Ilaha illallahu' is the most excellent of all sorts of remembrance of Allah and 'Alhamdulillah' is the most excellent of all the prayers.

It is apparent that the entire basis and the fundamental of religion is the unity (oneness) of Allah. From this point of view '*Kalimah*-al-Tayyabah' i.e. 'La illallahu' illallahu is definitely the most excellent of all the remembrance of Allah. But 'Alhamdulillah' is regarded the most excellent of all the prayers because it is the highest praise of Allah and is liked by Him (Allah) very much. As such Allah showers His mercy and grants everything, to the person who recites 'Alhamdulillah'.

2. The Holy Prophet Muhammad (PBH) has stated that once Hazrat Musa (Alaihis Salam) prayed to the Almighty Allah to grant him some special prayer for the purpose of remembering Him. The Almighty Allah commanded him to repeat 'La ilaha Illallahu'. Hazrat Musa

replied that the entire Universe chants this verse. He received the same reply. Again, Hazrat Musa prayed that he wished something special and exclusive while the '*Kalimah*' was in general recited by everyone. The reply was "Let all the seven heavens and seven earths be put together on the one side of the balance and the '*Kalimah*' alone on the other, it would weigh heavier.

3. Hazrat Abu Hurairah (radiallahu anhu) once inquired of the holy Prophet Muhammad (PBH), "who will benefit more by your intercession on the Day of Reckoning? The Holy Prophet Muhammad (PBH) replied: In view of your extreme thirst for my sayings I had anticipated that none would inquire into it before you". Then the Holy Prophet Muhammad (PBH) replied: "The person who would recite 'La ilaha illallahu with sincerity of heart will benefit more than anybody else".

4. Hazrat Zaid bin Arqam (radiallahu anhu) quotes the Holy Prophet Muhammad (PBH) as saying that whoever recited 'La ilaha Illallahu' with sincerity entered into Paradise. Someone inquired as to the sign of sincerity in reciting the *Kalimah;* the Holy Prophet Muhammad (PBH) replied that it would stop him from doing forbidden acts".

5. The Holy Prophet Muhammad (PBH) has said that there is no servant of Allah who recites 'La ilaha illallahu' and the gates of Heavens are not opened for him, and that it soar as far up to the high Heaven, provided the person refrains from the deadly sins.

The virtue of the *Kalimah* is quite evident from the fact that it goes straight up to the *Arsh* and under no circumstances it is without benefit even if a man commits deadly sins. Mulla Ali Qari (rahmatullah alaihi) explains that refraining from deadly sins is related to the quickening acceptance of it by the Almighty Allah, and wide opening of the gates of Heavens otherwise its acceptance and reward are due without any pre-condition attached to it. There is a Hadith in which it is stated that for such a person, who recites the *Kalimah*, the gates of Heavens will be opened as a mark of respect at the time of his death.

6. It is reported by Hazrat Shaddad (radiallahu anhu) and confirmed by Hazrat Ubaidah (radiallahu anhu) that once they went to the Holy Prophet Muhammad (PBH) who was sitting in the midst of his other companions. The Holy Prophet Muhammad (PBH) inquired

if there was no non-believer (non-Muslim) in the gathering. When it was confirmed that there was none at that time he ordered to close the door. Then he asked all those present to raise hands and recite 'La ilaha illallahu'. All of them did the same for some time. After this he said "Alhamdulillah' and thanked Allah saying that He had send him with this *Kalimah* and promised paradise for the same. Then he communicated the happy tiding to them that Allah had forgiven them all.

7. The Holy Prophet Muhammad (PBH) has asked his followers to renew their faith occasionally. When the companions inquired as to how to renew their faith (*Iman*)? The Holy Prophet, Muhammad (PBH) advised them to recite 'La ilaha illallahu' as frequently as they could.

8. In a Hadith it is mentioned that four things ruin one's spiritual being:

   i. Competition with fools;

   ii. Excess of sins

   iii Excessive mixing up with women and

   iv Remaining in the company of the 'dead'

When inquired what was meant by 'the company of the dead' the Holy Prophet Muhammad (PBH) referred to those wealthy people whom their wealth turned arrogant.

9. The Holy Prophet Muhammad (PBH) has enjoined on every believer to repeat 'La ilaha illallahu' with much frequency before one loses his power of speech.

10. There are many Hadith in which this topic has figured out and the Almighty Allah has Himself assured that all the sins except shirk would be forgiven.

11. The Holy Prophet Muhammad (PBH) has said the admittance of 'La ilaha illallahu' is tantamount to "keys to Paradise". The plural number is used because there are many gates of Paradise and the key

to every gate is the same '*Kalimah*'. Besides this, the *Kalimah* has two parts, 'La ilaha illallahu and Muhammadur Rasulullah'. In all such traditions where entry into Paradise or immunity from hell is discussed the '*Kalimah* Tayyibah' is mentioned or meant for in that context. There is another Hadith in which it is stated that 'La ilaha illallahu' is the price for Paradise.

12. The Holy Prophet Muhammad (PBH) has said "whoever recites 'La ilaha illallahu' any time during day or night the evil from his account of deeds are replaced by the good.

13. The Holy Prophet Muhammad (PBH) has said that those who recite 'La ilaha illallahu' are immune from the horrors of the grave and the court of Mehshar. The Holy Prophet (PBH) says that he is foreseeing those persons rising from their graves praising the Almighty Allah saying all praise is for Allah who has removed sorrow and grief from them forever.

14. There is yet another Hadith in which it is said that the persons reciting 'La ilaha illallahu' will have neither any anxiety at the time of their death or any dread of the grave.

15. Hazrat Ibn Abbas (radiallahu anhu) narrates that once Hazrat Gabriel (alaihis Salam) came to the Holy Prophet (PBH) and found him quite sad. After conveying the Almighty's Salam he said that He had inquired into the reason of the Holy Prophet (PBH)'s ill humour. The Holy Prophet (PBH) told angel Gabriel (alaihis Salam) that he was worried over the plight of Muslims on the Day of Qiyamah (Resurrection). There upon Hazrat Gabriel (alaihis Salam) took the Holy Prophet (PBH) to a tomb where the dead of the Banu Salmah were buried. The angel rustled his wings against a grave and said 'Qum bi iznillah' (rise by the order of the Almighty Allah); a very handsome youth came out of the grave, and he was reciting 'La ilaha illallahu Muhammadu Rasulullah Alhamdu lillahi Rabbil alamin'. Angel Gabriel (peace be upon him) bade him to go back to his place and the dead returned accordingly. And then went to another grave and repeated the same. From this grave a very ugly man bewailing excessively expressing sorrow, repentance and crying over the tortures of the grave. Hazrat Gabriel (peace be upon him) bade him too to go back to his place. After this he told the Holy Prophet (PBH) that

in whatever state a person died, he would rise in the same state or plight.

In this Hadith the people reciting 'La ilaha illallahu' refer to those who recite the *Kalimah* with utmost sincerity, deep interest and profound dedication.

16. In another Hadith it is mentioned that whoever recites the *Kalimah* one hundred (100) times every day will rise on the Day of Qiyamah (Resurrection) with his face shining like the full moon.

17. Hazrat Abu Darda (radiallahu anhu) has said that those whose tongues are always alive with the remembrance of Allah would enter into Paradise smilingly.

18. The Holy Prophet Muhammad (PBH) has said that on the Day of Reckoning Allah will call a person from his Ummah in the presence of the entire mankind and his record of deeds will be brought forward for reckoning. His record will consist of ninety nine consignments, and each consignment will be as long as eye can see far and wide. First of all he will be asked if he has to deny any of the entries of his record of deeds, or if he has to point out anything in the record which is contrary to the fact. The person would say that there is nothing as such in his record and that he has nothing to say in his favour. Neither any angel has made any false entry nor he has to deny anything, he would add. The Almighty Allah will ask if he has to make any excuse for his misdeeds. The person would plainly say that he has nothing to offer as an excuse either. Then Allah will say that there is one virtue in his record. And a piece of paper will be taken out on which 'Ashhadu an la ilaha illallahu wa ash haduanna Muhammadan abdahu wa rasuluhu' will be inscribed. Allah will ask him to go and get it weighed. The person would say that the piece of paper would not outweigh this long dark record of misdeeds. Allah will reply that 'today no unfairness would be shown to him. Now when that small piece of paper would be put against his entire record of misdeeds, the former would weigh heavier than the latter. The fact remains that nothing is heavier than 'La ilaha illallahu' (there is no deity to be worshiped except Allah).

19. The Holy Prophet Muhammad (PBH) says: "By Him in whose possession is my life. If the entire Heavens and the Earths and the people that are on them and things that are in between them and the things that are beneath them are put together on one side of the balance and admittance of 'La ilaha illallahu' on the other side of it, the latter would outweigh the former".

20. Once three non-believers came to the Holy Prophet Muhammad (PBH) and asked him if he did not believe in any other being worthy of worship than Allah. The holy Prophet (PBH) replied: "La ilaha illallahu" (there is no god beside Allah). I have been sent down to earth with this *Kalimah* and am called upon to invite the people towards it".

21. Hazrat Isa(*Jesus* Christ (alaihis Salam) has said that virtuous deeds of the followers of Muhammad (PBH) are the heaviest because their tongues are familiar with the *Kalimah* that the foregoing Ummahs were reluctant to recite and that *Kalimah*' is 'La ilaha illallahu'. The fact observed by Hazrat Isa (*Jesus* Christ alaihis Salam) emphasizes Muslims familiarity with the *Kalimah*. Every Prophet from Hazrat Adam down to the Holy Prophet Muhammad (PBH) was entrusted with the task of conveying this '*Kalimah*' and it is only the Muslims that the '*Kalimah*' is popular with as they recite it daily as much as they could. In Jamiaul Usool it is mentioned that recitation of the word Allah as remembrance is fixed at five thousand times (5,000 times) for an ordinary person and twenty five thousand times for saints (25,000 times) and five thousand times (5, 000 times) daily are also fixed as minimum for reciting 'La ilaha illallahu'.

Khalifa Daudu Mahmud Ibn Salihun (Rahamatullahi Alaihi) enjoined his followers in the auspices of Ayuele Progressive Association to always recite:

"La ilaha illallahu' at least one hundred times in the morning and evening. Astaghfirullah" one hundred times in the morning and evening. Alhamdulillah, one hundred times, in the morning and evening every day.

He himself recites La ilaha illallahu at least 35,000 times before sun rise, and 35, 000 (thirty five thousand times at sun set. Before reciting la ilaha illallahu he used to recite:

i. Bismillahir Rahamanr Rahim – 1000times

ii. Astaghfirullahal Azim – 1,000 times

iii. Allahumma Salli Ala sayyidina Muhammadin Wa sallim – 1,000 times

iv. Qul Huwallah Ahad (To the end) – 1,000 times.

After completing the recitation of La ilaha illallahu 35,000 times, he used to conclude by reciting:

i. La ilaha illallahu illahu Wahidun Rabbil *Arsh*il Azim – 1,000 times

ii. La ilaha illallahu Alhamd lillahi – 1,000 times

So that in 3 years, he recites La ilaha Illallahu at least 70 million times.

22. The Holy Prophet (PBH) quotes Angel Gabriel (peace be upon him) as saying that the Almighty Allah proclaim "I am the only Allah there is none worthy of worship except Myself, (hence) worship Me alone. And whoever comes to Me sincerely bearing witness to 'La ilaha illallahu' he will enter into my castle and whoever has entered into my castle will be safe from any tribulation or chastisement".

23. The Holy Prophet Muhammad (PBH) has said that 'La ilaha illallahu' is the most excellent of all kinds of remembrances of Allah, and the highest prayer (Dua) is Istighfar (i.e. Astaghfirullah or Astaghfirullahal Azim (Seeking Allah's forgiveness). Then he recited an Ayat of Surah Muhammad 'Fa'a lam annahu La ilaha illallahu'. At the very onset of this work, it has already been mentioned that 'La ilaha illallahu' is the most excellent of all the remembrances of Allah as it purifies the heart. And when it is followed by Istighfar, then it is doubling rewarded. In a Hadith it is narrated that when the fish swallowed Hazrat Yunus (alaihis Salam), the latter recited 'La ilaha illa-anta subhanaka Inni Kuntu Minazzalimin. And who ever prays with these words his prayer, Insha'Allah is certainly granted by the Almighty Allah. It is reported at the onset of this work that 'Alhamdulillahi' had been mentioned as the most excellent prayer, but in the present case Istighfar is cited as the best one. Such variations are greatly due to particular circumstances. For one who is a sinner 'Istighfar' is more suitable because it is his foremost requirement.

24. Hazrat Abu Bakr (radiallahu anhu) quotes the Holy Prophet (PBH) that 'La ilaha illallahu' and Istighfar should be recited excessively. Satan says he ruined people with the help of sins and they ruined him with the help of 'la ilaha illallahu' and Istighfar. That is why he (Satan) often go the sophisticated way of leading people into the abyss of carnal desire (innovations) where they consider themselves to be on the right path and have no need for Istighfar.

25. The Holy Prophet Muhammad (PBH) has said that whoever dies bearing witness to 'La ilaha illallahu Muhammadu Rasulullahi' with firm heart, he will definitely enter Paradise. Another Hadith gives the happy tiding that such person will be forgiven by the Almighty Allah.

26. The Holy Prophet (PBH) has said that there is always a curtain between the Almighty Allah and the acceptance of a virtuous act, but no curtain hangs between Almighty Allah and 'La ilaha illallahu' and father's prayer for his son.

27. The Holy Prophet Muhammad (PBH) has said that there will be none on the Day of Reckoning who appears reciting 'la ilaha illallahu' exclusively for the pleasure of Allah and having no other motive behind it, will be immune from the fire of hell.

28. Once Hazrat Talha (radiallahu anhu) looked down cast and depressed. Some one inquired of him the reason. He said that he had heard from the Holy Prophet (PBH) about a '*Kalimah*' the recitation of which eased the pains of death, made the face shine and showed something delightful to departing person. But he could not, he added, muster up courage to inquire about it. Hazrat Umar (radiallahu anhu) informed him that he knew it. Hazrat Talha (radiallahu anhu) very eagerly inquired what that *Kalimah* was. Then Hazrat Umar (radiallahu anhu) said, 'we know that no *Kalimah* excels the one which the Holy Prophet (PBH) had presented to his uncle Abu Talib at the time of his death and that is 'Lalaha illallahu'. Talha (radiallahu anhu) exclaims 'It is the same!'.

29. When the Holy prophet Muhammad (PBH) expired, his companions were greatly upset and were over taken by whims, misconceptions and suspicions as a result of this unbearable shock. Hazrat Usman (radiallahu anhu) was also one of them. He states that Hazrat Umar

(radiallahu anhu) came to him and greeted him by saying 'assalamu alaikum' but he was completely lost and did not take notice of it. Hazrat Umar (radiallahu anhu) complained of it to Hazrat Abu Bakr Siddiq (radiallahu anhu). Both of them went together to Hazrat Usman (radiallahu anhu). Hazrat Abu Bakr (radiallahu anhu) asked Hazrat Usman (radiallahu anhu) as to why he did not answer back. Hazrat Usman denied and pleaded his innocence. Then Hazrat Abu Bakr (radiallahu anhu) said that the same must have happened. Hazrat Usman again denied and said that he did not notice his arrival, nor did he hear him saying 'assalamu alaikum'. There upon, Hazrat Usman (radiallahu anhu) admitted then to have been contemplating the issues of the Holy Prophet's (PBH) death and that he could not ask him the way to 'Salvation'. Hazrat Abu Bakr told him that he had already asked the Holy Prophet (PBH) about it and he had replied that the way to salvation was the '*Kalimah*' which had been suggested to Abu Talib at the time of his death and which he rejected unfortunately.

30. The Holy Prophet Muhammad (PBH) says that when Hazrat Adam (alaih is Salam) committed that breach of trust (sin) and was sent down to this world he wept excessively and begged Allah's pardon. Once he looked upon the sky and said 'I seek Thy forgiveness through Muhammad (PBH). Soon thereafter through a revelation he was asked who is Muhammad? (Through whom you are seeking my forgiveness) Hazrat Adam replied that when he had been created he had seen on the high Heaven inscribed 'La ilaha illallahu Muhammadu Rasulullah' and had understood that Muhammad (PBH) was the highest eminent personality whose name had been mentioned with His own name. Again another revelation came informing that He was the last of the apostle and that he would be from amongst his descendants and that is, if he had not been there Adam too would have not been where he was then.

31. Another Hadith mentions that whoever recites 'La ilaha illallahu Wahdahu Lasharika lahu ahadan Samadan Lam yalid Walam yulad Walam yakullahu Kufuwan ahad' would be benefited by two million virtues.

32. The Holy Prophet Muhammad (PBH) has said that whoever recites 'La ilaha illallahu one hundred times (100 times) will rise on the Day of Judgement with a face shining like full moon and on the day on

which he recites it none else would be more virtuous than him except the one who recites it more than he did.

33. The Holy Prophet Muhammad (PBH) has said "Do commit 'La ilaha illallahu' to the memory of child when he starts learning to speak and to induce a person to recite 'La ilaha illallahu' when he is about to die. He whose first and last utterances are 'La ilaha illallahu' will not be counted for any sin even though he has lived for a thousand years (either due to the reason that he may not be having any sin to his account or has secured forgiveness through repentance or Allah has pardoned him by His grace)".

34. Some Hadiths report the Holy Prophet (PBH) as having said "The sins of a person who recited 'La ilaha illallahu' at the time of his death, fall down as do the buildings due to flood". Some Hadiths say, "All the past sins of a person who has been blessed with the ability to recite this holy *Kalimah* at the time of his death are forgiven".

35. A Hadith says "A munafiq (hypocrite) is not blessed with the ability to recite this *Kalimah* at the time of death"

36. A Hadith says "Serve your dead ones with the provision of 'La ilaha illallahu".

37. A Hadith says: "An Angel visits a person at the time of his death who has been prompt in his *Salat*, drives away the Satan and induces him to recite 'La ilaha illallahu".

It has been frequently seen that, the inducement works only if the person concerned has been reciting this holy *Kalimah* plentifully in his life time. A story has been written of a person who used to sell grass. When he was lying on his death bed he was being induced by the people to recite *Kalimah* Tayyabah but would say, "This bundle is for this much and that bundle is for that much". Several such incidents have been written in the book 'Nuzhatul Basateen' and many others can be easily observed in daily life.

38. As a story goes, when a person was induced to recite *Kalimah* Shahadah at the time of his death he said, "Pray to Allah. My tongue is unable to recite it". The people asked him, "What is the reason"? He said, "I used to be careless while weighing". Another story has been narrated in this regard that when a person was induced to recite this *Kalimah*

at the time of his death, he said, "I am unable to do so". The people asked, "What is the matter?" He said, "Once a woman had come to buy a towel from me. She was pretty and I remained looking at her for sometime".

Many such incidents take place in the world some of them have been written in the book 'Tadhira-e-Qartabiah". Thus it is the duty of a person to keep on repenting for his sins and ask Allah for His blessings.

39. The Holy Prophet Muhammad (PBH) has said "No deed can be better than 'La ilaha illallahu' and this *Kalimah* does not spare any sin"

It is quit obvious that no deed can be more valuable than the recitation of *Kalimah* Tayyibah because nothing is acceptable without it. Thus *Salat*, fasting, *Zakat* and all other good deeds are dependent upon it.

40. A Hadith says, "if a person is in the practice of reciting 'La ilaha illallahu' at the time of going to bed and getting up, the world itself will prompt him for (the preparation of) the Hereafter and protect him from the calamities".

41. The Holy Prophet Muhammad (PBH) has said "There are more than seventy branches (in some narration it has been reported as seventy) of *Iman*. The highest of them all is to recite 'La ilaha illallahu' and the lowest is to remove a harmful thing from the path. 'Haya' (modesty) is also a prominent part of *Iman*".

42. In another Hadith the keys to Heavens and Earths are said to be 'Alhamdu lillahi La ilaha illallahu Allahu Akbar'.

43. Hazrat Ka'ab (radiallahu anhu) tells that these words echo around the *Arsh* and repeat the names of their reciter.

44. The Holy Prophet Muhammad (PBH) states that Nuhu (allaih-is-Salam) called his Sons and told them that he wished them to refrain from two things '*shirk*' and arrogance. The two things which were required to them to practice were, such as pleased Allah as well as the righteous one of them was the recitation of 'La ilaha illallahu' which broke through all the heavens and earths on the other hand, the *Kalimah* would be weightier than all of them and; heavier than

entire universes and all that is in them. The other things to do, Hazrat Nuhu recommended was the frequent recitation of Subhanallahi Wabi hamdihi, which was the prayer (Ibadah) of all the creatures and which constituted the resources of all creature's nourishment. That there was no creature which did not thank and praise Allah for His benevolence but that they were unable to understand.

The two things which Hazrat Nuhu forbade him to practice were polytheism and arrogance because they drew curtain between Allah and the righteous ones.

45. The Holy prophet Muhammad (PBH) says: (Allah pays every man in his own coin) that the Almighty Allah has said: "I treat My servants as he expects from Me. And when he remembers Me, I am with him. Thus if he remembers Me in his heart, I also remember him in my Heart, and if he remembers Me at any assembly (of men), I remember him at a far superior assembly of my angels (who are innocent and pure)... if he comes to Me walking, I come to him running".

46. One of the companions requested the Holy Prophet Muhammad (PBH), to assign him one specific act, out of the great lots of the *Shariat* which could be practiced and be made a rule of life and a pre-occupation. The Holy Prophet Muhammad (PBH) advised him to remember Allah abundantly. Hazrat Ma'az(radiallahu anhu) further says that the Holy Prophet Muhammad (PBH) told him that the most admirable act to Allah is that even at the time of one's death he should be busy in the remembrance of Allah.

47. The Holy Prophet Muhammad (PBH) once told his companions: "Should I disclose to you such a thing which is best of all virtuous deeds, which is most hallowed to your Lord (Allah), which raises your position and enhances your status and which is superior even to Jihad?" The companions requested the Holy Prophet Muhammad (PBH) "Do tell us O Apostle of Allah!". The Holy Prophet Muhammad (PBH) told them: "That is Remembrance of Allah."

48. Musanad Ahmad quotes the Holy Prophet Muhammad (PBH) as having said that: "Remembrance of Allah is seven lakh times better than spending in the path of Allah".

49. Hazrat Abu Darda (radiallahu anhu) has said: "Remember Allah is your triumph; it will help you in your trials".

50. Hazrat Abu Hurairah (radiallahu anhu) says that: such houses, in which Allah is remembered, shine to the denizens of Heavens in the same manner as to the dwellers of the Earth the Stars in the sky shine. And those who are blessed by Allah to see this light can also see these houses similarly in paradise".

51. The holy prophet Muhammad (PBH) was reported to have said that whoever is unable to undergo labour at night (Ibadah) and does not want to spend in the path of Allah (Sadaqah, Nafil) or is unable to participate in Jihad due to cowardice should remember Allah abundantly".

52. An eminent scholar and Mohaddith Hafiz Ibn Qayyim (rahamatullah alaihi), in his pamphlet 'Alwabil-ul-saiyyib' has narrated more than one hundred virtues of the remembrance of Allah out of which seventy-two are as follows:

    1. It drives away the evil forces and defeats them;

    2. It pleases Allah;

    3. Removes gloom and rancour from the heart;

    4. It refreshes heart and makes it blissful;

    5. Strengthens the body and heart;

    6. Imparts glow to face and lends luster to heart;

    7. It attracts livelihood;

    8. It makes the personality impressive and prestigious;

    9. Develops a love for Almighty (Allah)

    10. Gives access to Allah;

11. Attracts towards Allah;

12. Gradually draws you closer to Him (Allah):

13. It is the key to the realization of the Almighty Allah;

14. Inculcates the fear of Allah and the sense of disinterestedness (in immoral act).

15. Causes one to be remembered by Allah;

16. It resuscitates heart;

17. It nourishes heart and spirit;

18. It cleans and purifies heart;

19. It banishes flaws and faults;

20. Develops an affinity with Almighty Allah;

21. The remembrance of Allah itself remembers the man around the high heavens;

22. His remembrance in good times ensures His help in adversities;

23. It rids one of the wrath of Allah;

24. It causes 'Sakinah' and the choicest blessings of Allah to descend on one who remembers Him.

25. It saves the tongue from back-biting, lies and evil speech;

26. Assemblies of remembrance of Allah are attended by angels who recommend blessings of Allah for the participants;

27. It makes the person fortunate;

28. It keeps away frustration and anxiety on the Day of Reckoning;

29. Remembrance of Allah in loneliness and weeping during that period brings under the shade of His mercy on the Day of Reckoning;

30. It brings more than what is granted otherwise to the seekers from Him.

31. It is the simplest, easiest and the most virtuous of all the prayers;

32. Remembrance of Allah (each time) is a plant in paradise;

33. It is the most rewarding;

34. It relegates passions into oblivion and releases it from its clutches;

35. It adds to the glory of one's inner personality;

36. Its brilliance accompanies are in this world as well as in the grave and leads one on the bridge of *Sirat*;

37. It is the grass root of mystic meditation (Tasawwuf) and all the mystic orders practice it to open the gate way to reach the Almighty Allah;

38. There exist a corner in man's heart which is not filled except with the remembrance of Allah when practiced enlightens the entire personality;

39. It unites the disunited and disunite the united;

40. It awakens the heart and revitalizes it;

41. Remembrance of Allah is a tree which produces the fruits of knowledge; the mystics call it the tree bearing the fruits of realization and awareness. Excess of Remembrance, strengthens the root of this tree;

42. It brings one closer to Allah. A Hadith informs that such people who remember Allah are 'Men of Allah';

43. It is at par with charity, Jihad, and manumission of slaves in the path of Allah.

44. It is the root of gratefulness to Almighty Allah;

45. Those who remember Him all the time are the most respectable in the eyes of God (near Allah).

46. It makes the heart soft and pure;

47. It remedies all the ailment of heart;

48. It is the root of friendliness with God;

49. It attracts the blessings of the Almighty Allah,

50. One who remembers Him is blessed with His mercy and the benedictions of angels;

51. The assemblies of which He is remembered are the Orchards of paradise in this world;

52. Assemblies of remembrance of Allah are the assemblies of angels;

53. Allah is proud of such persons who remember Him in the presence of angels;

54 One who remembers Him perpetually would enter paradise smiling;

55. All virtuous acts are meant for His remembrance; of all the practices, the practice of His remembrance is most excellent;

56. This precedes all the Nafil (voluntary) Prayers;

57. It is conducive and wholesome to all other prayers;

58. It facilitates all difficulties;

59. It removes all fear and fright from heart;

60. It cultivates a special power in man which prepares him to perform difficult tasks;

61. Those who remember him all the time lead all those who are trying to get utmost benefit in the hereafter.

62. The Almighty Allah testifies to the person who remembers Him and confirms Him as truthful:

63. It raises quarters in paradise; whenever any person delays his remembrance, the construction in Paradise is also held up by the angels.

64. It is a protective shield against hell;

65. Angels plead to the Almighty Allah to forgive a person who remembers Him;

66. The place where Allah is remembered takes pride;

67. Excess of His remembrance guarantees protection from hypocrisy;

68. As compared with other virtues, His remembrance has a special favour which no other virtue contains;

69. The face of one who remembers Him is lent a grace in this world and a luster in the hereafter;

70. The man who remembers Allah everywhere and all the time will have many witnesses;

72. It saves the tongue from evil, mischief and lies; the forces of evil are defeated by His remembrance.

REMEMBRANCE OF ALLAH IN THE HOLY QURAN

Remembrance of the Almighty Allah constantly is the key to paradise. The nature of Paradise is given in subsequent chapters. Man has no reason to give why he should neglect the Remembrance of his creator. Man has no reason to give why he should indulge in what God Almighty willeth not. Job (i.e. prophet Ayub) dwelt in Uz among idolaters, and that did not prevent him from remembering God constantly. The same with Noah (prophet Nuhu) and Abraham whose fathers were without faith and worshiped false gods/idols. So was Lot whose abode was among the wicked men on earth. Daniel as a child, with Ananias, Azarias and Misael were taken captive by Nebuchadnezar in such wise that they were nurtured among the multitude of idolaterous servants, and they all grew up to let the Remembrance of God be their watch words. *Jesus* (Peace be upon him) say: "As God liveth, even as the fire burneth dry things and converteth them into fire, making no difference between olive and cypress and palm; even so our God hath mercy on every one that worketh righteously, making no difference between Jew, Scythian, Greek, or Ishmaelite ... "Verily I say unto you, that man ought to spend all the time of his life not in learning how to speak or to read, but in learning how to work well (i.e. how to remember God)[190] As God liveth in whose presence standeth my soul, it is lawful to sleep some what every night, but it is never lawful to forget God and His fearful Judgement.

Barnabas asked *Jesus*: "O master how can we always have God in memory? Assuredly, it seemeth to us impossible".

Jesus replied with a sigh: "This is the greatest misery that man can suffer, O Barnabas ... water cleaveth the hardest rock with a single drop striking there for a long time. Do ye know why ye have not overcome this misery? Because ye have not perceived that (it is the key to paradise and) is sin.[191]

Allah (subhanahu) wata'ala in Holy Qur'an say:

1. Therefore remember Me, I will remember you be grateful to Me, and reject not Me [192]

2. Remember thy Lord much and praise Him in the early hours of night and morning[193]

3. Allah's are the fairest names. Invoke Him by them[194]

4. Say (unto mankind): Cry unto Allah, His are the most beautiful names.[195]

5. Restrain thyself along with those who cry unto their lord at morn and evening, seeking His countenance, and let not thine eyes overlook them, desiring the pomp of the life of this world and obey not him whose heart we have made heedless of our Remembrance, who followeth his own lust and whose case hath been abandoned.[196]

6. A mention of the mercy of thy lord unto His servant Zachariah, When he cried unto his Lord a cry in secret.[197]

7. And be not faint in Remembrance of Me.[198]

8. And men who remember Allah much and women who remember Allah much, Allah hath prepared for them forgiveness and a vast reward[199]

9. O ye who believe! Remember Allah with much Remembrance.[200]

10. And glorify Him early and late[201]

11. Then woe unto those whose hearts are hardened against Remembrance of Allah such are in plain error [202]

12. And he whose sight is dim to the Remembrance of the Beneficent, we assign unto him a devil who becometh his comrade[203]

13. O ye who believe, let not your wealth nor your children distract you from Remembrance of Allah. Those who do so, they are the losers[204]

14. And (whosoever) turneth a way from the Remembrance of his Lord, he will thrust him into ever growing torment (Al Jinn).

15. So remember the name of thy Lord and devote thyself with a complete devotion.[205]

16. He is successful who growth and remembereth the name of his Lord, so prayeth[206]

CHAPTER SEVEN
THE IMPORTANCE OF *SALAT* AS AN ASPECT OF REMEMBRANCE OF ALLAH

1. *Salat* is the most important of all devotions to Allah. It is, in fact, the first and foremost item to be reckoned with on the Day of Judgement.

2. The Holy Prophet Muhammad (PBH said that Allah says: "My wrath descends upon a person who bears ill-will towards my friends, and those that are blessed with my love are those who implicitly carry out my injunctions. A person keeps on advancing in my esteem through '*NAFI*'; till I chose him as 'my beloved'. I then become his ears by which he listens, his eyes by which he looks, his hands by which he holds, and his feet by which he walks (i.e, his listening, looking, holding, and walking are all in perfect accord with my injunctions and he would never even dream of employing any part of his body in any action contrary to my commands). If such a person prays for anything, I grant it to him and if he seeks my protection I do protect him".[207]

3. Another Hadith has it: "All the people shall be gathered on the Day of Judgement, when it will be asked, 'who are those who glorified Allah in ease and adversity? A group will arise and enter Paradise without any reckoning. Again it will be asked 'who are those who left their beds and passed their nights in acts of worshipping their creator: Another group will arise and enter Paradise without any reckoning. The angel will ask yet again, 'where are those whom trade did not hinder from remembering Allah'. And yet another group will arise and enter Paradise without any reckoning. After these three groups have departed, reckoning would commence for the people in general'.[208]

4. Abdullah bin Umar (radiallahu anhu) narrates that he heard the Holy Prophet Muhammad (PBH) saying! "Islam is founded on five pillars; bearing witness that there is no God but Allah and Muhammad (PBH) is His servant and apostle, establishment of *Salat*, paying of *Zakat*, performance of *Hajj* and fasting in Ramadan".[209]

The Holy Prophet Muhammad (PBH) has compared Islam to a canopy resting on five supports. *Kalimah* is the central support and the other four pillar of Islam are, so to say, the remaining four supports, one at each corner of the canopy. Without the central support the canopy cannot possibly stand and if anyone of the corner supports is missing a collapse will result in the defective corner. Now, let us judge for ourselves how far we have kept up the canopy of Islam. Is there really any pillar that is being held in its proper places? Although a Muslim cannot do without anyone of them, yet *Salat*, in Islam, occupies a position next only to *Iman*. Abdullah bin Masood says: "Once, I inquired of the Holy Prophet Muhammad (PBH) which act (of man) was the dearest to Allah. The Holy Prophet Muhammad (PBH) replied, '*Salat*'. I then inquired which act came next (in order of merit) and the Holy Prophet Muhammad (PBH) replied, 'Kindness to parents'. I again asked what was next and he answered 'Jihad'.[210]

5. In another Hadith the holy Prophet Muhammad (PBH) is reported to have said "*Salat* is the best of all that has been ordained by Allah".

6. "Another Hadith relates that once the Holy Prophet Muhammad (PBH) came out of his house. It was autumn and the leaves were falling off the trees. He caught hold of a branch of a tree and its leaves began to drop in large numbers. At this he remarked O! Abzzar when a Muslim offers his *Salat* to please Allah, his sins are shed away from him as these leaves are falling off this tree".[211]

7. "Huzaifah (radiallahu anhu) says that whenever the Holy Prophet Muhammad (PBH) happened to face any difficulty, he would at once resort to *Salat*".

8. There are so many sayings of the Holy Prophet Muhammad (PBH) enjoining *Salat* and explaining its virtues that it is very difficult to cover all of them in this small book. A few quotations are, however, reproduced below for benediction![212]

    8.01 "*Salat* was the first and the foremost thing ordained by Allah and it shall be the first and the foremost thing to be reckoned for on the Day of Judgement"

    8.02 "Fear Allah in the matter of *Salat*; Fear Allah in the matter of *Salat*!; Fear Allah in the matter of *Salat*!!"

8.03 "*Salat* is the only partition between Man and shirk"

8.04 "*Salat* is the mark of Islam; A person who says his *Salat* at fixed hours with sincerity and devotion observing all its regulation including the mustahabbat, is surely a Mumin'.

8.05 "Of all that have been ordained by Allah *Iman* and *Salat*; are the most valued. If there were any other thing better then *Salat*, Allah would have ordain it for his Angels. Some of whom are always in *Ruku* and others in *Sajdah*".

8.06 "*Salat* is the Pillar of Islam".

8.07 "*Salat* abase the devil".

8.08 "*Salat* is the light of Mumin".

8.09 "*Salat* is the best Jihad".

8.10 "Allah keeps relenting towards a person so long as he is engaged in *Salat*".

8.11 "When a calamity befalls from the heaven people frequently in the *Masjid* are spared and saved".

8.12 If some major sins of a Muslim place him in hell, the fire would not burn the part of his body which has touched the ground while he was in *Sajdah* during his *Salat*".

8.13 "fire has been forbidden on those parts of the body which torch the ground in humility".

8.14 "Of all the practices *Salat* made at fixed hours is most loved by Allah".

8.15 "Allah likes most the postures of a person when he is in *Sajdah* rubbing his forehead on the ground in humility".

8.16 "A person in *Sajdah* is the nearest to Allah".

8.17 "*Salat* is a key to paradise".

8.18 "When a person stands in *Salat*, the gates of paradise are let open and all the veils between him and Allah are lifted (provided that he spoils not *Salat* by committing any *Makrooh*)".

8.19 "A person in *Salat* (so to say) knocks at the door of the sovereign Lord and the door is always opened for him who knocks".

8.20 The position of *Salat* in Islam is as the position of head in the body".

8.21 "*Salat* is the light of heart. Let those who wish, kindle their hearts (through *Salat*).

8.22 "If a person wishes to have his sins forgiven by Allah, he should perform the al wudhu properly, offer with devotion two or four Raka'ts of *Fardh* or Nafl and then pray to Allah his wish. Insha Allah, Allah will forgive him.

8.23 "Any pieces of earth of which Allah is remembered in *Salat* feels proud over the rest of the earth".

8.24. "Allah accepts the prayer of a person who prays to Him after performing two *Raka'ats* of *Salat*. Allah grants him what he prays for, sometimes immediately and sometimes (in his own interest) later".

8.25 "A person who performs two rak'ats of *Salat* in Seclusion where nobody except Allah and His Angels see him receives the writ of deliverance from the fire of Hell"

8.26 "Grant of one's prayer becomes due to a person from Allah after each Fard *Salat* performed by him"

8.27 "Fire of hell is forbidden and the Paradise becomes due to a person who performs his Al Wudu properly and says his *Salat* conscientiously according to its regulation".

8.28 "Devil remains scared of a Muslim so long as he is particular about his *Salat* but no sooner does he neglect it than the devil gets hold upon him and aspires for success in reducing him".

8.29 "*Salat* at its early hours is the most excellent practice".

8.30 "*Salat* is the offering of the pious".

8.31 "*Salat* at its early hours is a practice most liked by Allah"

8.32 "At dawn some people go to the *Masjid* and some to the market. Those going to the *Masjid* are the flag-bearers of *Iman* and those leaving for the market are the flag bearers of devil".

8.33 "The four *Raka'ats* before *Zuhr* are counted equal (in reward) to the four *Raka'ats* of *Tahajjud*"

8.34 "Mercy of Allah relents toward a person standing in *Salat*".

8.35 "*Salat* at dead of night is more valued but there are very few who do it"

8.36 "Jibril came to me and said, 'O Muhammad! However long thou livest thou shalt die one day and thou may lovest whoever, thou shalt depart from him one day. Surely thou shalt receive the recompense of whatever (good or evil) thou doest. No doubt the dignity of a Mumin is in *Tahajjud* and his honour is in contentment and the position of head in a body"

8.37 "Two *Raka'ats* in late hours of the night are more valuable than all the riches of this world. But for fear of hardship to my followers, I would have made them obligatory"

8.38 "Keep offering *Tahajjud* for it is the path of the righteous and the means of approach to Allah. *Tahajjud* keeps away from sins, causes forgiveness of sins and improves the health of the body."

8.39 "Allah says: 'O son of Adam! Do not be helpless in offering four *Raka'ats* in early part of the morning for I shall suffice thee in thy jobs in the rest of it".

SELECTED DEAD OF NIGHT SALAT FROM HADITH

Ikiramat (Radiallahu anhu) reports that he heard it from Ibn Abbas (Radiallahu anhu) who said he heard it from Abu Hurairah (Radiallahu anhu); and Abu Hurairah took an oath that he heard it from the Holy Prophet Muhammad (PBH). The Holy Prophet Muhammad (PBH) said that he heard it from Malaika Jibril, and Malaika Jibril took an oath that he heard it from the Almighty Allah. And the Almighty Allah Ta'ala, took oath with His Greatness and said: Any Muslim who rise up on Friday night and perform 12 *Raka'ats* as follows:

1ST RAKA'AT

a. Recite – Fatihah - once

b. Inna an zalnahu (complete) once

c. Qulhuwallahu (complete) 12 times

2ND RAKA'AT Same as first.

Then make *Tashahhud*, the same with the rest 10 *Raka'ats*.

ALLAH'S REWARDS:

i. Your flesh from that night has been forbidden to the torment of fire.

ii. The first 2 *Raka'ats* will prevent any form of suffering at the time of death

iii. The 2nd two *Raka'ats* will protect you from the ordeal of the grave.

iv. The third two *Raka'ats* will prevent the darkness of the grave.

v. The balance six *Raka'ats* will escort you to the Day of Judgement.

NIGHT: FRIDAY

1.01 (2) Two Raka'at as follows:

1st Raka'at Recite

a. Fatihah once

b. Idha Zulzi (complete) 15 times

2nd Raka'at same as first Raka'at then make *Tashahhud* and recite

"YAHAYYU YAQAYYUM YA ZAL JALALI WAL IKRAM" – 100 TIMES.

ALLAH'S REWARDS:

i. You will see your Paradise from this world.

ii. Before your death, you will see 30 Angels of the Almighty Allah with the good news of your Paradise.

iii. The Almighty Allah promise to assign 30 Angels to protect you from hell fire on the day of Judgement.

The Almighty Allah also promised to assign 30 Angels to protect you against all forms of evils of this world.

1.02 (2) two *Raka'ats* as follows:

1st Raka'at Recite:

a. Fatihah once

b. Qulhuwa 7 times.

2nd Raka'at same as first Raka'at. Then make *Tashahhud* and recite – Astaghfirullah al Azim 70 times.

ALLAH'S REWARDS:

i. You will not die until your Paradise is ready for you.

ii. Every of your prayers will always be accepted by the Almighty Allah.

iii. You will be favoured with blessings as much as the leaves upon the trees on earth during the rise of the sun and the setting of the sun.

iv. You will be favoured with blessings as much as what exist on earth and in Heavens.

1.03 Two (2) Raka'at as follows;

1st Raka'at Recite:

a. Fatihah once

b. Qul a uz bi Rabbi Nas once

2nd Raka'at, same as the first Raka'at. Then make *Tashahhud.*

ALLAH'S REWARDS:

i. God will descend light onto your personality and your appearance.

ii. God promised to protect you with His light from the front of you and from behind your back.

iii. You will receive your account on the day of Judgement with your right hand.

iv. You will not go to hell.

1.04 Two (2) *Raka'ats* as follows:

1st Raka'at Recite:

a. Fatihah once

b. Ayat al Kursiyyu (complete) once

c. Qul ya Aiyuhal Kafirun (complete) once

d. Qulhuwa (complete) 3 times.

2nd Raka'at same as the 1st Raka'at. Then make *Tashahhud.*

ALLAH'S REWARDS:

i. If you had earlier committed sins that would have lead you to the punishment of hell, your situation has been changed to that of access to God's vast Paradise unexamined.

ii. God Almighty will descend His Angels to shower His blessings on you.

iii. Your access to God's vast Paradise becomes debt owing you by the Almighty Allah that must be paid, for God never fail in His promise.

1.05 Two (2) *Raka'ats* as follows:

1st Raka'at Recite

a. Fatihah once

b. Ayatal Kursiyu (complete) once

c. Qulhuwa (complete) 100 times.

2nd Raka'at same as 1st Raka'at. Then make *Tashahhud* and Recite:

Yanuru, Ya'allahu, Yarahman, Yarahim, Yahayyu, Yaqayyum, Iftahli, Abwaba Rahmatika, Wa'ali, Bidkhali Jannat, Wa'atqini, Minannari; - 7 Times.

ALLAH'S REWARDS:

i. Your sins are all forgiven;

ii. You have been accepted into God's Kingdom;

iii. Your greatness will be elevated both in this world and in the hereafter.

1.06 Six (6) *Raka'ats* as follows:

1st Raka'at Recite:

a. Fatihah once

b. Qulhuwa (complete) 3 times;

2nd Raka'at Recite:

a. Fatihah once

b. Qulhuwa (complete) 10 times then make *Tashahhud*

3rd Raka'at Recite:

a. Fatihah once

b. Qulhuwa (complete) 20 times

4th Raka'at Recite

a. Fatihah once

b. Qulhuwa (complete) 30 times. Then make Tashahhud

5th Raka'at Recite

a. Fatihah once

b. Qulhuwa (complete) 40 times

6th Raka'at Recite

a. Fatihah once

b. Qulhuwa (complete) 50 times

Then make final *Tashahhud* and Recite:

1. Salatun Nabi 50 times
2. Lahawla 50 times

ALLAH'S REWARDS:

i. If you are poor and struggling, your condition will be changed immediately to that of ease, progress and prosperity by the Almighty Allah.

ii. Your sins are all forgiven.

iii. If you have problem of bearing children, your condition will be changed to that of bearing children blessed by God Almighty.

Hazrat Adam (alaihis Salam), Hazrat Nuhu (alaihis Salam) Hazrat Ibrahim (alaihis Salam) and the holy Prophet Muhammad (PBH) all offered this prayer as directed above during their difficult period in life, and their conditions were changed to the better for them by the Almighty God.

1.07 Friday after *Maghrib* (sun set) Prayers and before *Ishai* prayers:

2 *Raka'ats* as follows:

1st Raka'at Recite

a. Fatihah once

b. Qulhuwa(complete) 11 times.

2nd Raka'at: Same as 1st Raka'at. Then make *Tashahhud.*

ALLAH'S REWARD:

i. God will bless you with blessings as much as one who performs fasting for 12 years.

ii. God will also bless you with blessings as much as the blessing of one who performs mid-night *Salat* for 12 years.

1.08 Friday and any other day after *Maghrib* prayers and before *Ishai* prayers:

Two (2) *Raka'ats* as follows:

1st Raka'at Recite

a. Fatihah once

b. Quliya (complete) once

c. Qul'Auzu Birabbil Falaka (complete) 3 times

2nd Raka'at: Same as 1st Raka'at. Then make *Tashahhud*.

ALLAH'S REWARDS:

i. You have been blessed by the Almighty Allah with the blessings of 60 nights.

ii. You have been blessed by the Almighty Allah with the blessings of all the Prophets of God.

iii. You will not leave your place of prayers without receiving from God Almighty (100) one hundred blessings.

iv. If you were to die at the time of your plan to offer this prayer, you will see your Paradise instantly.

If you eventually in your life die between *Maghrib* and *Ishai*, you have died a *Shahid* death. (Death of a Martyr)

1.09 Friday and any other day after *Maghrib* and before *Ishai Salat* perform the following prayers.

1st Raka'at Recite:

a. Fatihah once

b. Kursiyyu(complete) once

c. Idha ja'a(complete) once

2nd Raka'at Recite:

a. Fatihah once

b. Kursiyyu(complete) once

c. Idha Zulzi(complete) once. Then make *Tashahhud.*

ALLAH'S REWARDS:

i. You have been blessed with the blessings of *Shahid*

ii. God Almighty will build for you a high quality building in Paradise.

iii. If you die in the same year your will die a pious person (i.e. sinless person).

1.10**ON FRIDAY AFTER SUN RISE:**

4 *Raka'ats* as follows:

1st Raka'at Recite:

a. Fatihah once

b. Qulhuwa 25 times

2nd Raka'at Recite

a. Fatihah once

b. Idha Zulzionce

c. Qulhuwa 25times. Then make *Tashahhud.*

3rd Raka'at Recite:

a. Fatihah once

b. Al'ha kumu once

c Qulhuwa 25 times.

4th Raka'at Recite:

a. Fatihah once

b. IZAJIA'A once

c. Qulhuwa 25 times.

Then make final *Tashahhud* and Recite.

1. Astaghfirullah 25 times

2. Alla humma Salli Ala Sayyidina Muhammad an Wasalli (i.e. *Salat*i Anabi) 50 times.

ALLAH'S REWARDS:

i. You have done what is required of you on a Friday.

ii. Your sins for 56 years will be forgiven by God Almighty.

iii. All your good wishes will be realized and fully fulfilled by God Almighty

iv. You will not experience the difficulties of the grave.

v. You will be in the Company of the Prophet of God Almighty to enter God's vast Paradise on the Day of Judgement.

vi. You will enter Paradise unexamined.

1.11 **ON FRIDAY**

4 Raka'at as follows,

1st Raka'at Recite:

a. Fatihah once

b. Sabi hisma(complete) once

The same with the rest 3 *Raka'ats*, but after every two *Raka'ats*, make *Tashahhud*.

ALLAH'S REWARDS:

i. You will enter Paradise unexamined.

ii. You have been blessed by God Almighty with the powers to rescue 1,000 inhabitants of hell. God Almighty promised to assign Angels to you to accomplish this task.

iii. God Almighty also promised to deal with you directly in granting you the powers to carry out the rescue operations.

2. **SATURDAY DEAD OF NIGHT *SALAT*:**

4 *Raka'ats* as follows:

1st Raka'at Recite:

a. Fatihah once

b. Quliya (complete) 3 times.

The same with the rest 3 Raka'at, but you must make *Tashahhud* after every 2 *Raka'ats*. After the final *Tashahhud*, Recite Ayat al Kursiyyu 50 times.

ALLAH'S REWARDS:

i. You have been blessed by God Almighty with the blessings as much as Jews that have lived in this world and years of good deed they did.

ii. God will descend light into your heart.

iii. You have been blessed with the blessings contained in the *ATTAURA*, *ZABURA* and *INJIL*.

iv. You will be made to sit close to the Throne of God on the day of Judgement with the Holy Prophet Muhammad (PBH).

v. You will be in the Company of the followers of the Holy Prophet (PBH) on the day of Judgement.

vi. You have been listed among those who will eat dinner with the Holy Prophet Muhammad (PBH) in Paradise.

vii You have been blessed with the blessings of 6000 years day and night.

2.01 **SATURDAY AFTER SUN RISE**

12 Raka'at as follows:

a. 1st Raka'at Recite:

i. Fatihah once

ii. Al-Falaq once

iii. Al-Nas once

b. 2nd raka'at same as the first Raka'at. Then make *Tashahhud*

c. The same with the rest 10 *Raka'ats.*

d. After the final *Tashahhud*, make Sujada and recite "LAHAWLA" to the end, then rise up from *Ruku'*u to your sitting position; and pray for paradise.

ALLAH'S REWARD:

i. Allah Subhanahu Wata'ala will say to you, "You have been welcomed into my Kingdom. You have been welcomed into my Kingdom. I have grant you, from now forward access to my vast Paradise unexamined. Enter it from the gate of your choice".

ii. You will be in the company of the Holy Prophet Muhammad (PBH) with his pious followers on the day of Judgement.

3. **SUNDAY DEAD OF NIGHT *SALAT*:**

3.01 4 *Raka'ats* as follows:

1st Raka'at Recite:

a. Fatihah once

b. Ayat al Kursiyyu once

2nd Raka'at same as first Raka'at. Then make *Tashahhud* and recite Qulhuwa -10 times

3rd Raka'at Recite:

a. Fatihah once

b. Ayatal Kursiyyu once

4th Raka'at same as 3rd Raka'at. Then make *Tashahhud* and recite Qulhuwa 10 times.

ALLAH'S REWARDS:

i. The Angels of God Almighty will call you and say to you, well done for your good work. Your sins are all forgiven by God Almighty.

ii. You will enter God's vast Paradise unexamined.

3.02 4 *Raka'ats* as follows:

1st Raka'at recite:

a. Fatihah once

b. Amanar Rasulu(complete) once

The same with the rest 3 Raka'at but after two *Raka'ats*, make *Tashahhud*.

ALLAH'S REWARDS:

i. You have been blessed with the blessings from the Almighty God as much as NASARA that lived in this world.

ii. You will receive the blessings of all the believers among them for (1,000) one thousand years.

iii. One thousand (1,000) Angels will be assigned to protect you from hell fire on the day of Judgement by the Almighty God.

iv. The gates of Paradise will be opened to you on the day of your death, and you will enter into it from the gate of your choice.

3.03 Sunday after sun rise perform 2 *Raka'ats* as follows:

1st Raka'at recite:

a. Fatihah once

b. Falaqi and Nasi twice each.

2nd Raka'at same as first, Then make *Tashahhud* and Recite LAHAWLA to the end. 99 times

ALLAH'S REWARDS:

i. Your sins even if as much as waters in River Nile, they are forgiven by the Almighty God.

ii. Your prayers will always be answered instantly.

iii. You have been accepted into the Kingdom of God Almighty.

4. **MONDAY DEAD OF NIGHT *SALAT***

4.01 2 *Raka'ats* as follows:

1st Raka'at Recite

a. Fatihah once

b. Ayat al Kirsiyyu once

c. Qulhuwa once

d. Falaqi and Nasi once each

2nd Raka'at same as 1st Raka'at. Then make *Tashahhud* and Recite:

a. Astaghfirullah 10 times

b. *Salat* Anabi 10 times

ALLAH'S REWARD:

i. All your sins are forgiven.

ii. You will receive uncountable blessings in Paradise from God Almighty Himself.

4.02 6 *Raka'ats* as follows

1st Raka'at recite:

a. Fatihah once

b. Quliya once

c. Qulhuwa 11times.

The same with the rest 5 *Raka'ats*, but after every 2 Raka'at; make *Tashahhud* after the final *Tashahhud* recite: Yahayyu Yaqayyumu, Yazul Jalali Wal Ikram. Ya Wahhabu Yasawabu 7times

ALLAH'S REWARDS:

i. A voice will call you at the bottom of the Throne of the Almighty God and say to you, that you have truly showed devotion to the Almighty God. Your sins are all forgiven, the same with the sins for the rest of your life.

ii. Your access to paradise has been guaranteed by God Almighty. these are the assurances from God Almighty to you.

4.03 **MONDAY AFTER SUN RISE**

Two (2) *Raka'ats* as follows:

1st Raka'at Recite:

a. Fatihah once

b. Qulhuwa 5 times.

c. Falaki And Nasi – 15 times each

2nd RAKA'AT same as the 1st Raka'at. Then make *Tashahhud* and recite:

1. Astaghfirullah 15 times

2. Ayat Kursiyyu 15 times.

ALLAH'S REWARDS:

i. You have been listed among those to enter Paradise no matter the amount of your sins (excluding shirk).

ii. Both your known sins and unknown sins have all been forgiven by God Almighty.

iii. You will not die with sins.

4.04 Two (2) *Raka'ats* as follows:

1st Raka'at Recite:

a. Fatihah once

b. Ayat al Kursiyyu once

c. Qulhuwa once

d. Ina'atainaka 10 Times

2nd RAKA'AT same as the 1st Raka'at. Then make *Tashahhud* and recite

a. Qulhuwa 11 times

b. Amanar Rasulu 3 times, for the forgiveness of your parents.

ALLAH'S REWARDS:

i. If your parents are in hell punishment, they will be instantly released and will be forgiven of all their sins.

ii. You will be blessed by God Almighty with an honoured Paradise.

5. **TUESDAY DEAD OF NIGHT SALAT:**

5.01 12 *Raka'ats* as follows:

1st Raka'at Recite:

a. Fatihah once

b. Qulhuwa 3 times

The same with the rest 11*Raka'ats* but at the end of 2 *Raka'ats* make *Tashahhud*

ALLAH'S REWARDS:

i. Each sin committed by you will be changed to become 10 times of virtues by God Almighty.

ii. You will be granted access to God's vast Paradise unexamined.

iii. All the gates to hell have been permanently closed against you forever and ever.

iv. You will be blessed like the pious men of God Almighty in this world and in the hereafter.

6. **WEDNESDAY AFTER SUN RISE**

12 *Raka'ats* as follows:

1st Raka'at Recite:

a. Fatihah once

b. Qulhuwa 3 times.

The same with the rest 11 *Raka'ats* but make *Tashahhud* after every 2 *Raka'ats* . After the final *Tashahhud* recite;

a. Astaghfirullah Azim 3 times.

ALLAH'S REWARDS:

i. You will be called by the angels at the bottom of the Throne of the Almighty Allah and give you the good news that all your sins (except shirk) have been forgiven by God Almighty.

ii. Both the sins you have committed in the past and those you will ever commit again in the future, have all been forgiven.

iii. You will not experience the difficulties of the grave.

6.01 2rd Raka'at Recite as follows:

1st Raka'at Recite

a. Fatihah once

b. Idha Zulzi once

c. Qulhuwa 3 times.

2nd Raka'at same as 1st Raka'at. Then make *Tashahhud.*

ALLAH'S REWARDS:

i. You will not experience the darkness of the grave.

ii. You will not experience the difficulties, fears and anxiety of the day of Judgement.

iii. You will shine tremendously on that day of Judgement.

iv. You will receive your account with the right hand on the day of Judgement.

7. **THURSDAY DEAD OF THE NIGHT SALAT**

7.01 8 *Raka'ats* as follows:

1st Raka'at Recite:

a. Fatihah once

b. Qulhuwa 10 times.

The same with the rest 7 *Raka'ats* but make *Tashahhud* at the end of every 2 *Raka'ats* . After the final *Tashahhud* recite:

'La Ilaha Illallahu Mulikun Haqqun Mubin, Muhammadu Rasullulahi, Sadiqun Wahidun Amin.'100 times

ALLAH'S REWARDS:

1. All your sins have been washed away by God Almighty.

2. You will be honoured (1,000) one thousand times in Paradise called *Firdausi* by God Almighty.

7.02 2 *Raka'ats* after *Zuhr* payer:

1st Raka'at Recite:

a. Fatihah once

b. Qulhuwa 5 times.

2nd *Raka'ats* same as 1st Raka'at, then make *Tashahhud* and recite: Astaghfirullah Azim 100 times.

ALLAH'S REWARDS:

1. You will not leave the place of your prayers without all your sins been forgiven by God Almighty.

2. You will receive the blessings as much as those who perform fasting during the month of Sha'aban, Ramadan, and those who performed *Hajj*i and *UMRA* since the beginning of the world.

3. You will receive the blessings as much as the blessings of SAFA, MARWA and TAWAF performed by the angels of God Almighty since the beginning of the universe.

OTHER VERY IMPORTANT PRAYERS

1. **AFTER SUN RISE** (Between 9 am and 11 am) prayers.

1.01 4 *Raka'ats* as follows:

a) 1st Raka'at Recite:

1. Fatihah 10 times
2. Ayat al Kursiyyu 10 times
3. Qulhuwa 10 times
4. Al-falak 10 times
5. al-Nas 10 times

b) 2nd Raka'at same as the first Raka'at

c) 3rd and 4th Raka'at same as 1st and 2nd *Raka'ats.*

d) After final Tashhud, recite

1. "Subhanallahi, Waliamdulillahi, wa La illaha Illallahuu, Allahu Akbar, Walahawla, Walaqu wata, ILLa billahi Alaliyul Azim" once.

2. *Salat* an Nabiy 10 times

ALLAH'S REWARDS:

1. You are hence forth shielded away from the evils of men, women and Jinn.
2. Your sins are all forgiven by Allah.

3. 70 of your needs in this world and in the hereafter have been fulfilled and guaranteed.

4. Your day and night desires will be fulfilled by Allah.

5. You will be in the company of the Angels on the day of Judgement who will be singing the songs of praises of you on that dreadful day of your good works on earth.

2 AFTERNOON PRAYERS

After afternoon obligatory prayers, recite:

Allahumma salli Ala Muhammadan, Wa'Ala'Ali Muhammadin, Kama sallaita ala Ibrahim, Wa Ala Ali Ibrahima, Innak hameed Majeed" once.

ALLAH'S REWARD:

1. Your sins are all forgiven together with your sins for the next 70 years.

2. You will be made great among the followers of the Holy Prophet Muhammad (PBH)

3. 7 gates to paradise will be opened to you at the time of your death and you will enter paradise from the gate of your choice.

4. The gates of successes are opened to you in this world.

3 AFTER ANSAR PRAYERS

Recite: "Astagfrullaha, Azim" 70 times

ALLAH'S REWARD:

1. Your sins are all forgiven including your sins for the next 70 years.

2. You will receive blessings as much as 70 accepted *Hajj* and *UMRA*.

3. You will receive blessings of Jihad

4. Your repentance each time you make a mistake will easily be accepted by Allah.

5. Allah will always like your prayers for acceptance and your sins are forgiven and made pure all the time.

4 AFTER MAGHRIB PRAYERS

Recite: "La ilaha Illallahu Muhammad Rasulullahi" 70 times

ALLAH'S REWARD:

1. You have been given the blessings of a believer that performs 40 *Raka'ats* reciting in each raka'at, the Holy Qur'an, *Zabura* and *Attaura.*

2. You have been given the blessings of a believer that sincerely worshipped God for 70 years.

3. Allah has blessed you with blessing as much as the leaves upon the trees on earth and those that have fallen from them.

4. If you die between *Maghrib* and *Ishai* prayers, you will die a *Shahid* death. (death of a Martyr)

5 ISHAI PRAYERS:

Recite LAHAWLA to the end 70 times

ALLAH'S REWARD:

1. You will be raised from the grave among the Angels that have never sinned on the day of Judgement.

THE USE OF SELECTED SURATS OF THE HOLY QUR'AN

A THE USE OF YASIN

1. According to one Hadith, Allah Subhanah wata'ala recited *SURAT* YASIN and *SURAT* TAHA for one thousand years before creating Heaven and Earth. On Hearing this, the Angels said: "Blessing is for the Ummat unto whom the Qur'an will be sent down, blessing is for

the hearts which will bear it, i.e. memorise it, and blessing is for the tongue which will recite it".

According to another Hadith, YASIN is named in *ATTAURA* as Mun'imah (giver of good things), because it contains benefits for its reader in this life as well as in the hereafter. It removes from him the affliction of this world and the next and takes away the dread of the next life.

2. Hadrat Ata Ibn Abi Ribah says that the Holy prophet Muhammad (PBH) is reported to have said:

2.01 Whoever reads YASIN, Almighty Allah records for him a reward equal to that of the reading the whole Qur'an ten times.

2.02 Everything has a heart, and the heart of the glorious Qur'an is *Surat* YASIN.

2.03 Whoever reads *Surat* YASIN for the pleasure of Allah only; all his earlier sins are forgiven. Therefore make a practice of reading this *Surat* YASIN over your dead relations or friend.

2.04 Anyone that recites *Surat* YASIN every night, and then dies, he dies as *Shahid* (martyr).

2.05 Whoever reads *Surat* YASIN in the beginning of he day, all his needs for that day are fulfilled.

2.06 Whoever reads *Surat* YASIN, his or her sins are forgiven.

2.07 Whoever reads it in hunger, is satisfied.

2.08 Whoever reads it having lost his or her way, finds it.

2.09 Whoever reads it on losing an animal, finds the same.

2.10 Whoever reads it apprehending that his food will run short, that food becomes sufficient.

2.11 If one reads it beside a person who is in the agonies of death, the same are made easy for him.

2.12 If one reads it on a woman experiencing difficulty in child birth, the delivery becomes easy.

2.13 If *Surat* YASIN is read by one who fears the ruler or an enemy; he gets rid of this fear.

2.14 If somebody reads *Surat* YASIN and *Surat* WA SAFFAT on Friday and begs Allah Sub hallah Wata'allah of something, his prayers are granted.

B **THE USE OF SURAT AL-WAQI'AH**

As directed by the Holy Prophet Muhammad (PBH)

1. If you recite this *Surat* every night, starvation shall never afflict you.

2. If you recite *Surat* AL WAQIAH and AR RAHMAN, you are reckoned amongst the dwellers of Jannat ul Fridaus (the best story of paradise).

3. Teach *Surat* Al Waqiah to your wife and children. If it is recited for the contentment of the heart and for the sake of the next world, then worldly gains will come to us automatically.

C **THE USE OF *SURAT* TABARAKA-AL-LADHI**

The uses of this *Surat* as directed by the Holy Prophet Muhammad (PBH):

1. It intercedes for a person (its reader) until he is forgiven.

2. The Holy Prophet Muhammad (PBH) said "my heart desires that this *Surat* should be in the heart of every believer"

3. Any believer who reads this *Surat* and *Surat* Alif lam mim (*Sajdah*) between the *Maghrib* (dusk) *Salat* and Isha *Salat*, is like a person who stands in *Salat* through out the night called "Lailat al Qadr"

(the 27th night of Ramadan the month of fasting and the 9th month of the Islamic calendar).

4. Any believer that reads these two *Surats*, 70 virtues are added to his account, and 70 sins are condoned.

5. If one reads these two *Surats*, reward equal to that of standing in *Salat* through out Lailatul Qadr is written for him.

6 The Holy prophet Muhammad (PBH) would not go to bed to sleep until he had recited *Surat* Alif lam mim (sajdah) and *Surat* Tabaraka ladhi.

7. Khalid Ibn. Ma'dan (Radiallahu anhu) has said that he heard it narrated thus "There was a man who was a great sinner, but he used to recite *Surat Sajdah*. He never read anything else. This *Surat* spread its wing over the man and submitted to Allah, 'O my sustainer! This man used to recited me very frequently: so that intercession of that *Surat* was accepted. All his sins were changed to virtues".

8. This *Surat* pleads for its reader in the grave and says 'O, Allah! If I am contained in Thy Book, then accept my intercession; otherwise write me off from Thy Book!

9. "This *Surat* appears in the form of a bird spreads its wings over the dead and guards him against the punishment in the grave". The same applies to *Surat* Tabaraka ladhi.

D FATIHA: THE USE AND METHODS

1. The Holy prophet Muhammad (PBH) said to his followers "I tell you of a *Surat* which is the greatest that is the most virtuous in the Holy Qur'an. It is AL-HAMD (the first Surah of the Qur'an) which has seven *Ayats*. It is said by some *ULAMA*, that whatever was in the earlier Divine books is condensed in the Glorious Qur'an and the contents of the Qur'an are condensed into Suratal Fatihah.

2. The Mashaika have stated that the reading of Suratal Fatihah with firm belief cures all maladies whether spiritual or worldly, external or internal.

3. In the 6th books of Hadidth, Sahabah used to read Suratal Fatihah and blow upon those bitten by a snake or a scorpion and even on the epileptic and on the mentally deranged.

4. When going to bed recite Suratal Fatihah and *Surat* Ikhlas and blow on yourself, you will be immune from all dangers except death.

5. According to a Hadith, Suratal Fatihah is equivalent to 2/3rd of the Holy Qur'an in reward.

6. The Holy Prophet Muhammad (PBH) was reported to have said "I have been given four things from the special treasure of *'Arsh'* from which nothing has ever been given to any one before:

    1. Suratal Fatihah

    2. Ayat ul Kursiy

    3. Amanar Rasulu

    4. Suratal Kauthar.

7. Hadrat Hasan Basri (rahmatullah Alaih) reports the saying of the Holy prophet Muhammad (PBH) that whoever read Suratal Fatihah is like one who read the Torah, the gospel, the Psalms and the Glorious Qur'an.

8. It is reported in one Hadith that the Devil lamented, wept and threw dust on his head on four occasions:

    1. When he was cursed;

    2. When he was thrown out of Heaven

    3. When the Holy Prophet Muhammad (PBH) was given prophethood; and

    4. When Suratal Fatihah was revealed.

9. It is written in the established practices of Mashaikh that Suratal Fatihah is Ism al A'zam the most Glorious Name of Allah and it should be read for the achievement of all objectives.

There are two ways of reading it:

1. One method is to read this Suratal Fatihah 41 times for 41 days after 2 *Raka'ats* before *Subhu Salat*. Each should be recited with "Bismillahir Rahmanir Rahim". What ever the objective may be, it will, Insha Allah (if Allah wills) be fulfilled.

2. The Second method is to read it 70 times after 2 *Raka'ats* before *Subhu Salat* on the 1st Sunday of a new moon, after which the number is reduced by 10 every day until the course ends with a reading of 10 times on the 7th day. Repeat this weekly course for 4 weeks. If the purpose is achieved at the end of the 1st month, well and good; otherwise this course should be repeated for the second month and if necessary for the third month.

10. In the treatment of a patient or one who is bewitched, it should be recited and blow on water and be used for drinking.

11. To cure chronic diseases write the Suratal Fatihah 41 times on a porcelain dish, and the writing is washed into a container, and add to the water the following:

    1. Water of Rose

    2. Musk; and

    3. SAFFRON

The water is given to the patient for drinking for 40 days.

12. To tooth ache, head ache, and stomach pain, read it 7 times and then blow on the patient.

13. The readers of Suratal Fatihah and Amanar Rasulu are called Nur, because on the day of Judgement these will travel in front of their readers (illuminating their parth).

E THE USE OF INNA ANZALNAHU

The following use of INNA ANZALNAHU FILAILATIL Quadir (chapter 97 of the Holy Qur'an is confirmed by IKIRAMAT (Radiyallahu anhu) That he heard it from Ibn Abas who said he heard it from Abu Hurairah; and Abu Hurairah took an oath that he heard it from the Holy Prophet Mohammed (PBH). The Holy prophet Muhammad (PBH) said that he heard it from Malaika Jibril; and Malaika Jibril (Angel Gabriel) took oath that he heard it from the Almighty Allah. And the Almighty Allah Ta'ala, took oath with His Greatness and said:

1. Any Muslim who rise up at the (dead) of Friday night and perform 12 Raka'at, and each raka'at recites Fatihah once, - Inna Anzalnahu once, and Qulhuwallahu 12 times, his or her flesh will from that night be forbidden to the torment of fire.

    a. The first 2 *Raka'ats* will prevent any form of suffering at the time of death.

    b. The 2nd 2 *Raka'ats* will protect him or her from the ordeal of the grave.

    c. The 3rd 2 *Raka'ats* will prevent the darkness of the grave

    d. the balance 6 raka'at will escort him or her to the day of Judgement.

2. Any one who recites INNA ANZALNAHU 1,000 times at night will gain access to paradise unexamined.

3. Any Muslim that recites it 3 times (at any time) God Almighty will bless him or her with the blessings as much as the number of people that existed in this world and in the hereafter.

4. He who recite it once, and write it and drink it, will never be a munafiqun through out his or her life.

5. He who recites it (regularly) 11 times before Al zuhur *Salat*, will not die until he or her sees the Holy Prophet Muhammad (PBH) asleep.

6. Any Muslim who recite it at the appearance of the early morning star (i.e after 2 *Raka'ats* before *Subhu Salat*) 7 times and *Salat* Anabi (i.e Alahuma Sali, alah Muhammad Wasali) 70 times, the Holy Prophet Muhammad (PBH) said that he or she will gain access to paradise without any doubt. That any one who doubts it is an unbeliever (Kafir).

7. He who recites it 1,000 times on Friday night, will see his paradise before his or her death.

8. He who recites it on a Friday 50 times will be blessed (with blessings equivalent) to the greatness of the following prophets of the Almighty God:

    a. Prophet Ibrahim (Alaihis Salam)

    b. Prophet Ishaqa (Alaihis Salam)

    c. Prophet Ya'kub (Alaihis Salam)

    d. Prophet Musa (Alaihis Salam)

    e. Prophet Isa (Alaihis Salam)

9. He who recites it (regularly) on Saturday 11 times will be loved by God Almighty. He or she will be loved by all the prophets of the Almighty God, the angels and human beings.

10. He who recites it (regularly) 11 times on Sunday before Al zuhur *Salat* will be elevated by God Almighty in this world and in the hereafter and will be given special gifts in paradise.

11. He who recites it (regularly) on Monday 11 times all his or her sins will be forgiven.

12. He who recites it (regularly) on Tuesday 30 times will not suffer from hunger in this world, and the Devil and the Jinn will have no power to cause harm through out one's life.

13. He who recites it (regularly) on Wednesday 12 times, all his sins are forgiven and will not indulge in the habit of stealing throughout his or her life.

14. He who recites it (regularly) on Thursday 30 times all his or her sins are forgiven by the special Grace of the almighty God.

15. Waliyi Shaib Ibn Mohammed (Rahmat ullah Alaihis) used to saythat any Muslim that wants to see Lailatul Qadir, or gain closeness to God Almighty or a good and Godly wife to marry, should embark on 6 months course as follows:

    (a) Every Friday night before going to sleep, should recite:

        1. INNA ANZALNAHU 1,000 times

        2. Sharbazu, Kharbazu, Rabzu Ibn Abdullahi – 510 times.

COMMENTARY AND CONCLUSION

You can see for yourself that God Almighty does not want any one to be sentenced to hell; for eternal punishment. All that is required of us is what is contained in the last portion of verse 186 of Surahat Baqara "... Let them also with a will listen to my call, and believe in Me: That they may walk in the right Way" The call of God Almighty is contained in Surah AL-Mumin verses 1,2,;3,4,5,6,52,58,59,60, etc.

The point is that refraining from sinful act is not enough, you should also with a will practice restraining others from misdeeds. ALLAMA Sherani writes "... Simply guarding ones *Salat* is not enough, because when a calamity befalls, it does not befall on the wrong doers alone. It affects everybody in that locality. Once the Sahabah asked the Holy Prophet Muhammad (PBH) "can we perish when there are pious people among us? The Holy Prophet Muhammad (PBH) replied "yes, if the vice becomes predominant".

In another Hadith it was reported that the Holy prophet Muhammad (PBH) was sitting comfortably, when he suddenly became emotional and said "I swear by Allah that you people (the Muslims) cannot obtain salvation, unless you prevent the Tyrants from tyranny".

Hazrat Jareer Ibn Abdallah says I heard the messenger of Allah saying "when a sin is committed before an individual or a party, and they do not prevent it in spite of having power, then Allah inflicts a severe punishment on them before their death (Targhib).

There is another Hadith to the same effect "The Almighty Allah ordered that a certain village should be overturned. Angel Jibril (Alaihis Salam) submitted that there was a person who had never committed any sin. The Almighty Allah said that it was true, but that he witnessed so much disobedience to Me (around him) and never did appear a frown on his face (in disapproval).

In fact it is because of this Hadith that *Ulamas* do not hesitate to express their disapproval when they see any disobedience to the Almighty God being committed. It has to be understood that it is not the duty of *Ulamas* alone to check disobedience to the commandments of Allah. It is the duty of every Muslim who wants his or her prayers answered by God Almighty. Bilal Ibn Sa'd (radiallahu anhu) has said "If evil deeds are committed secretly only the evil doer suffers for it, but if they are committed openly and nobody prevent them, all the people are punished.

I therefore call on you today to rise up against evil doers in your locality. Challenge them where ever you find them. Call people to the oneness of God Almighty. 'LA ILAHA ILLALLAH' so that mankind can be saved from himself. Death is fast approaching. Do something today, so that God Almighty can take notice of your effort no matter how small, before the arrival of the Death Train in your station; i.e. before you commence the unavoidable journey to meet the Almighty Allah.

Of no profit to you will be your relatives and your children on the Day of Judgement. He will judge between you for Allah sees all ye do.[213]

O ye who believe! Fear Allah and let every soul look to what provision he has sent forth for his morrow. Yea fear Allah for he is well acquainted with all that ye do. And be ye not like those who forgot Allah. And He made them forget themselves! Such are the rebellious transgressors.[214]

Allah is He, who knows (all things) both secret and open; He (is) most Gracious, most Merciful. He is very severe in punishment.

Allah is He, than whom there is no other God; the sovereign, the Holy ONE, the source of peace (and perfection), the Guardian of Faith, the preserver of safety, the Exalted in might, the irresistible, the Justly Proud: Glory to Allah (High is He) above all things and the partners they attribute to Him.

He is Allah, the creator, the originator and nothing existed before Him. He is the present and nothing is possible without Him. He is the end of everything and nothing comes after Him. He is from ever lasting to ever lasting. He is the sustainer, the fashioner and nourisher of all things. To Him belong the most Beautiful names: Whatever is in the heavens and on earth Doth declare His praises and Glory and He is the Exalted in might, the wise. His mercy exceeds His wrath, therefore no matter your previous sins, begin today to use this book to release you from the chains of the accursed Devil and accelerate your advancement to salvation: Flee onto Allah; O ye flee onto Allah for He is waiting to receive you.

May the Almighty Allah bless you, your family and your parents and your community Amen. I still plead with you to remember me my family and my parents in your prayers. My name is MAHMUD SALIHU UMORU the slave of the Almighty God.

CHAPTER EIGHT
END OF TIME

Jesus says: "The Judgement day will be so dreadful that, verily I say unto you, the reprobates would sooner choose ten hells than go to hear God speak in wrath against them. Against whom all things created will witness. Verily I say unto you, that not alone shall the reprobates fear, but the saints and the elect of God, so that Abraham, shall not trust in his righteousness and Job shall have no confidence in his innocence. And what say; even the messenger of God shall fear, for that God, to make known His Majesty, shall deprive His messenger of memory, so that he shall have no Remembrance how that God hath given him all things. Verily I say unto you that speaking from the heart, I tremble because by the world I shall be called God, and for this I shall have to render an account. As God liveth, in whose presence my soul standeth, I am a mortal man as other men are, for although God has placed me as prophet over the house of Israel for the health of the feeble and the correction of sinners, I am the servant of God, and of this ye are witness, how I speak against those wicked men who after my departure from the world shall annul the truth of my Gospel by the operation of Satan. But I shall return towards the end, and with me shall come Enoch and Elijah, and we will testify against the wicked, whose end shall be accursed".[215]

Before that day shall come, great destruction shall come upon the world, for there shall be war so cruel and pitiless that the father shall slay the son, and the son shall slay the father by reason of the fraction of peoples. Wherefore the cities shall be annihilated, and the country shall become desert. Such pestilences shall come that none shall be found to bear the dead to burial, so that they shall be left as food for beasts. To those who remain upon the Earth, God shall send such scarcity that bread shall be valued above gold, and they shall eat all manner of unclean things. O miserable age, in which scarce any one shall be heard to say: "I have sinned, have mercy on me, O God", but with horrible voices they shall blaspheme Him who is glorious and blessed for ever. After this, as that day draweth nigh, fifteen days, shall come every day a horrible sign over the inhabitants of the Earth. The first day the sun shall run its course in Heaven without light but black as the dye of cloth, and it shall give groans as a father who groaneth for a son nearing to Death. The second day the moon shall be turned into blood, and blood shall come upon the Earth like dew. The third day the stars shall be seen to fight among themselves like an army of enemies. The forth day the stone and rocks shall dash against each other as cruel enemies. The fifth day every plant and herb shall weep blood. The sixth day the sea shall rise without leaving its place to the height of one hundred and fifty cubits, and shall stand all day like a wall. The seventh day it shall on the contrary sink so low as scarcely to be seen. The eight day the birds and the animals of the Earth and of the water shall gather themselves close together, and shall give forth roars and cries. The ninth day then shall be a hail of storm so horrible that it shall kill such wise that scarcely the tenth part of the living shall escape. The tenth day shall come such horrible lightening and thunder that the third part of the mountains shall be split and scorched. The eleventh day every river shall run backwards and shall run blood and not water. The twelfth day every created thing shall groan and cry. The thirteenth day the Heaven shall be rolled up like a book, and it shall rain fire, so that every living thing shall die. The fourteenth day there shall be an Earth quake so horrible that the tops of the mountains shall fly through the air like birds and all the Earth shall become plain. The fifteenth day the holy Angels shall die and God do alone shall remain alive, to whom be honour and glory".[216]

A number of Hadith told, that the holy prophet (PBH) says: "The last hour will not be established until you see before it ten incidents: The smoke, Ad-Dajjal (antichrist); the beast, the rising of the sun from the west, the descent of *Jesus*, son of Mary (may peace be upon him), the Gog and Magog; the three collapses: one in the east one in the west, and one in Arabia. At the end, fire would come out of Al-Yemen and expel people to their assemblage and a gale throwing the people into the sea. There would be turmoil from the east from where the horns of Satan would appear.

People would return to the worship of idols i.e AL-Lat and Al-Ouzza. Then Allah would send an agreeable wind. Every one who has in his heart a mustard grain of faith in Allah would die. Those who have no goodness in them would survive. These are the ones that would revert to their parents' religion. I say unto you, the last hour would not come until a man passes by a grave of another man and would say: I wish I were in his place because of calamity. A time when the murderer would not know why he had committed the murder and the murdered would not know why he had been killed. It would be the time "the Muslims would fight the Jews. The Muslims would kill them, until the Jew hides behind the stone and the tree. The stones or the trees would say: O Muslim, O Abdullah here behind me is a Jew come and kill him. But the 'Ghargad' a Jewish tree would not say this" it would be a period "around thirty imposters and liars would be resurrected; all of them claiming that he is the messenger of Allah.

The issues to be carefully considered in these prophecies are some of them will happen exactly as foretold, and some of them may be parables. For example the Hadith of the holy prophet Muhammad (PBH) says: "... then Allah would send an agreeable wind. Every one who has in his heart a mustard grain of faith in Allah would die. Those who have no goodness in them would survive. These are the ones that would revert to idolatry. Obviously these are the people, that will witness the last fifteen days prophesized by *Jesus* (Peace be upon him). *Jesus* also prophecised that after his departure the truth of his Gospel shall be annulled by wicked people by the operation of Satan. This prophecy has been fulfilled by the Almighty God; The Nicolaitan conspiracy which led to the establishment of Gentile Christianity is a good example *Jesus* (peace be upon him) prophecised that he would return from Heaven back to Earth towards the end of time. The Hadith of the holy prophet Mohammed (PBH) confirms this prophecy: "On the authority of Hudaifa Bin Qusaid Al Ghafari... The holy prophet (PBH) mentioned ten incidents that would happen before the establishment of the last hour, and one of them is the return of *Jesus*, son of Mary back to Earth. And on the authority of Abu Hurairah (radiallahu anhu), *Jesus* (peace be upon him) would return from Heaven to Earth as "A just judge". He will break crosses, kill swine, abolish Jizya, and the wealth will pour forth to such an extent that no one will accept it". In another Hadith, the holy prophet says: "The antichrist would appear in my nation and he would stay for forty". I do not know if it is forty days or forty months or forty years. Allah the exalted would then send *Jesus* son of Mary as though he is Urwa Bin Masud. He (*Jesus* Christ) would chase him and kill him. Then people would live for seven years that there would be no hostility between two persons. Then Allah would send cold wind from the side of Syria that no one would survive on the surface of the Earth, (i.e. all people of faith no matter how small in their hearts)". Only the wicked people would survive and would witness the horrors of the last 15 days foretold by *Jesus*, son of Mary.

The invasion of Iraq by the forces of America and Great Britain appear as fulfillment of this prophecy of the holy prophet (PBH) and the return of *Jesus*, son of May from Heaven to Earth is around the corner.

The appearance of Gog and Magog as one of the signs of last hour, prophesized by the holy prophet (PBH) seems also to fit in very well by the aforementioned recent invasion of Iraq by America and British forces, in complete violation of the UN Charter. Some believe that Gog and Magog are wild beasts that would be let loose to cause havoc on the globe as sign of the nearness of the day of Judgement. Others believe that they are two nations that will dominate the world. The holy Qur'an confirmed that Gog and Magog are two nations.[217]

The appearance of Gog and Magog is also clearly foretold in another chapter of the holy Qur'an "At length when Gog and Magog are let loose and they will sally forth from every point of eminence"[218]

The domination of the world by two nations as evidence of, the last hour is spoken of in the Hadith: In various ways according to one Hadith "No one will have the power to fight against them".[219] According to another Hadith, "They will drink the waters of the whole world.[220] According to a third Hadith, the Almighty God said: "I have created some of my servants whom no one can destroy but myself".[221] The holy Bible says: "A mighty conflict will engulf the world: Nation shall rise against nation and kingdom against kingdom; and there shall be famines, pestilences and Earthquakes in diverse places. All these are the beginning of sorrows[222] Again, these two nations are already drinking the water of the whole world through the instrumentality of their financial cabals: IMF and the world Bank. There is no power that can stand against them as foretold by a Hadith of the holy prophet Muhammad (PBH). Right now where ever IMF and World Bank go with their economic reform programmes they leave the country in worse state than prevailed before the introduction of their economic reform programmes. They have succeeded in creating poverty in every nation in the developing world. And the two nations effectively sidelined the United Nations Organisation recently by their illegal invasion of Iraq. However a Hadith says that Allah has said: "I have created some of my servants whom no one can destroy, but myself". This is true, as there is no power on Earth today that can destroy the forces of America and Great Britain, except the Almighty God that has created them. All these are signs of the last hour. Therefore do not delay your Repentance and Amendment. *Do it now; before been overtaken by the inevitable – Death.*

THE NATURE OF ANTICHRIST (AD-DAJJAL)

Antichrist is what is called Ad-Dajjal in Islam, a Hadith of the holy prophet Muhammad (PBH) tells us that Ad-Dajjal's right eye is blind and "would be like a floating grape". Every prophet of God Almighty "warned his people of the one-eyed liar". He can easily be identified, because between his eyes would be written the letters K.F.R (i.e. Kafir, Unbeliever). He would bring along with him an image of paradise and fire. The holy prophet (PBH) says: "what he would call paradise is fire. I warn you of him, as Noah warned his people of him. I know better about him than he knows about himself. Along with him would be two flowing canals: One seen with the naked eye, flowing with clear water, and the other, also seen with the naked eye flowing with blazing fire". From this description, Ad-Dajjal has been foretold by all the

124,000 prophets of the Almighty God. Democracy is now being preached as a religion, and those preaching and forcing it on mankind have successfully floated a satellite in space, the one eyed equipment spying on all nations of the world. There is a cult dominating the world to day whose symbol of worship is "one eye object". The cult has multiplied in various forms some of its branches slaughter newly born babies for money and wealth, others slaughter old and young for the same purpose, and even exhumed newly died and buried loved ones from their graves, cut off their heads for sale to ready buyers. Father and mother do not spare sons and daughters, and similarly sons and daughters do not spare their parents. Brothers no longer spare their sisters and sister no longer spare their brothers. They are all engaged in worse rebellious act against God Almighty. These are the ones that wallow in wealth and power. Unless you join the unholy alliance against God Almighty you are denied all access of escape from poverty, sorrows, pains, damned anguish, and penury unheard of in the annals of history. It is the unholy alliance against The Almighty God they present to you as paradise while in actual fact is fire.

Those already in it know what they are facing which they cover up with pretended ease and affluence. Beneath the flowing garment the richly furnished homes and offices, etc is fire. They are in a state of perpetual torment because the accursed Satan can never give you access to his evil wealth and power without paying a price. Therefore the canal of fresh water that the Ad-Dajjal presents is fire. The canal of fire which he presents, difficulties, penuries, sorrows and dammed anguish that is the canal of fresh water, and the straight way to salvation; therefore stay in it, the lord God Almighty is watching and will come to the rescue at His own time. He only allows the Satan to fool himself for the last time before the Judgement day. Therefore what people see as wealth, position or power etc is fire, and what people see as hardship of all sorts, is sweet pure water. The holy prophet (PBH) enjoin on all believers to frequent themselves in the recitation of the opening verses of *Surat* "Al-Kahf"; when the Ad-Dajjal surfaces. Now that we know that he has surfaced, we should frequent ourselves in the recitation of the opening verses of *Surat* "Al Kahf".

The holy prophet (PBH) says "that the Ad-Dajjal (antichrist) would appear on the way between Syria and Iraq and would ravage right and left. He would stay on Earth for forty days, the first day would be like a year, the second day like a month, the third day like a week, and the rest of the days would be like ordinary days of our reckoning". That prayer during the period would be by estimate of time. That Ad-Dajjal would walk on Earth like cloud driven by the wind. He would come over to people and mislead them (with wealth, power and positions). They would affirm their faith and respond to him. He would command the sky to rain, and the Earth would grow crops. In the evening, the animals would come covered with their humps very high and their udders full of milk and their flanks stretched. He would then come to a people and call them to his way. But they would reject him, and he would turn away from them, and drought would befall them. Nothing would be left with them in form of wealth. He would pass by the ruins and would say to it: bring forth your treasures, and it would come out and would collect them like the swarms of bees". The kind of situation in Iraq; after destroying the country, America and his allies descended on the oil reserves of Iraq and plundered it. The holy prophet (PBH) says: "Mean while, Allah would send *Jesus*, son of Mary and he will descend at the white minaret, in the eastern side of Damascus wearing two garments lightly dyed with saffron and placing his hands on the wings of two Angels. Beads of pearl would drop of him if he lowered his head and also if he raised his head. Every unbeliever who would smell the odour of his body would die. His breath would reach as far as he would be able to see. Then he would search for him (antichrist) until he would catch hold of him at the gate of Ludd and kill him. Those who rejected Ad-Dajjal would come to *Jesus*, son of Mary and he would wipe their faces and would inform them of their ranks in paradise.

Another Hadith says: "the antichrist would be accompanied by seventy thousand Jews of Isfahan wearing Persian shawls". May the Almighty God, save us and join us with the righteous. Amen.

CHAPTER NINE
DEATH: A BRIDGE TO ETERNAL LIFE

In the previous chapters, I tried to remind you of the straight path to Allah: the Beneficent, the Merciful, who forgives sins again and again. The holy Qur'an says: "If ye do love Allah, follow me: Allah will love you and forgive your sins: For Allah is oft-forgiving, most merciful".[223] If Allah forgives your sins through Repentance and Amendment, you are assured of success when Death takes the strong hold of you; For Death is not the end of our souls as scientists would want us to believe. Death is the bridge through which mankind and Jinn cross to eternal life. However prolonged this worldly life may be, it is mortal and must end one day. And however great may be the possessions of this world, one day is one day, and that day these possessions are bound to be left behind.

Poverty and/or hunger are ill-companions in this life. It is worse in the eternal life, for Death can take us out of the sorrows, penury, pains and damned anguish of this life, but without Repentance and Amendment in this life, all those ills and much more will abide with the rebellious ones in the next life forever. The life of this world is transitory. Therefore do not let your reasons to be clouded by stupor. We are enamored of the embellishments of the waiting room of a station where the period of our stay ends, with the arrival of the train (Death). This book has taught you of the kind of preparations you should make: arrangements of goods for the journey and provisions for those things which will prove useful on arrival at the eternal home. There is no need to waste your precious and short time dusting and furnishing the waiting room: Purchasing mirrors and maps for hanging in this room for the eternal life is immortal, its blessings are everlasting. "O those who keep faith! Let not your goods and your offspring make you heedless towards the Remembrance of God Almighty."[224] When Death comes, "God certainly grants no respite to any man, for God is well aware of all our deeds". The accumulation of wealth, power and valuable goods and the pride of family and offspring that have made us indifference in carrying out the commands of the Almighty Allah; cannot save us in the Hereafter. Let mankind and jinn be warned, that all these things would be left behind without notice when Death comes.

Therefore avoid negligence, *Repent and make Amends now*; wake up from your slumber before the shout goes around that you have fallen ill, and in a critical state and all effort of physicians and skilled doctors have failed. At this stage, the dieing person becomes speechless and the soul begins to escape from his body and at last crosses over to eternal life. The kith and kin at once start to prepare the funeral. The cries and laments of the sympathisers are over and they have calmed down. The enemies all jubilant; the kinsmen are busy dividing the estate, and as for the dead man, he lies entrapped by his own deeds. Such is the reality of mortal life. The case of Death is severe indeed, and by and large we fail to realize its gravity. In all our daily-day- to day activities, we seldom hint at Death and even when we do we just bring it in as a piece of conversation. This will not avail us. Instead, let us get our hearts clear from the thought of all other pursuits, and think of Death as if it were facing us. The realization can be brought about by recalling how you participated in the preparation of the funerals of friends and relatives and bore them in the Earth. Imagine their faces, their high stations in life, and reflect how Earth would have disfigured the beauty of their faces, their bodies disintegrated into pieces; how they departed leaving behind their worldly possessions and power, how they have turned their children into orphans and wives into widows, relations and loved ones into mourning. Let it come down on you seriously today that one day you are inevitably going to meet this doom.

The dead, what plans had they conceived, they entertained thoughts of making provisions for years ahead. And yet, when they were planning for years ahead, Death was hovering over their heads. The final day of their lives had come; but they knew not, that tonight they would be no more. Hadrat Ibn Abbas (May God be pleased with him) says: Qaroon belonged to the family of Moses (Mercy and Blessings of Allah be upon him) and was his cousin. He made great progress in the worldly knowledge and was jealous of Hadrat Moses. One day Moses said to him: "The Almighty and Glorious God hath commanded me to take poor due (*Zakat*) from you. He refused to give *Zakat* and said to the people that Moses wanted "to eat up your wealth on the pretext of *Zakat*. He ordered for the prayer and you tolerated. He gave other commandments and you obeyed them. Now he orders you to pay *Zakat* (poor due) ask you to submit to it". The people said: "We cannot tolerate it. You should yourself tell us some plan" He told them: "I have thought out a plan and that is to induce a corrupt woman to put blame on Moses that he wants to attack her chastity".

The people succeeded in influencing her on promise of some great reward that she should bring this calumny against Hadrat Moses (alaihis salam) when Qaroon got her assent, he went to Hadrat Moses (Alaihis Salam) and said to him: "Reveal to the children of Israel the commandments of Allah, which He hath sent unto you, by gathering them at one place. Hadrat Moses liked this proposal and got all the children of Israel assembled at one place and when all were present; Hadrat moses delivered to them commandments of the Almighty Allah". He told them: "Allah hath commanded you to worship Him only, not to ascribe any partner to Him, treat your relatives with kindness and then inform them about other commandments through which it was revealed that if a married man commits fornication, he must be stoned to Death". Upon this the people said: "And if you commit fornication!" Hadrat Moses replied: If I commit this offence I should also be stoned to Death". The people said: "You have fornicated". Hadrat Moses enquired from them in utter amazement: "Have I committed fornication?" The people replied: "You have done so". And, after saying this they called for the woman and asked her: "What do you say about Moses? Hadrat Moses adjured her to state the fact. The woman said: "Since you are asking me something on Oath, I dare not tell a lie. The fact is that these people have promised me so much reward for casting upon you this blame. You are however, innocent. On hearing this, Hadrat Moses fell down in prostration with tears in his eyes. In prostration, the Almighty and Glorious God sent unto him a divine revelation: "There is no cause for you to worry about it. We have favoured ye with a mighty power to rule over Earth so that you award punishment to these people whatever order you will give to the Earth about them, it will submit to it. Hadrat Moses raised his head from prostration and ordered the Earth to swallow them up. The Earth engulfed them up to their heels, when they begin to implore Hadrat Moses to spare their lives. Hadrat Moses again ordered the Earth to engulf them. When they had sunk into the Earth up to their necks, they again started imploring Moses to spare their lives. Moses again ordered the Earth to engulf them. The Earth swallowed them all. There upon, The Almighty and Glorious God sent a Divine revelation onto Mose: "They begged and implored you to spare their lives. I swear by My Honour that if they had called Me and begged Me, I would have acceded to their request.[225]

The point of all this is that when Qaroon was poor and wretched he approached Hadrat Moses to beseech Allah on his behalf to favour him with wealth. Hadrat Moses did and The Almighty Allah accepted his (Hadrat Moses) prayers, Allah instructed Moses what Qaroon should do. Moses came out of his prayers and told Qaroon that Allah, the Bountous giver has accepted the prayers. That Qaroon should build a farm and plant only calabash seedlings during the planting season. Qaroon did as directed by Moses. At the time of harvest, every calabash broken by Qaroon was gold. Qaroon became a wealthy man.

The commandment of Allah required the payment of *Zakat*. The collection of a very small fraction from the earnings of the wealthy men in the community to cater for the poor. This, Qaroon refused to do, instead hatched a plot not only to defame Moses (his source of wealth) but to eliminate him completely.

Worldly power, glory, wealth, position, and all that man scramble for are but a fleeting show. The possession or want of them does not betoken a man's real value or position in the coming world that will endure forever. Yet they have their uses: They test a man's sterling quality. He who becomes their slave, loses rank in the next world. He who uses them if he gets them, and does not fall into despair if he does not get them, shows his true mattle and quality, and his conduct proclaims him.

There is a story told of one of the rulers of Bukhara who was a tyrannical ruler. One day he was going on his ride when he happened to see a dog suffering from itch, cold and was thus in serious trouble. As soon as that cruel king saw it, tears welled up his eyes, and asked his servant to bring the dog to his home, and to look after it, until he returns. After giving this instruction he took his way. When he returned, he ordered them to bring the dog and got it tied in a corner of his house. He fed the dog and gave it water to drink, rubbed the body with oil, and covered it with a sheet. Fire was lit around in order to protect it from cold. Two days later, the cruel king died. A pious man – a saint who was well aware of his cruelties and atrocities, saw him in a dream. He asked him: "What has happened to you?" The cruel king replied: "The Almighty God caused me to stand before Him and said to me "You were a dog (i.e. ye did works like dogs and not like human-beings). Despite these faults, because you were kind to a dog that was in trouble your sins have all be forgiven by Me".[226]

This means if He is pleased even with an insignificant deed of a person, that person is successful. Therefore we should always try to seek Allah's pleasure, as no one knows when for a small liking of His, one may attain salvation.

BARZAKH

When the train of Death takes man from the waiting room, i.e. from this transitory world, it goes straight to the station of Barzakh, where he will disembark into the kind of home the man built for himself while he was in this transitory world. The literal meaning of the word Barzakh is "barrier between two things". From religious point of view, Barzakh is the period which intervenes between this transitory world and the life of Hereafter which commences immediately after the Death of a man, and it ends on the Day of Resurrection. This means that as soon as a man dies, he enters Barzakh to wait for the Day of Judgement.

The Almighty God created Adam, from dust and taught him the name of everything, glorified his position by enjoining upon the Angels to fall down before him in prostration and He made his abode in paradise, caused him to fall down to the Earth with a view to fulfilling the purpose for which He had created him. In this way, his first lodging was paradise the second was the world, the third was Barzakh and the fourth again is paradise. Similarly, the first dwelling place of his offspring is the womb of mother, the second place is the world, the third place is Barzakh, and the fourth is either paradise or hell. The Almighty God allotted appropriate functions for each abode and called the world a field for practical work and a cultivation ground for the Hereafter. He bestowed a great favour upon man by sending prophets for guidance in order to enable humanity to discriminate between right and wrong. Those who follow the teachings of the prophets are known as believers and those who reject the teachings of the prophets are called unbelievers. The interval between Death and resurrection is called Barzakh. During this period a believer feels happy whereas unbelievers suffer torments. The real reward or punishment will be given on the day of Judgement after due reckoning.

The Importance Of Islam

Jesus says: verily I say unto you, that every prophet when he is come hath borne to one nation only the mark of the mercy of God. And so their words were not extended save to that people to which they were sent. But the messenger of God, when he shall come, God shall give to him as it were the Seal of His hand, insomuch that he shall carry salvation and mercy to all the nations of the world that shall receive his doctrine. He shall come with power upon the ungodly , and shall destroy idolatry, insomuch that he shall make Satan confounded: For so promised God to Abraham, saying : "Behold in thy seed I will bless all the tribes of the Earth; and as thou hast broken in pieces the idols O Abraham even so shall thy seed do"[227]

"I therefore say unto you that the messenger of God is a splendour that shall give gladness to nearly all that God hath made, for he is adorned with the spirit of understanding and of counsel, the spirit of wisdom and might, the spirit of fear and love, the spirit of prudence and temperance, he is adorned with the spirit of charity and mercy, the spirit of justice and piety the spirit of gentleness and patience, which he hath received from God three times more than He hath given to all His creatures. O blessed time, when he shall come to the world! Believe me that I have seen him and have done him reverence even as every prophet hath seen him. Seeing that of his spirit God giveth to them prophecy. And when I saw him my soul was filled with consolation saying: "O Mohammed, God be with thee, and may He make me worthy to untie thy shoelatchet, for obtaining this I shall be a great prophet and holy one of God" And having said this, *Jesus* rendered his thanks to God".[228] ... As for me I am now come to the world to prepare the way for the Messenger of God, who shall bring salvation to the world. But beware that ye be not deceived for many false prophets shall come who shall take my words and contaminate by Gospel".[229]

All these mean that Mohammed (PBH) is the living exponent of the message of Allah as a whole. If any one desires a religion, other than Islam (i.e. Submission to Allah), never will it be accepted of him; and in the Hereafter, he will be in the ranks of those who have lost[230] on such people rests the curse of Allah, of His Angels and of all mankind.[231] Therefore fear Allah as he should be feared, and die not except in a state of Islam.[232]

Situation Under The Grave

When a pious man dies, he is made to sit by the Angels. He attains a position that neither anxiety nor grief overtakes him. First of all, a question pertaining to Islalm is put to him. After that he is asked about the messenger of God, the holy prophet Muhammad (PBH). He confirms that the holy prophet (PBH) brought clear signs from God to the entire world and that he believed those signs to be true in their entirety. Thereafter he is shown a place in hell which presents a scene of pandemonium. Then diverting his attention from the scene, he is told that God has saved him from that punishment. After that he is shown a place in paradise, richly bedecked and elegantly adorned, where he observes pleasant sights. Then he would be told that he would be granted access to it after the Judgement day.

When a wicked man dies, he is seated in the grave overwhelmed with anxiety and grief. The same questions that have been mentioned above, are put to him. He says that he knows nothing about anything. At first the gate of Paradise is opened for him to see. After seeing its adornment and elegance, and all riches contained therein, he is told that it was his original dwelling place, but has now been denied to him. Then a spectacle of hell is shown to him. He observes there a state of pandemonium. Then he is informed that he would be given that abode to dwell in it forever after the Judgement day. Then he is informed that it was a reality which he doubted when he was alive.

Hadrat Abu Qatada (radiallahu anhu) reports that the holy prophet(PBH) once said: "The Death of a wrong doer is a great relief and pleasure to the inhabitant of towns and villages, trees and animals: They are relieved of the calamities which fall upon the Earth on account of him: The evil shadow of his sins create troubles for every one, including riots and draughts. In the case of a believer, he feels pleasure when he is relieved of the worldly worries and troubles to find a place in the neighborhood of the Almighty God. The holy prophet (PBH) says: "The grave is either one out of the gardens of paradise or one of the pits of hell.[233] The nature of paradise and hell shall be discussed in the next chapters of this book.

The poor, the rich, all are lying on the same ground. The wealth of the wealthy is left behind and some of it falling into the hands of the enemies. The eyes that used to roll in their sockets in all directions have gotten out, necks separated, limbs disembodies, mouths filled with water and pus, and the worms and insects crawl in all parts. Wives bound to nuptial ties with another and enjoying themselves. O Death! Why can't man remember you always: Why does man allow himself to be deceived by the demands of this transitory world? Why can't man busy himself with the provisions and preparations for the inevitable journey towards the grave? Why should man entangle himself with the allurements of this mortal world? Why should man waste his time on all these while Death is hovering over his head? I wonder indeed! Repent today and make Amendment, Remember Allah frequently, for without them, there will be no happy journey to the grave. The procedures to follow are already detailed out in the previous chapters of this book. Remember this brief life span is not the sum total of man's existence. Man takes off this body of flesh, as he does to his clothes and is alive still in another guise, though its nature is beyond our ken. No one knows what awaits him in the life that is fast approaching and the state mankind will find itself after the dissolution of this mortal life; nor can mankind read the hand which holds that destiny in its determination. It is for this reason that Almighty God choose prophets among men, blessed them with the insight into the unseen world to learn what it holds for man. So by their noble office they mediate between the two worlds: They stand on the frontier.

Why is the Almighty God so concerned about mankind? The reason is simple: He intended a very high destiny for man, and placed him in his uncorrupted state even above the Angels. Due to corruption man has made himself even lower than the beast. What was it that made man so high and noble? The differentiating quality which the Almighty God gave man was that He breathed something of His own spirit into man. This means that man was given a limited choice between good and evil and that he was made capable of forbearance, love and mercy. And in himself man summed up Allah's great world: Man is in himself a microcosm.

Prophets after prophets of God came with a religion from the Almighty Allah to remake the world in the image of the Almighty God, but ended up being remade in the image of the world except Islamic religion. R.H. Dufty says that scientists have now agreed with Islamic position, that "eventually the whole Universe will collapse on itself and there is no knowing what the outcome will be; what the nature of any subsequent existence will be".[234]

Therefore, every scholarly enquiry must not stray too for from its moral and social base: prosperity must not be measured by wealth and worldly gains alone, but most importantly, by the health of the mind and the spirit. But if men deliberately put away the Remembrance of Allah from their minds, the natural consequence under Allah's Decree is that they join on with evil. The down-ward course in evil is rapid. But the most tragic consequence is that evil persuades its victims to believe that they are pursuing good. They think evil to be their good. They go deeper and deeper into it and become more and more callous[235] they remain in that state until Death over take them.

As mentioned already in previous chapters of this book, in order for mankind to rise above the mere animal part that it is now inclined, and achieve dignity as spiritual being, and noble destiny there is the indispensable need to constantly Remember Allah, the Almighty. If inspite of Allah's loving care, any particular men or group of men decide or chose to misuse their powers or willfully disobey Allah's law; it is the promise of Allah to set them aside and substitute others in their place with like powers. Although Allah's gifts are free, let no one think that he can monopolise them, or misuse them without being called to answer for the trust in the grave and on the day of reckoning. The man of God should not be discouraged by the seeming stupendous prosperity of the wicked, because Allah's will and plan work in their own good time.[236] History tells us that the Persian Empire crumbled for many reasons; Chief among them was the corruptions of the Zoroastrian religion which had crept in under the Parsian Dynasty of the Arsacids. The Sasanians that over threw Arsacids failed to purify the Old Persian belief in the dual principle of good and evil. They only adhered to fire worship as the Chief feature of their cult. In manners and morals they succumbed to the vices of arrogance, luxury, sensuality and monopoly of power and privilege which the office of religion was to denounce and root out.

The fact that our forefathers were righteous cannot help us, unless we are ourselves are righteous. The doctrine of personal responsibility is a cardinal feature of Islamic religion. Every soul draws the need of its acts on none but itself. No bearer of burden can bear the burden of another.[237] It is true that Adam and Eve sinned but Allah forgave them.[238] They repented and made Amendment and Allah in His infinite mercy, had mercy upon them and washed away their sins. Therefore 'the concepts of original sin and some one dying for another persons sins' is stupid and frivolous, even the holy Bible distance itself from these concepts in Exodus 20: 6 which reads: "... And showing mercy on thousands of them that love Me and keep My Commandment".

CHAPTER TEN
THE DAY OF JUDGEMENT

The holy *Jesus* (peace be upon him) says: "On fifteenth day (of dreadful events) the holy Angels shall die and God alone shall remain alive, to whom be honour and glory". The holy Qur'an confirms it in Surat 55 v. 26 – 28: "All that is on Earth will perish, but will abide (forever) the face of thy Lord, full of Majesty, Bounty and Honour. Then which of the favours of your Lord will ye deny?" And having said this, *Jesus* smote his face with both hands and then smote the ground with his head. And having raised his head he said: "cursed be every one who shall insert, into my sayings that I am the son of God" At these words the disciples fell down as dead. Where upon *Jesus* lifted them up, saying: 'Let us fear God now, if we would not be affrighted in that.[239] The Holy Qur'an says; "O ye who believe, fear Allah as He should be feared, and die not except in a state of Islam".[240]

Fear is of many kinds:

(1) The abject fear of the coward;

(2) The fear of a child or an inexperienced person at the face of an unknown danger;

(3) The fear of a reasonable man, who wishes to avoid harm to himself or to the people whom he wishes to protect; and

(4) The reverence which is akin to love; that is the fear to do something which is not pleasing to the object of love.

The first fear, is unworthy of a man, the second is necessary for immaturity, the third is a manly precaution against evil as long as it is unconquered and the fourth is what is required of a Muslim, as it is the seed-bed of righteousness. This is the fear the holy *Jesus* referred to and is confirmed by the holy Qur'an.

The holy *Jesus* said that after the fifteen calamitous days "there shall be darkness over the world (for) forty years. God alone being alive, to whom honour and glory is due forever. When the forty years be passed, God shall give life to His messenger (Muhammad (PBH) who shall rise again like the sun, but resplendent as a thousand suns. He shall sit, and shall not speak, for he shall be as it were beside himself. God shall raise again the four Angels, favoured of God who shall seek the messenger of God (Mohammed PBH) and having found him, shall station themselves on the four sides of the place to keep watch upon him. Next shall God give life to all the Angels, who shall come like bees circling round the messenger of God (i.e. Mohammed (PBH). Next shall God give life to all His prophets, who following Adam, shall go every one to kiss the hand of the messenger of God (Mohammed (PBH) committing themselves to his protection. Next shall God give life to all the elect, who shall cry out! "O Mohammed, be mindful of us!" At whose cries pity shall awake in the messenger of God, and he shall consider what he ought to do, fearing for their salvation. Next shall God give life to every created thing, and they shall return to their former existence, but every one shall besides possess the power of speech. Next shall God give life to all the reprobates, at whose resurrection, by reason of their – hideousness, all creature of God shall be afraid, and shall cry: "Let not thy mercy forsake us, O Lord our God". After this shall God cause Satan to be raised up, at whose aspect every creature shall be as dead, for fear of the horrid form of his appearance. May it please God said *Jesus* that I behold not that monster on that day. The messenger of God alone shall not be affrighted by such shapes because he shall fear God only.

Then the Angel, at the sound of whose trumpet all be raised, shall sound his trumpet again, saying: "Come to the Judgement O creatures, for your creator willeth to judge you". Then shall appear in the midst of Heaven over the valley of Jehoshaphat a glittering throne, over which shall come a white cloud, whereupon the Angels shall cry out: "Blessed be thou our God, who hast created us, and saved us from the fall of Satan". Then the messenger of God (Mohammed (PBH) shall fear, for that he shall perceive that none hath loved God as He should. For he who would get in change a piece of gold must have sixty mites; wherefore, if he have but one mite he cannot change it. But if the messenger of God shall fear, what shall the ungodly do who are full of wickedness?"[241]

"The messenger of God shall go to collect all the prophets, to whom he shall speak praying them to go with him to pray to God for the faithful. And everyone shall excuse himself neither for fear; nor as God liveth, would I go there, knowing what I know. Then God, seeing this, shall remind his messenger (Mohammed (PBH) how he created all things for love of him, and so his fear shall leave him, and he shall go nigh unto the throne with love and reverence while the Angels sing: "Blessed be thy holy name O Lord, our God".

'And when he hath drawn nigh unto the Throne, God shall open (His mind) unto His messenger, even as a friend unto a friend when for a long while they have not met. The first to speak shall say: "I adore and love Thee, O my God, and with all my heart and soul I give Thee thanks for that thou didst vouchsafe to create me to be thy servant, and madest all for love of me so that I might love thee for all things and in all things and above all things, therefore let all thy creatures praise Thee, O my God". Then all things created by God shall say: "We give Thee thanks, O Lord and bless Thy holy name". Verily I say unto you, the demons and reprobates with Satan shall then weep so that more water shall flow from the eyes of one of them than is in the river of Jordan. Yet shall they not see God.

'And God shall speak unto His messenger (Mohammed (PBH), saying: "Thou art welcome, O my faithful servant; therefore ask what thou wilt, for thou shalt obtain all". The messenger of God (i.e. Mohammed (PBH) shall answer, "O Lord, I remember that when thou didst create me, thou sayeth that thou hadst willed to make for love of me the world and paradise, and Angels and men, that they might glorify thee by me thy servant. Therefore, Lord God, merciful and just. I pray Thee that thou recollect thy promise made unto thy servant".

'And God shall make answer even as a friend who jesteth with a friend, and shall say: "Hast thou witnesses of this, my friend Mohammed?" and with reverence he shall say: "Yes, Lord". Then God shall answer: "Go call them, O Gabriel". The Angel Gabriel shall come to the messenger of God, and shall say: "Lord who are thy witnesses?" The messenger of God shall answer: "they are Adam, Abraham, Ishmael, Moses, David, and *Jesus* son of Mary".

'Then shall the Angel depart, and he shall call the aforesaid witnesses, who with fear shall go thither. And when they are present, God shall say unto them: "Remember ye that which my messenger affirmeth?" They shall reply: "what thing, O lord?" God shall say: "That I have made all things for love of him, So that all things might praise me by him". Then every one of them shall answer: "There are with us three witnesses better than we are, O Lord". And God shall reply: "Who are these three witnesses?" then Moses shall say: "The book that thou gavest to me is the first" and David shall say: "The book that thou gavest to me is the second" and he who speaketh to you (i.e. *Jesus*) shall say: Lord, the whole world, deceived by Satan, said that I was Thy son and Thy fellow, but the book that thou gavest me said truly that I am thy servant and that book confesseth that which thy messenger of God speak, and shall say: "Thus saith the book that thou gavest me, O Lord". And when the messenger of God hath said this, God shall speak, saying: "All that I have now done, I have done in order that every one should know how much I love thee". And when He hath thus spoken, God shall give unto his messenger a book, in which are written all the names of the elect of God. Wherefore every creature shall do reverence to God saying: "To Thee alone, O God, be glory and honour, because thou hast given us to thy messenger" [242]

'God shall open the book on the hand of His messenger, and his messenger reading therein shall call the Angels and prophets and all the elect and on the forehead of each one shall be written the mark of the messenger of God. And in the book shall be written the glory of paradise'.

'Then shall each pass to the right hand of God: Next to whom shall sit the messenger of God, and the prophets shall sit near him, and the saints, and the Angel shall then sound the trumpet, and shall call Satan to Judgement."[243]

'Then that miserable one shall come, and with greatest contumely shall be accused of every creature. Wherefore God shall command the Angel Michael, who shall strike him one hundred thousand times with the sword of God. He shall strike Satan, and every stroke is heavy as ten hells, and he shall be the first to be cast into the abyss. The Angels shall call his followers and they shall in like manner be abused and accused. Wherefore the Angel Michael, by commission from God, shall strike some a hundred times, some fifty, some twenty, some ten, some five. And then shall they descend into the abyss because God shall say to them: "Hell is your dwelling place O cursed ones".

'After that shall be called to Judgement all the unbelievers and reprobates, against whom shall first arise all creatures inferior to man, testifying before God how they have served these men, and how the same have outraged God and His creatures. And the prophets every one shall arise testifying against them; wherefore they shall be condemned by God to enternal flames. Verily I say unto you, that no idle word or thought shall pass unpunished in that tremendous day. Verily I say unto you that the hair-shirt shall shine like the sun, and every louse a man shall have borne for love of God shall be turned into pearl. O, thrice and four times blessed are the poor, who in true poverty shall have served God from the heart, for in this world are they destitute of worldly cares, and therefore be freed from many sins, and in that day they shall not have to render an account of how they spend the riches of the world, but they shall be rewarded for their patience and their poverty. Verily I say unto you, that if the world knew this, it would choose the hair-shirt sooner than purple, lice sooner than gold, fasts sooner than feasts".

'When all have been examined, God shall say unto His messenger: "Behold, O my friend, their wickedness, how great it has been for I their creator did employ all created things in their service, and in all things have they dishonoured Me. It is most just, therefore, that I have no mercy on them. The messenger of God shall answer: "It is true, Lord, our glorious God, not one of thy friends and servants could ask Thee to have mercy on them nay, I thy servant before all ask justice against them".

'And He having said these words, all the Angels and prophets, with all the elect of God-nay, why say I the elect? Verily I say unto you, spiders and flies stones and sands shall cry out against the impious, and shall demand justice.

'Then shall God cause to return to Earth every living soul inferior to man, and He shall send the impious to hell. Who, in going, shall see again that Earth, to which dogs and horses and other vile animals shall be reduced. Wherefore shall they say: "O Lord God, cause us also to return to that Earth." But that which they ask shall not be granted to them.[244]

'While *Jesus* was speaking the disciples wept bitterly. And *Jesus* wept many tears. Then after he had wept, John spake: O master two things we desire to know. The one is, how it is possible that the messenger of God, who is full of mercy and pity, should have no pity on reprobates that day, seeing that they are of the same clay as himself? The other is how is it to be understood that the sword of Michael is heavy as ten hells, and then is there more than one hell? *Jesus* replied; "Have ye not heard what David the prophet saith how that the just shall laugh at the destruction of sinners, and shall deride him with those words saying: "I saw the man who put his hope in his strength and his riches, and forgot God". Verily, therefore, I say unto you, that Abraham shall deride his father, and Adam all reprobate men; And this shall be because the elect, shall rise again so perfect and united to God that they shall not conceive in their minds the smallest thought against justice, therefore shall each of them demand justice and above all the Messenger of God. As God liveth, in whose presence I stand, though now I weep for pity of mankind, on that day I shall demand justice without mercy against those who despise my words, and most of all against those who defile my Gospel".[245]

The holy Qur'an has the following to say about the last hour and the Judgement day: The inevitable will come to pass that day, and no soul will any longer deny its coming. That is the day the Earth shall shake to its depths and flattened out and graves turned upside down. Mountains shall crumbled to atoms and scattered to the winds as dust, and shall vanish as if they were a mirage. The oceans shall boil over with swells and shall be suffered to burst forth. The sun with its spacious light shall be folded up, the sky cleft asunder, and the stars scattered. Heavens shall be opened as if there were doors. Everything will be in violent commotion, followed by repetition of commotions. Hearts, that day will be in serious agitation, and all eyes will be cast down: Those of the blessed ones in humble modesty, and those of the rejecters of Allah, in utter humiliation, sorrow and shame for their arrogance and insolence in this probationary life. That day, each soul shall know what it hath sent forward.

The Earth is a globe enclosing within it many secrets and mysteries; gold and diamond in its mines, heat and magnetic forces in its entrails and the bodies of men and women of countless generations buried within its soil. At its dissolution, all these contents will be disgorged: It will lose its shape as a globe, and cease to exist. So as man and his possessions dissolve into the Earth, and the Earth itself dissolves into a truer reality.

On the day of Judgement there will be a sorting out of Good and Evil. This means mankind will be sorted out into three categories:

i. The first category among the Good will be the specially exalted class as they are the ones that the holy Qur'an calls "those nearest to Allah[246] which *Jesus* son of Mary (may peace be upon him) said would sit next to the messenger on the right hand of God. The righteous people are the ones the holy Qur'an calls "the companions of the right Hand.[247] *Jesus*, son of Mary (May peace be upon him) described them as saints and/or elect of God, and would sit next to those of the exalted class, before the Angels take their seat on the Judgement day.

This will be the position of the High table on the Judgement day. We should therefore repent of our sins, O Lord our God; have mercy upon us, forgive our sins, and favour us with a seat with the righteous on the High-table on the inevitable day of Judgement. The third category or class will be those in agony, which the holy Qur'an calls the companions of the Left Hand.[248] Many who were high and mighty in this life and were negligent in Remembrance of Allah, and deny the day of Judgement, and worked iniquities in this probationary life will be brought low for their sins, and many who were lowly but virtuous, will be exalted to various ranks and degrees.

Why should man forget his creator while himself is a created being? The seed of his body, out of which physical life starts, is not created by man, no matter the foolish arguments of some scientists, it is created by Allah. Why will man not recognize and bear witness of this fact by living a life of obedience to Allah's law? Just as Allah has created this life that we see, so He has decreed that Death should be the common lot of all of us. Surely, if He can thus give life and Death as we see it, why should we refuse to believe that He can give us other forms, when this mortal life is over? The future life as indicated by what we now know, is to be on a wholly different plane. Abu Hurairah reports that the holy prophet (PBH) said: "Allah the exalted and glorious said". "I have prepared for my servants (something) which no eye (has ever) seen, no ear (ever) heard, and no human heart has ever perceived".[249] This is testified in the Holy Qur'an. The holy prophet (PBH) then recited thus "No soul knows what (comfort) is concealed from them as a reward for what they did".[250]

May Allah keep us steadfast in His command, forgive us our sins, and join us with the righteous on the day of Judgement - Amen.

On the question of the Right Hand of God and left hand of God, *Jesus* was once asked by Matthew one of his disciples thus: "O master, thou hast confessed before all Judaea that God hath no similitude like man; and now thou hast said that man receiveth from the hand of God accordingly, since God hath hands He hath a similitude with man".

Jesus answered: "Thou art in error, O Matthew and many have so erred, not know the sense of the words. For man ought to consider not the outward (form) of the words, but the sense; seeing that human speech is as it were an interpreter between us and God. Now know yet not, that when God willed to speak to our fathers on Mount Sinai, our fathers cried out: "Speak thou to us, O Moses, and let not God speak to us, lest we die? And what said God by Isaiah the prophet, but that so far as the Heaven is distant from the Earth, even so are the ways of God distant from the ways of men, and thoughts of God from the thoughts of men.[251]

The holy Qur'an tells us that on the Day of Judgment those nearest to Allah will be in Gardens of Bliss, seating on couches encrusted (with gold and precious stones). They will recline on them facing each other. Round about them shall be youths of perpetual (freshness) who will serve them with goblets (shining) beakers, and cups (filled) out from clear flowing fountains. They shall suffer no after – ache, nor will they suffer intoxication. They shall be served with fruits of their choice, eat flesh of fowls as they desire. Their companions shall be beautiful, with big and lustrous eyes,, like unto pearls well guarded. A reward for the deeds of their past (life). No frivolity will they hear therein, nor any mischief; Only the saying peace, peace and peace will they be hearing.

The companion of the Right Hand will be among the lot-trees without thorns. And tall trees with flowers and fruits piled one above another. They shall be in extended shade with water flowing constantly and all Season fruits in abundance. They shall relax on couches raised high and all about them shall be pure virgins created from special creation, equal in age and full of love. A Hadith says that in paradise there is a tree, where the rider can travel under its shadow for a hundred years.[252] Abu Hurairah added that the inhabitants of paradise would not make water, not void excrement. They would neither suffer from catarrh, nor would they spit. Their combs will be made of gold, their sweat will be musk. The fuel of their brazier will be aloes, and their wives will be large eyed maidens. Their shaping would be as the shape of a man in the form of their father Adam, and of sixty cubits tall. They will be made to enjoy such an everlasting bliss that they would not become destitute, nor would their clothes wear out, nor their youth wear away. There would be an announcer saying: verily, you have health, and would never be ill again, you would live for ever, and never to experience Death again, you would remain young and never to grow old and you would always live in affluent circumstances and never to become destitute. The words of Allah the exalted and glorious are: "This is the paradise, you have inherited it for what you used to do". A Hadith says that the Muslims shall constitute half of the inhabitants of paradise. Another Hadith says: "Allah would admit the inhabitants of paradise to paradise, and the inhabitant of fire to fire. Then announcer would come between them and would say: O inhabitants of paradise, no Death, and you inhabitant of fire, no Death. Every one is immortal in what he is in" Allah would say to the inhabitants of paradise "O citizens of paradise". They would respond: "our Lord, we are at your service, luck and goodness are in thy hands. Allah would say: "Are you satisfied (now)? They would reply: "why should we not be satisfied Lord, Thou hast given us what thou hast not given to any of thy creatures. Allah would say: "Should not I give you even better than that?" They would say: "Our lord, what is better than this? "Allah would say: "To settle down my warm heart (on you) and should not ever befall my wrath on you afterwards. He Allah would lift the veil. They would discover that they were not given something dearer to their hearts, better than looking at their Lord" Imam Muslim added that the holy prophet (PBH) recited a verse from the holy Qur'an: "*Those who do good will have the best reward and even more*".[253]

CHAPTER ELEVEN
THE NATURE OF PARADISE

Jesus said to his disciples: "God is so immeasurable that I tremble to describe Him. But it is necessary that I make unto you a proposition. I tell you, then, that the Heavens are nine and that they are distant from one another even as the first Heaven is five hundred years journey. Wherefore the Earth is distant from the highest Heaven four thousand and five hundred years journey. I tell you, accordingly, that the Earth is in proportion to the first Heaven as the point of a needle and the first Heaven in like manner is in proportion to the second as a point, and similarly all the Heavens are inferior each one to the next. But all the size of the Earth with that of all the Heavens is in proportion to paradise as a point, nay, as a grain of sand. Is this greatness immeasurable? The disciples answered: "Yea, surely". Then said *Jesus*: "As God liveth, in whose presence my soul standeth, the Universe before God is small as a grain of sand, and God is as many times greater (than it) as it would take grains of sand to fill all the Heavens and paradise, and more. Now consider ye if God hath any proportion with man, who is a little piece of clay that standeth upon the Earth. Beware then, that ye take the sense and not the bare' words, if ye wish to have eternal life." The disciples answered: "God alone can know himself and truly it is as said by Isaiah the prophet". He is hidden from human senses. *Jesus* answered: "So is it true; wherefore when we are in paradise we shall know God, as here one knoweth the sea from a drop of salt water. Returning to my discourse, I tell you that for sin alone one ought to weep, because by sinning man forsaketh his creator. But how shall he weep who attendeth at revelings and feasts? He will weep even as ice will give fire! Ye needs must turn revelings into fast, if ye will have lordship over your senses, because even so hath our God lordship". Thaddaeus, one of the disciples asked: "So then, God hath sense over which to have lordship?" *Jesus* replied: "Go ye back to saying: "God hath this, God is such". "Tell me, hath man sense?" "Yes answered the disciples. Then *Jesus* said: "Can a man be found who hath life in him, yet in him sense worketh not?" "NO" said the disciples. "Ye deceive yourselves" said *Jesus* "for he that is blind, deaf, dumb and mutilated, where is his sense? And when a man is in a swoon?

Then, were the disciple perplexed, when *Jesus* said: "Three things there are that make up man: that is the soul, the sense and the flesh, each one of itself separate. Our God created the soul and the body as ye have heard, but ye have not yet heard how He created the sense. Therefore tomorrow, if God please, I will tell you all.[254]

The holy Qur'an tells us that life after Death takes two forms: a life in paradise for those in whom the good preponderates over the evil and a life in hell for those in whom the evil preponderates over the good. Paradise is the abiding place of the righteous who are generally described as those who believe and do good deeds.[255] These are the people on the right hand who will abide in 'Gardens in which rivers flow, the rivers corresponding to faith, and the trees of the garden corresponding to the good which a man does.

The description of Paradise as a garden with rivers flowing in it, is however, only a parable: "A parable of the Garden which the righteous are promised: Therein are rivers of water".[256] The blessings of paradise cannot be conceived in this life, and are not, therefore, things of this world: "No soul knows what is hidden for it of that which will refresh the eyes: a reward for what they did"[257] An explanation of these words by the holy prophet(PBH), is given in Bukhari as fellows: "Allah says, I have prepared for my righteous servants that which no eye has seen and no ear has heard, and what the heart of man has not conceived".[258] Therefore paradise and what it contains cannot even be conceived by the mind of man. Ibn Abbas is reported to have said that "nothing that is in paradise resembles anything that is in this world except in name"[259] For instance, a "shade" is mentioned in several places of the holy Qur'an in connection with the blessings of paradise, but a shade is not what is really meant, for there shall be no sun: "They shall see therein neither sun, nor intense cold"[260] The word is there, but the significance underlying it is different. Nor are the fruits of paradise like the fuits of this life because these shall be the fruits of deeds done: "Whenever they shall be given a portion of the fruits thereof, they shall say: "why, this is what we were fed with before".[261] Evidently the fruits of the deeds are meant here, and not the fruits that the Earth grows, because the latter are not given to all the faithful here while the former are. Similar is the case with the water, the milk, the honey, the cushions, the thrones, the clothes, and the adornments of the next life; these descriptions are of the nature of similes as the Qur'an calls them similes.

In fact, a little consideration would show that even our ideas of place and time are not applicable to the next life. It is said in the holy Qur'an that Paradise extends over the whole of the Heavens and the Earth: "And hasten to forgiveness from your Lord and a Garden the extensiveness of which is as the Heavens and the Earth."[262] and when the prophet was asked where hell was, if paradise extends over the whole of the Heavens and the Earth, he replied: "Where is the night when the day comes?"[263] This shows clearly that paradise and hell are more like two conditions than two places. Again, not withstanding that the two are poles as under, the one being the highest of the high and the other the lowest of the low, they are separated only by a wall "then a separation would be brought between them by a wall having a door in it; on the inside of it shall be mercy and before the outside of it there shall be chastisement.[264] Elsewhere, speaking about the inmates of paradise and inmates of hell, the holy Qur'an says: "And between the two there shall be a veil".[265] Again a "Vehement raging and roaring" of hell fire is mentioned repeatedly,[266] but those in paradise shall "not hear its faintest sound"[267] while we are told that those in hell shall talk with those in Heaven and the two shall hear each other.[268] The concluding verse reads "And the inmates of the fire shall call out to the dwellers of the Garden saying: 'Pour on us some water of that which Allah has given you'. They shall say: 'Allah has prohibited them both to the disbelievers".

The greatest of all the achievements in Paradise is Allah's goodly pleasure – that is the grand achievement [269]. May Allah make us to be among of those to be favoured with it – Amen.

CHAPTER TWELVE
THE NATURE OF HELL

Jesus (Peace be upon him) says: "Hell is one, O my disciples and in it the damned shall suffer punishment eternally. Yet hath it seven rooms or regions, one deeper than the other and he who goeth to the deepest shall suffer greater punishment. Yet are my words true concerning the sword of the Angel Michael, for he that committeth but one sin meriteth hell, and he that committeth two sins meriteth two hells. Therefore in one hell shall the reprobates feel punishment as though they were in ten, or in a hundred or in a thousand, and the omnipotent God, through His power and by reason of His justice, shall cause Satan to suffer as though he were in ten hundred thousand hells, and the rest each one according to his wickedness".

Then Peter one of the disciples of *Jesus* said: "O master, truly the justice of God is great, and today this discourse hath made thee sad; therefore, we pray thee, rest and tomorrow tell us what hell is like."

Jesus replied: "O Peter thou tellest me to rest; O Peter, thou knowest not what thou sayest, else thou hadst not spoken thus. Verily, I say unto you, that rest in this present life is the poison of piety and the fire which consumeth every good work. Have ye then forgotten how Solomon, God's prophet with all the prophets, hath reproved sloth? True it is that he saith: "The idle will not work the soil for fear of the cold, therefore in summer shall he beg! Wherefore he said: "All that thy hand can do do it without rest". And what saith Job, the most innocent friend of God: "As the bird is born to fly, man is born to work". Verily I say unto you, I hate rest above all things".[270]

Jesus said: "Hell is one, and is contrary to Paradise, as winter is contrary to summer and cold to heat. He therefore who would describe the misery of hell, must needs have seen the paradise of God's delights".

'O place accursed by God's justice for the malediction of the faithless and reprobates of which said Job, the friend of God: "There is no order there, but even lasting fear!" And Isaiah the prophet against the reprobate saith: "Their flame shall not be quenched nor their worms die". And David our father, weeping said: "Then shall rain upon them lightening and bolts and brimstone and great tempest. "O miserable sinners, how loathsome then shall seem to them delicate meats, costly raiment, soft couches and concord of sweet song! How sick shall make them raging hunger, burning flames, scorching cinders, and cruel torments with bitter weeping! Truly it is better never to have been formed than to suffer such cruel torments. For imagine a man suffering torments in every part of his body, who hath no one to show him compassion, but is mocked of all, tell me, would not this be great pain?

The disciples answered: "The greatest" then said *Jesus*; "Now this is a delight (in comparison) of hell. For I tell you in truth, that if God should place in one balance all the pain which all men have suffered in this world, and shall suffer till the day of Judgement, and in the other one single hour of the pain of hell, the reprobates would without doubt choose the worldly tribulations, for the worldly come from the hand of man, but the others from the hand of devils, who are utterly without compassion. O what cruel fire they shall give to miserable sinners! O what bitter cold, which yet shall not temper their flames! What gnashing of teeth and sobbing and weeping! For the Jordan has less water than the tears which every moment shall flow from their eyes. And here their tongues shall curse all things created, with their father and mother, and their creator, who is blessed forever".[271]

The Hadith of the holy prophet (PBH) tells us that Hell would be brought on that day (Judgement day) with seventy bridles, with every bridle seventy Angels dragging it. The fire, which sons of Adam burn, is only a part of seventy parts of the fire of Hell: The distance of the two shoulders of an infidel in Hell, will be a three days journey for a swift rider. They would get up in the morning under the wrath of Allah; and they would get into the evening with the anger of Allah. The fire would cause them to burn till they would be into charcoal and would return to the original form and punishment process continues without end, except those granted intercession.

May God make us repent and make amend before Death overtakes us, and save us from His wrath – Amen.

THE EPILOQUE

Question (1): Did God Almighty ever say as credited to John in the Bible, "This is my Son with whom I am well pleased?"

Answer: ".... *Jesus* departed and went to the mount Tabor with Peter, James, John and Barnabas. Whereupon there shone a great light above him and his garments became white like snow and his face glittered as the sun and Lo! There came Moses and Elijah speaking with *Jesus* concerning all that needs must come upon our race and upon the holy city"

'Peter spake, saying: "Lord it is good to be here. Therefore if thou wilt, we will make here three tabernacles, one for thee, one for Moses and the other for Elijah".

'And while he spake, they were covered with a white cloud, and they heard a voice saying: "Behold my servant in whom I am well pleased hear ye him".

'The disciples were filled with fear, and fell with their face upon the Earth as dead. *Jesus* went down and raised up his disciples, saying; "Fear not for God loveth you, and hath done this in order that ye may believe on my words"[272]. The Lord, our God did not say: "Son", He said "my servant" according to the Gospel of *Jesus*.

The Christian doctrine that *Jesus* was the son of God was borrowed from earlier pagan people. Recent research has established the fact beyond all doubt: when St. Paul saw that the Jews would on no account accept *Jesus* Christ as a messenger of God, he introduced the pagan doctrine of sonship of God into the Christian religion, so that it might become more acceptable to the pagans.

Question (2): Did *Jesus* say: "I will come back to the world again from Heaven, as contained in the holy Qur'an and Hadith?

Answer: In discussing Judgement day with his disciples, *Jesus* said: "... I am a mortal (man) as other men are, for although God has placed me as prophet over the house of Israel for the health of the feeble and the correction of sinners, I am the servant of God, and this ye are witness, how I speak against those wicked men who after my departure from the world shall annul the truth of my Gospel by the operation of Satan. But I shall return towards the end and with me, shall come Enoch, and Elijah, and we will testify against the wicked whose end shall be cursed".[273]

Question (3): *Jesus,* son of Mary said he would come back again to Earth from Heaven, towards the end of time, and this claim has been authenticated by the Holy Qur'an and the Hadith of the Holy prophet Muhammad (PBH), what is the credibility of the claim by one Ghulam Ahmad, founder of Ahmadiya movement in Islam, that *Jesus* never went to Heavens that he lived and died at the age of 120 years in India?

Answer: A Hadith says the return of *Jesus,* Son of Mary from Heaven to Earth shall be one of the signs of the last hour. Another Hadith says after the Antichrist (Ad-Dajjal) has committed atrocities on Earth, "Allah would send *Jesus*, son of Mary, and he will descend at the white minaret, in the eastern side of Damascus, wearing garments lightly dyed with saffron and placing his hands on the wings of two Angels... Then he would search for him, until he would get hold of him at the gate of Ludd and kill him". (Imam Muslim). Any one that contradicts the Hadith is not a Muslim and Ghulam Ahmad falls into this category.

Question (4): *Jesus*, son of Mary said: "I am not God, and I am not son of God. God our creator is God alone and I am God's servant...[274] What is the position of the holy Qur'an in this matter?

Answer: The holy Qur'an says: "The likeness of *Jesus* with Allah is surely as the likeness of Adam. He created him from dust, and then said to him "Be" and he was."[275] "And the Jews say: Isa is the son of Allah and the Christians say, the Messiah is the son of Allah. These are the words of their mouths. They imitate the saying of those who disbelieved before Allah's curse be on them! How they are turned away".[276] "They take their doctors of law and their monks for Lords besides Allah, and (also) the Messiah son of Mary. And they were enjoined that they should serve one God only; there is no God but He. Be He glorified from what they set up (with him)[277]

Most of the commentators agree that by following blindly the doctors of law and monks in what they enjoined and what they forbade; different from what Allah has Decreed, they have attached to them Divine dignity. It is related in a Hadith that when this verse was revealed, 'Adi' Ibn Hatim, a convert from Christianity, asked the holy prophet (PBH) as to the significance of this verse for he said: "We did not worship our doctors of law and monks". The holy prophet (PBH) replied: "Was it not that the people considered lawful what their priests declared to be lawful, though it was forbidden by God?" Ibn Hatim replied: "Yes that is true". The holy prophet (PBH) said: "that is what the verse means".[278] Muslims who accord a similar position to their pirs or saints are guilty of the same error, and the curse of Allah is upon them.

Question (5): *Jesus* said in his Gospel: "I was not crucified, and I was not killed by my enemies and I have not died at all.[279] What is the position of the holy Qur'an in this matter?

Answer: "And for their saying: "We have killed the Messiah, son of Mary, the messenger of Allah, and they killed him not, nor did they cause his Death on the cross, but he was made to appear to them as such. And certainly those who differ therein are in doubt about it. They have no knowledge about it, but only follow a conjecture, and they killed him not for certain'. "Nay, Allah exalted him in His presence. And Allah is ever mighty, wise". [280]

Deut 21: 23 Explains that "he that is hanged is cursed of God". If *Jesus* had died on the cross, he would have been accursed; hence the statement "he was not killed on the cross and accursed, but he was exalted in the Divine presence of God".

Both the Jews and the Christians believe in the Death of *Jesus* on the cross, while according to the Holy Qur'an, they have really no sure knowledge of it. The Jews reject the Messiahship status of *Jesus* on the basis of [281] "He that is hanged is accursed of God". Their belief is that since *Jesus* died on the cross, he was accursed and no one who is accursed of God can be a prophet. The Christians believe in the contrary, although agree that *Jesus* having died on the cross was accursed according to the truth of Deut. 21: 23, but that *Jesus* had to die on the cross in order to take away the sins of those that believe in him. As in [282]"Christ hath redeemed us from the curse of the law, being made a curse for us for it is written, cursed is every one that is hanged on the tree'.

The holy Qur'an explains the absurdity of this belief. The irony is that because "they have no sure knowledge at all, they will all believe before their Death that "*Jesus* died on the cross".

Question (6): Before Judgement Day, *Jesus* gave details of the signs that would reveal it in his Gospel[283] What does Islam say regarding the signs of the Judgement Day?

Answer: The Hadith of the holy prophet (PBH) tells that "The last hour' would not come until the Euphrates deteriorates from a mountain of gold. People would fight each other (for it). Ninety nine, out of each one hundred would die, and every man among them would say: Perhaps I would be the one who would be saved.

The Last hour will not be established until you see before it, ten events:

i. The smoke

ii. Ad-Dajjal (antichrist), the beast

iii. The rising of the sun from the west,

iv. The return of *Jesus*, Son of Mary (from Heaven),

v. The Gog and Magog,

vi The three collapses: one in the east, one in the west, and one in Arabia. At the end, fire would come out of Al-Yemen expelling people to their assemblage;

vii. A gale throwing the people into the sea.

viii. The last-hour would not come until a man passed by a grave of another man and would say, I wish I were in his place.

ix. The world would not end until a day would come on people, (there would be so much murder) and the murderer would not know why he had killed, nor the murdered would know why he had been killed.

x. The Last-Hour would not come until the Muslims fight the Jews. The Muslims would kill them, until the Jew hides behind the stone, and the tree. The stone or the tree would say: O Muslim, O Abdullah here behind me a Jew, come and kill him. But the Ghargad tree (would not say this). It is of Jewish trees.

Question (7): Ghulam Ahmad, founder of Ahmaddiyya movement in Islam said in page 52 in the book published by the mission "Titled: *Jesus* in India". That it was false that *Jesus* ascended to Heaven and that "There was no evidence in the Gospel that any one saw *Jesus* ascend to the Heavens". How true is Ghulam Ahmad's statement?

Answer: Ghulam Ahmad was a poor researcher, other wise he would not have limited himself to "according to Matthew etc" in the Bible and the history of Hinduism published by uninspired people, before laying claim to his false prophethood. His claim to prophethood is one of the signs of the last hour as the holy prophet (PBH) say: "The last hour would not come until about thirty imposters and liars would be resurrected, all of them claiming that he is the messenger of Allah.[284]

Because of the importance of this matter, the following details are given as answer to this question thus:

(i) "Having gone forth from the house, *Jesus* retired into the garden to pray, according as his custom was to pray, bowing his knees an hundred times and prostrating himself upon his face. Judas, accordingly, knowing the place where *Jesus* was with his disciples went to the high priest, and said: "If ye will give me what was promised this night will I give into your hand *Jesus* whom ye seek: for he is alone with eleven companions.

The high Priest answered: "How much seekest thou?"

Judas said: "Thirty pieces of gold". Then straight way the high Priest counted unto him the money and send a Pharisee to the governor to fetch soldiers and to Herod, and they gave a legion of them, because they feared the people; wherefore they took their arms and with torches and lanterns upon staves went out of Jerusalem".[285]

(ii) "When the soldiers with Judas drew near to the place where *Jesus* was, *Jesus* heard the approach of many people, wherefore in fear he- withdrew into the house. And the eleven were sleeping". "Then God, seeing the danger of His servant commanded Gabriel, Michael, Rafael, and Uriel his minister to take *Jesus* out of the world".

"The holy Angels came and took *Jesus* out by the window that looketh toward the south. They bare him and placed him in the third Heaven in the company of Angels blessing God for ever more"[286]

iii) "Judas entered impetuously before all into the chamber whence *Jesus* had been taken up. And the disciples were sleeping; whereupon the wonderful God acted – wonderfully, insomuch that Judas was so changed in speech and in face to be like *Jesus*, that we believed him to be *Jesus*. And he, having awakened us, was seeking where the Master was whereupon we marveled, and answered: "Thou, Lord art our Master, hast thou now forgotten us?" 'And he (Judas), smiling said: "Now are ye foolish, that know not me to be Judas Iscariot".

"And as he was saying this, the soldiery entered, and laid their hands upon Judas, because he was in every way like to *Jesus*".

"We having heard Judas saying, and seeing the multitude of soldiers fled as beside ourselves".

"And John, who was wrapped in a linen cloth, awoke and fled, and when a soldier seized him by the linen cloth he left the linen cloth and fled naked. For God heard the prayer of *Jesus*, and saved the eleven from evil".[287]

"The soldiers took Judas and bound him not without derision. For he truthfully denied that he was *Jesus*; and the soldiers mocking him said: "Sir, fear not for we are come to make thee king of Israel, and we have bound thee because we know that thou dost refuse the kingdom".

"Judas answered; 'Now have you lost your senses! Ye are come to take *Jesus* of Nazareth, with arms and lanterns as a robber; and ye have bound me that have guided you, to make me king!"

"Then the soldiers lost their patience, and with blows and kicks they began to flout Judas, and they led him with fury into Jerusalem".

"John and Peter followed the soldiers afar off; and they affirmed to him who writeth (i.e. Barnabas) that they saw all the examination that was made of Judas by the high Priest, and by the council of the Pharisees, who were assembled to put *Jesus* to Death. Whereupon, Judas spake many words of madness, insomuch that every one was filled with laughter believing that he was really *Jesus*, and that for fear of Death he was feigning madness. Whereupon the scribes bound his eyes with a bandage and mocking him said: "*Jesus* prophet of the Nazarenes; (for so they called them who believed in *Jesus*), tell us who was it that smote thee?" And they buffeted him and spat in his face".

'When it was morning, there assembled the great council of scribes and elders of the people, and the high priest with the Pharisees sought false witness against Judas, believing him to be *Jesus*, and they found not, that which they sought. And why say I that the Chief Priests believed Judas to be *Jesus*? Nay, all the disciples with him who writeth (i.e. Barnabas) believed it and more, the poor virgin mother of *Jesus* with her kinsfolk and friends, believed it, insomuch that the sorrow of every one was incredible. As God liveth, he who writeth (i.e. Barnabas) forgot all that *Jesus* had said (i.e. prophesized); how that he should be taken up from the world, and that he should suffer in a third person, and that he would not die until near the end of the world. Wherefore he who writeth (i.e. Barnabas) went with the mother of *Jesus* and with John to the cross".

"The high priest caused Judas to be brought before him bound, and asked him of his disciples and his doctrine".

"Whereupon Judas as though beside himself answered nothing to the point. The high Priest then adjured him by the living God of Israel that he would tell him the truth".

"Judas answered: 'I have told you that I am Judas Iscariot, who promised to give into your hands *Jesus* the Nazarene; and ye, by what art I know not are beside yourselves, for ye will have it by every means that I am *Jesus*".

"The high Priest answered: 'O perverse seducer, thou hast deceived all Israel, beginning from Galilee even unto Jerusalem here, with thy doctrine and false miracles; and now thinkest thou to flee the merited punishment that befiteth thee by feigning to be mad? As God liveth, thou shall not escape it!" And having said this he commanded his servants to smite him with buffeting and kicks, so that his understanding might come back into his head…but the chief priest the Pharisees and the elders of the people had their hearts so exasperated against *Jesus* that believing Judas to be really *Jesus* they took delight in seeing him so treated".

"Afterwards they led him bound to the governor, who secretly loved *Jesus*. Whereupon he, thinking that Judas was *Jesus*, made him enter into his chamber, and spake to him, asking him for what cause the Chief Priests and the people had given him into his hands".

"Judas answered: "If I tell thee the truth, thou wilt not believe me; for perchance thou art deceived as the chief priests and the Pharisees are deceived".

"The governor answered (thinking that he wished to speak concerning the law): 'Now knows thou not that I am not a Jew? But the chief priests and the elders of the people have given thee into my hand; wherefore tell us the truth, that I may do what is just. For I have power to set thee free and to put thee to Death".

"Judas answered: 'Sir, believe me, if thou put me to Death, thou shall do a great wrong, for thou shalt slay an innocent person; seeing that I am Judas Iscariot, and not *Jesus*, who is a magician, and by his art hath so transformed me".

"When he heard this the governor marveled greatly, so that he sought to set him at liberty. The governor therefore went out and smiling said; "In the one case, at least, this man is not worthy of Death, but rather of compassion. This man saith, said the governor, 'that he is not *Jesus*, but a certain Judas who guided the soldiery to take *Jesus* and he saith that *Jesus* the Galilean hath by magic art so transformed him. Wherefore, if this be true, it were a great wrong to kill him, seeing that he was innocent. But if he is *Jesus* and denieth that he is, assuredly he hath lost his understanding, and it were impious to slay a madman"

Alas! They prevailed on the governor and "they led him to mount Calvary, where they used to hang malefactors and there they crucified Judas naked for the greater ignominy" "Judas truly did nothing else but cry out: "God, why hast thou forsaken me, seeing the malefactor hath escaped and I die unjustly?'

"Verily I say that the voice, the face and the person of Judas were like to *Jesus*, that his disciples and believers entirely believed that he was *Jesus*, where some departed from the doctrine of *Jesus*, believing that *Jesus* had been a false prophet and that by magic art he had done the miracles which he did: for *Jesus* had said that he would not die till near the end of the world; for that at that time he should be taken away from the world".

"But they that stood firm in the doctrine of *Jesus* were so encompassed with sorrow, seeing him die[288] who was entirely like to *Jesus*, that they remembered not what *Jesus* had said (i.e. prophesized). And so in company with the mother of *Jesus* they went to mount Calvary, and were not only present at the Death' of Judas, weeping continually, but by means of Nicodemus and Joseph of Abarimathia they obtained from the governor the body of Judas to bury it. Whereupon they took him down from the cross with such weeping as assuredly no one would believe, and buried him in the new sepulchre of Joseph, having wrapped him up in an hundred pounds of precious ointment". [289]

"Then returned each man to his house, He who writeth (i.e. Barnabas) with John and James his brother went with the mother of *Jesus* to Nazareth".

"Those disciples who did not fear God went by night (and) stole the body of Judas and hid it, spreading a report that *Jesus* was risen again. Whence great confusion arose. The high priest then commanded, under pain of Anathema, that no one should talk of *Jesus* of Nazareth. And so there arose a great persecution, and many were stoned and many beaten and many banished from the land, because they could not hold their peace on such matter".

"The news reached Nazareth how that *Jesus*, their fellow citizen, having died on the cross was risen again. Whereupon, he that writeth (i.e. Barnabas) prayed the mother of *Jesus* that she would be pleased to leave off weeping because her son, was risen again. Hearing this, the Virgin Mary weeping said: 'Let us go to Jerusalem to find my son I shall die content when I have seen him".

'The Virgin returned to Jerusalem with him who writeth (i.e. Barnabas), and James and John on that day on which the decree of the high Priest went forth... We with the mother of *Jesus* were consumed in grief". And returned to Nazareth, So the Angels that were guardians of Mary ascended to the third Heaven where *Jesus* was in the company of Angels and recounted all to him.[290]

"Wherefore *Jesus* prayed to God that he would give him power to see his mother and his disciples. Then the merciful God commanded his four favourite Angels, who were Gabriel, Michael, Rafael, and Uriel, to bear *Jesus* into his mother's house, and there keep watch over him for three days continually, suffering him only to be seen by them that believed in his doctrine".

"*Jesus* came, surrounded with splendour, to the room where abode Mary the virgin with her two sisters and Martha and Mary Magdalene and Lazarus and him who writeth (i.e. Barnabas), John, James and Peter. Whereupon, through they fell as dead. And *Jesus* lifted up his mother and others from the ground, saying: "fear not, for I am *Jesus*; and weep not for I am alive and not dead. They remained every one for a long time beside himself at the presence of *Jesus*, for they altogether believed that *Jesus* was dead. Then the virgin weeping said: "Tell me my son, wherefore God, having given thee power to rise the dead, suffered thee to die to the shame of thy kinsfolk and friends, and the shame of thy doctrine. For every one that loveth thee hath been as dead". [291]

"*Jesus* replied embracing his mother: 'Believe me mother, for verily I say to thee that I have not been dead at all; for God hath reserved me till near the end of the world". And having said this he prayed the four Angels that they would manifest themselves and give testimony how the matter had passed… Then the four Angels (manifested themselves and narrated to the virgin how God had sent for *Jesus*, and had transformed Judas, that he might suffer the punishment to which he had sold another…"

The third day *Jesus* said: Go to the Mount of Olives with my mother for there will I ascend again into Heaven and ye shall see who shall bear me up".

"So there went all save twenty-five of the seventy-two disciples, who for fear had fled to Damascus. And as they all stood in prayer at mid-day, came *Jesus* with great multitude of angels who were praising God: and the splendour of his face made them sore afraid, and they fell with their faces to the ground. But *Jesus* lifted them up, comforting them, and saying: 'Be not afraid, I am your master".

'And he reproved many who believed him to have died and risen again, saying: "Do ye then hold me and God for liars? For God hath granted to me to live almost unto the end of the world, even as I said unto you. Verily I say unto you, I died not, but Judas the traitor. Beware for Satan will make every effort to deceive you, but be ye my witnesses in all Israel, and through out the world, of all things that ye have heard and seen".

"And having thus spoken, he prayed God for the salvation of the faithful and the conversion of sinners. And, his prayer ended, he embraced his mother, saying: "Peace be unto thee, my mother, rest thou in God who created thee and me". 'And having thus spoken, he turned to his disciples, saying: "May God's grace and mercy be with you".

"Then before our eyes, the four Angels carried him up into Heaven." [292]

Ghulam Ahmad, the founder of Ahamadiya movement in Islam, therefore lied that "there was no evidence in the Gospel that anyone saw *Jesus* ascend to the Heavens" He was a false prophet for contradicting the Gospel of *Jesus*, the Hadith of the holy prophet (PBH) and above all the holy Qur'an.

Question (8): It is said that there is a curse on Israel, what was the nature of this curse of God, and can Repentance and Amendment clear this curse from them?

Answer: *Jesus* weeping said to his disciples: "O Jerusalem, O Israel, I weep over thee for thou knowest not thy visitation; because I would fain have gathered thee to the love of God thy creator, as a hen gathered her chickens under her wings, and thou wouldst not wherefore God saith thus unto thee: "O city, hard-hearted and perverse of mind, I have sent to thee my servant, to the end that he may convert to thine heart, and thou mayest repent; but thou, O city of confusion, hast forgotten all that I did upon Egypt and upon Pharaoh for love of thee, O Israel. Many times weepest thou that my servant may heal thy body of sickness: and thou seekest to slay my servant because he seeketh to heal thy soul of sin".

"Shall thou, then, alone remain unpunished by me? Shalt thou, and then live eternally? And shall thy pride deliver thee from my hands? Assuredly not, For I will bring princess with an army against thee, and they shall surround thee with might and in such wise will I give thee over into their hand that thy pride shall fall down into hell".

"I will not pardon the old men or the widows, I will not pardon the children, but I will give you all to famine, the sword, and derision and the temple whereon I have looked with mercy, I will make desolate with the city, in somuch that ye shall be for a fable, a derision and a proverb among the nations. So is my wrath abiding upon thee and mine indignation sleepeth not".[293]

"If Jerusalem shall weep for her sins and do penance, walking in my ways, I will not remember her iniquities any more, and I will not do unto her any of the evil which I have said. But Jerusalem weepeth for her ruin and not for her dishonouring of Me, wherewith she hath blasphemed my Name among the nations. Therefore is my fury kindled much more. As I live eternally, if Job, Abraham, Samuel, David and Daniel my servants with Moses, should pray for this people my wrath upon Jerusalem will not be appeased." [294]

Arrogance that made Satan to remain accursed for ever, the same arrogance is the problem of the Jews. If they can reflect, and become sober, and Repent and make Amend; by following what they know already i.e the teachings of Islam, the Almighty God who promised to pardon Satan if he Repents and make Amend will pardon them, because the Almighty God loves Repentance: of this I bear witness.

Question (9): From the account given by Barnabas of the crucifixion of Judas, which they thought was *Jesus*, is there any proof that *Jesus* prophesied this event before it happened?

Answer: *Jesus* said: "... Believe me Barnabas; that I cannot weep as much as I ought. For if men had not called me God I should have seen God here as He will be seen in Paradise and should have been safe not to fear the Day of Judgement. But God knoweth that I am innocent because never have I harboured thought to be held more than a poor slave(i.e. a poor and humble servant of God). Nay, I tell thee that if I had not been called God, I should have been carried into Paradise when I shall depart from the world, where as now I shall not go thither until the Judgement".

"Now thou seest if I have cause to weep. Know, O Barnabas, that for this, I must have great persecution, and shall be sold by one of my disciples for thirty pieces of money. Whereupon I am sure that he who shall sell me, shall be slain in my name, for that God shall take me up from the Earth and shall change the appearance of the traitor so that every one shall believe him to be me; nevertherless, when he dieth an evil Death, I shall abide in that dishonour for a long time in the world. But when Mohammed shall come, the sacred messenger of God, that infamy shall be taken away. And this shall God do because I have confessed the truth of the Messiah, who shall give me this reward, that I shall be known to be alive and to be a stranger to that Death of infamy".

“Then asked Barnabas: “O master, tell me who is that wretch, for I fain would choke him to Death.”

Jesus replied: “Hold thy peace for so God willeth, and you cannot do otherwise; but see thou that when my mother is afflicted at such an event thou tell her the truth in order that she may be comforted”.

‘Barnabas replied: “All this will I do, O master, if God please”.

Question (10): Despite all these glaring facts and evidences, why do Christians and some people still believe in Gospel of *Jesus* “according” to individuals, instead of “according” to the Gospel of *Jesus*?

Answer: The malice of the scribes, the doctors and rabbis corrupted the Bible: consider the statement of the Almighty God when he said to *Jesus* and his disciples at Mount Tabor: “Behold my servant in whom I am well pleased, hear ye him”. This statement is contained in the Gospel of *Jesus*. In the Bible, the story changed from “servant” to “son” in John 3:16; and many more...

Another example is the lineage of the promised Messiah: The disciples asked *Jesus*: “O master, it is thus written in the book of Moses that in Isaac was the promise made”

Jesus replied: “It is so written, but Moses wrote it not, nor Joshua, but rather our rabbis, who fear not God. Verily I say unto you that if ye consider the words of the Angel Gabriel, ye shall discover the malice of our scribes and doctors. For the Angel said to Abraham: “Abraham all the world shall know how God loveth thee; but how shall the world know the love that thou bearest to God? Assuredly it is necessary that thou do something for love of God”.

‘Abraham replied: “Behold the servant of God, ready to do all that which God shall will”.

Then spake God saying to Abraham: “Take thy son, thy first born, Ishmael, and come up the mountain to sacrifice him”.

Jesus asked his disciple: “How is Isaac first born, if when Isaac was born Ishmael was seven years old?”

"Then said the disciples: "Clear is the deception of our doctors: Therefore tell us thou the truth, because we know that thou art sent from God".

Jesus replied: "Verily I say unto you, that Satan ever seeketh to annul the laws of God, and therefore he with his followers, hypocrites and evil doers, the former with false doctrine, the latter with lewd living today, have contaminated almost all things, so that scarcely is the truth found. Woe to hypocrites! For the praises of this world shall turn for them into insults and torments in hell.

It is left for the Christians in particular and mankind in general to seek the truth with the greatest diligence, because it is the truth that will secure Us in the Judgement of God. They kept on referring to *Jesus* as "Lord God,and son of God, contrary to the Gospel of *Jesus.*

Jesus said: "As God liveth in whose presence my soul standeth, I am a mortal man as other men are, for although God has placed me as prophet over the house of Israel for the health of the feeble and the correction of sinners, I am the servant of God and of this ye are witness, how I speak against those wicked men who after my departure from the world shall annul the truth of my Gospel by the operation of the Satan. But I shall return towards the end, and with me shall come Enoch and Elijah and we will testify against the wicked whose end shall be accursed".

'And having thus spoken, *Jesus* shed tears, whereat his disciples wept aloud and lifted their voices saying: "Pardon, O Lord God, and have mercy on thy servant" '*Jesus* replied: "Amen".[295]

Question (11): Is the word "Servant" in mankind's relationship with God a degrading word, because Christians claim that the term "Servant of God which the Muslims call themselves is an insult, and that they are children of God, and that fact makes them superior to the Muslims. What is the truth of the matter?

Answer: *Jesus*"... Blessed be the holy name of God who created the splendour of all the saints and prophets before all things to send him for the salvation of the world, as He spake by His servant David saying: "Before Lucifer in the brightness of the Saints I created thee..." Here, Prophet David is described as "Servant" of God in the Gospel of *Jesus.*[296] In prayers *Jesus* said: "O Lord, (our God), I know that the scribes hate me and the priests are minded to kill me thy servant, therefore Lord God Almighty and Merciful in mercy hear the prayers of thy servant, and save me from their snares for thou art my salvation …"[297]

The holy Bible itself says:

i) 1st Corinthians 7: 20 – 23; Christians addressed as Servants of God.

ii) Roman 6: 16; you are servants of the person you owe allegiance to.

iii) Romans 6: 22; being servant of God makes one holy.

iv) Isaiah 43: 10 – You are my servants whom I have chosen.

The holy Qur'an says: "And I have not created the jinn and the men except that they should serve Me".[298] And the servants of the Beneficent are they who walk on the Earth in humility, and when the ignorant address them, they say "Peace! Allah further says: "And when my servants ask thee concerning Me, surely I am nigh. I answer the prayer of the supplicant when he calls on Me, so they should hear my call and believe in Me that they may walk in the right way"

A good Christian and a good Muslim must seek the truth, and follow the path of truth to salvation. Truth is the spear that pierced the heart of Satan, and send him and his followers to oblivion.

Question (12): *Jesus* in his Gospel says: "I am not God, and I am not son of God. Wherefore when God shall come to judge my words like a sword shall pierce each one of them that believes me to be more than man". Why does the Bible teach Christians to believe that *Jesus* is God and or son of God?

Answer: The holy Bible does not teach Christian that *Jesus* is God:

i) Isaiah 43: 10 No other God except God.

ii) Isaiah 44: 8 No other God.

iii) Isaiah 44: 5 – 6 No other God

iv) Isaiah 45: 21 No God except the Only God.

v) Matthew 4: 10 *Jesus* said: Thou shall worship only one God.

vi) Mark 12: 29 – 33 *Jesus* said Our God is one.

vii) Mark 10: 17 – 18 *Jesus* said Only God is good, he is not.

viii) 1 Timothy 6:16 God is immortal

ix) Matthew 27: 50 *Jesus* died

x) John 20: 17 *Jesus* said my God and your God, my father and your father.

xi) 1 John 17:3 There is only one God. Therefore any Christian that claims that the Bible taught him to regard *Jesus* as God has lied against the Bible and against the Gospel of *Jesus*.

Question (13): The Christians say: "*Jesus* is the saviour, and no good work can save man" How true is this statement what does the Gospel of *Jesus*, the Bible and the holy Qur'an say regarding this matter?

Answer: Saviourship is a doctrine built on the crucifixion of *Jesus*. The Christian faith is founded on the crucifixion of *Jesus* that he died for their sins. Let us examine the Gospel of *Jesus* regarding this matter: '*Jesus* said; "… Know, O Barnabas that for this I must have great persecution, and I shall be sold by one of my disciples for thirty pieces of money. Whereupon I am sure that he who shall sell me, shall be slain in my name, for that God shall take me up from the Earth, and shall change the appearance of the traitor so that every one shall believe him to be me; nevertheless when he dieth an evil death, I shall abide in that dishonour for a long time in the world. But when Mohammed shall come, the sacred messenger of God, the infamy shall be taken away. And this shall God do because I have confessed the truth of the Messiah, who shall give me this reward, that I shall be known to be alive and to be a stranger to that Death of infamy".[299]

When the event foretold by *Jesus* happened, the virgin Mary and others including Barnabas forgot the prophecy of *Jesus*, and they were so overwhelmed with sorrows, and believed that it was *Jesus* that was crucified. When eventually *Jesus* returned from the third Heaven to console his mother and his disciples with four Angels; *Jesus* said to his mother: "Believe me mother, for verily I say to thee that I have not been dead at all, for God hath reserved me till near the end of the world". And having said this he prayed for the four Angels to manifest themselves and give testimony how the matter had passed. Then the four Angels manifested themselves and narrated to the virgin in the present of John, James, Peter and the two sisters of the Virgin Mary and Barnabas how God had sent for *Jesus*, and had transformed Judas, so that he could suffer the punishment to which he had sold another.[300]

Despite these glaring facts, Christians refuse to believe that *Jesus* was never crucified and never died on the cross; talk less of dying for any body's sins.

The holy Bible tells us that *Jesus* prayed against Death,[301] and that the Lord answers the prayer of the righteous.[302] Therefore *Jesus* was never crucified, and never died on the cross. This means that God sent for *Jesus* at the time Judas the traitor led the enemy soldiers to arrest *Jesus*, narrated by the four Angels to the Virgin Mary and others with her and transformed Judas "that he might suffer the punishment to which he had sold another" is the authentic account of what happened. Christians chose to believe in a contaminated account of the event but Jesus in his Gospel said "… I am the servant of God of this ye are witness how I speak against those wicked men, who after my departure from the world shall annul the truth of my Gospel by the operation of the Satan. But I shall return toward the end and with me shall come Enoch and Elijah and we will testify against the wicked whose end shall be accursed".

Let us see what the Bible says about saviourship at its contaminated state:

i) Isaiah 43: 11 God is the only Saviour

ii) Isaiah 45: 21 – 22 God is the only Saviour

iii) Hosea 13: 4 No saviour except God

iv) James 2: 14 – 26 Faith without good work is nonsense.

The holy Qur'an tells that righteousness does not consist in formalities, but in faith, kindness, prayer, charity, probity and patience under suffering.[303] Saviourship therefore depends on man's righteousness.

Therefore the Christians belief that *Jesus* was crucified for their sins is nonsense and is outrageously stupid. The wicked cannot screen itself behind a sacred relic, nor can sacred relic help the enemies of faith. The fact that our forefathers were righteous cannot help us, unless we are ourselves righteous. The doctrine of personal responsibility is a cardinal feature of Islam. The holy Qur'an says: "Every soul draws the need of its acts on none but itself. No bearer of burden can bear the burden of another.[304]

It is true that Adam and Eve sinned, but Allah forgave them.[305]

Question (14): Are Christians belief about *Jesus*, not due to; (1) his miraculous birth and (2) the wonders he worked?

Answer: These are no grounds for excuse. The reason is that Adam the origin of man had neither father nor mother. And the holy Bible tells us that Melchizedek had no father nor mother.[306]

In the case of miraculous work, *Jesus* confessed in several places in the Bible, even at its contaminated state thus:

i) John 5:20 I can of myself do nothing

ii) John 5:36 The work given to me I do

iii) John 5: 37 The father that sent me

iv) John 6:38 I come to do the will of the person who sent me.

v) John 7:16, 17 My doctrine is not mine.

vi) John 9:4 I must work the work of Him that sent me.

vii) John 10:25 The work I do is in my father's name.

In the Gospel of *Jesus*, *Jesus* said:

(1) "Moses with a rod made the water turn into blood, the dust into fleas, the dew into tempest and the light into darkness. He made the frogs and mice to come into Egypt, which covered the ground, he slew the first born, and opened the sea, wherein he drowned Pharaoh" Of these things I have wrought none. And of Moses, every one confesseth that he is a dead man at this present

(2) Joshua made the sun to stand still, and opened the Jordan which I have not yet done. And Joshua every one confesseth that he is a dead man at this present.[307]

(3) Elijah made fire to come visibly down from Heaven, and rain, which I have not done.[308] And of Elijah, every one confesseth that he is a man, and (in like manner), very many other prophets, holy men, friends of God, who in the power of God have wrought things which cannot be grasped by the mind of those who know not our God Almighty and Merciful, who is blessed for ever more.[309]

Even the Bible in its contaminated state admits thus:

1. Ezekiel 37:1-4 God commanded Ezekiel to tell skeletons to have flesh and rise from dead.

2. 2 Kings 6:17 Elisha caused the blind to see.

3. 2 Kings 4:31-37 Elisha resurrected the dead.

4. 2 Kings 4:1-7 Elisha used a pot of groundnut oil to produce many pots of oil.

5. 2 Kings 13:21 A man resurrected after his body touched the grave of Elisha.

Therefore, it is completely foolish to believe that the working of miracle makes one God.

Question (15): The Christians say that *Jesus* was sinless and apart from him nobody, not even the prophets of God before him were righteous and that is why he alone and none else can atone for others sins. How true is this assumption and what does the Gospel of *Jesus* and the holy Qur'an say regarding this matter?

Answer: The first sermon of *Jesus* to the people of Jerusalem when he entered the temple to pray reads in part "... Blessed be the holy name of God, who of his goodness and mercy willed to create his creatures that they might glorify Him. Blessed be the holy name of God, who created the splendour (i.e. Mohammed) of all the saints and prophets before all things to send him for the salvation of the world, as He spake by His servant David saying: "Before Lucifer, in the brightness of the saints I created thee..." Those Christians with the view that apart from *Jesus* no body not even the prophets of God before him were righteous, such is a belief in vain doctrines.

Jesus in his first sermon in Jerusalem vehemently rebuked the people for that they had forgotten the word of God, and gave themselves only to vanity; he rebuked the priests for their negligence in God's service and for their worldly greed; he rebuked the scribes because they preached vain doctrine, and forsook the law of God; he rebuked the doctor because they made the law of God of no effect through their traditions. And in such wise did *Jesus* speak to the people that all wept, from the least to the greatest crying mercy, and beseeching *Jesus* that he would pray for them, save only the priests and leaders who on that day conceived hatred against *Jesus* for having thus spoken against the priests, scribes and doctors. And they meditated upon his Death, but for fear of the people, who had received him as a prophet of God, they spake no word.[310]

Some days having passed, *Jesus* having in spirit perceived the desire of the priest, ascended the Mount of Olives to pray. And having passed the whole night in prayer, in the morning *Jesus* praying said: "O Lord I know that the scribes hate me, and the priest are minded to kill me, thy servant; therefore, Lord God Almighty and Merciful, in Mercy hear the prayers of thy servant and save me from their snares, for thou art my salvation. Thou knowest Lord that I thy servant seek Thee alone, 'O Lord and speak thy word; for thy word is truth, which edureth forever'.

'When *Jesus* had spoken these words behold there came to him the Angel Gabriel, saying: "Fear not O *Jesus* for thousand, thousand who dwell above the Heaven guard thy garments, and thou shalt not die till everything be fulfilled, and the world shall be near its end".

'*Jesus* fell with his face to the ground saying: "O great Lord God how great is thy mercy upon me, and what shall I give thee, Lord for all that thou hast granted me?'

The Angel Gabriel answered: "Arise, *Jesus*, and remember Abraham, who being willing to make sacrifice to God of his only begotten son Ishmael, to fulfill the word of God, and the knife not being able to cut his son, at my word offered in sacrifice a sheep. Even so therefore shalt thou do, O *Jesus*, servant of God."

Jesus answered: "Willingly; but where shall I find the lamb, seeing I have no money and it is not lawful to steal it?"

'Thereupon the Angel Gabriel showed unto him a sheep, which *Jesus* offered in sacrifice praising and blessing God who is glorious forever.[311]

Therefore the assumption is a fabrication, as *Jesus* accepts that righteous people exist apart from himself [312]

i) Luke 1:70 As he spoke by the mouth of His holy prophets of old.

ii) Matt 5:10-12 Prophets persecuted for righteousness

iii) Mark 6:20 Herod feared John because he was righteous

iv) Matt 11:11 *Jesus* acknowledged John's righteousness

v) Matt 25:35 Abel was righteous

vi) Daniel 6:21-27 Daniel was righteous

vii) 2 Kings 22:2 Josiah was righteous

viii) Luke 1:6 Zachariah and his wife were righteous

ix) 1 Samuel 12:3-5 Samuel was up right

x) Luke 2: 25 Simeon was righteous

xi) Luke 13:28 All the prophets to be in the kingdom of God.

Therefore, John 10: 8 "That all the prophets that came before him were thieves is a fabrication and an evidence of the contamination of the Bible by wicked people through the operation of the Satan.

The holy Qur'an[313] says: O children of Israel ... guard yourselves against a day when one soul shall not avail another nor shall compensation be accepted from her, nor shall intercession profit her, nor shall any one be helped (from outside). Every one shall reap the fruit of what he did.[314]

On the day of Judgement each soul would have to answer for its own deeds, it cannot claim merit from other, nor be answerable for the crimes or sins of other. I am repeating the fact that our forefathers were righteous men cannot help us unless we all ourselves righteous. That is why it is pointed out earlier that the doctrine of personal responsibility is a cardinal feature of Islam. Muslims believe in Allah and the revelation given to the holy prophet (PBH); to Abraham, Ishmael, Isaac, Jacob and the Tribes and that given to Moses and *Jesus,* and that given to (all) prophets from their Lord. We make no difference between one and another of them and we submit absolutely and completely to Allah.

In the process, if we make mistake, we repent our sins and beseech our Lord God for forgiveness. May He in His Mercy, forgive us our sins- *Amen.*

GLOSSARY

1. *Salat* – Obligatory prayers
2. *Zakat* – Obligatory tax on wealth
3. *Hajj* – Holy Pilgrimage to Mecca required for believers even once in a life time for those who can afford it.
4. *Kalimah* – Acceptance that non is worthy of worship says Allah
5. *Mumm* – Righteous or Righteousness
6. *Iman* – Absolute faith in God
7. *Ruku* – Bending posture in *Salat*
8. *Sajdah* – Prostration posture in *Salat*
9. *Masjid* – Mosque
10. *Makrooh* – A deed which is not permissible but not punishable, not approved, the deed which is not accepted.
11. *Raka'ats* – A unit of *Salat.*
12. *Fardh* – Obligatory deed
13. *NAFI* – Non- obligatory deed.
14. *Al-wudhu* – Ablution
15. *Zuhr* – Afternoon
16. *Tahajjud* – *Salat* after midnight
17. *Tashahhud* – Glorification of Allah in sitting posture in *Salat.*
18. *Maghrib* – Obligatory *Salat* after sun set.

19. *Ishai* – Obligatory *Salat* about one hour after sun set or obligatory *Salat* when darkness replaces the reddish colour of sun set.

20. *Shahid* – Death of a martyr

21. *Attaura* – The Book of Moses

22. *Zabura* – The Book of David

23. *INJIL* – The Gospel of Jesus Christ

24. *UMRA* – Lesser holy pilgrimage to Mecca.

25. *Surat* – A chapter of the Holy Qur'an.

26. *Ayats* – A verse of the Holy Qur'an

27. *Ulama* – Muslim theologians or scholars

28. *Arsh* – The Sublime Throne of Allah.

29. *Subhu* – Early morning Sulat, i.e before sun-rise

30 *Alzuhur* – Afternoon *Salat*

31. *Sirat* – Straight path

32. *Sadagah* – Charity

33. *Shariat* – Islamic law

34. GB. – Gospel of Barnabas

ENDNOTES

[1] Q. 3 v. 87

[2] Q 2 v. 4; 35 v 20 and 10 v 47

[3] Q. 16 v. 63 – 64

[4] Q. 35 V. 2, and 5 – 6

[1] Matt 23:33-34

[2] Q 15:15-84

[3] Q32:1-30

[4] Q36:51-83

[5] Q 37: 1-74

[6] Q 37: 139-182

[7] Q 38: 65-88

[8] Q 39: 1 - 21

[9] Q 30: 20-40

[10] Q 2: 177

[11] Q 89: 1-30

[12] Q 99: 1-8

[13] Q10:1-20

[14] Q 10: 93-109

[15] Q 11: 1-5

[16] Q 16: 101-128

17Q 18:45-59

[17] Q 21: 1-29

[18] Q 23: 93-118

[19] Q 22: 1-25

[20] Q28:61-88

[21] Q.29:41

[22] Q 35:1-26

[23] Q.35:27-45

[24] Q.38:1-26

[25] Q.38:27-64

[26] Q.39:53-75

[27] Q 40:1-20

[28] Q 41:1-32

[29] Q.46:1-35

[30] Q.52:1-49

[31] Q.55:76

[32] Q.70:1-40

[33] Q.87:1-19

[34] John 16:12

[35] Q.91:1-15

[36] Q.94:1-8

[37] Q.102:1-8

[38] Q.113:1-5 and 114:1-6.

40 Q.11:25-49

[39] Q.40:51-88

[40] Q.77:1-50

[41] Q.21:1-29

[42] Q 11:5-68

[43] Q. 6:31 – 30

[44] Q. 6:31 -60

[45] Q. 25:15 – 16

48 Q 11:69- 95

[49] Q. 7:32 – 58

[50] Q.7: 172 – 206

[51] Q.11:96 – 123

[52] Q.13:32 – 43

[53]Q.8: 20 – 37

[54]Q.9:30 – 42

[55] Q.9:73 – 99

[56] Q.13: 1 – 18 and Q. 16:26 – 50

[57] Q.16:51 – 83

[58] Q.16: 81 - 100

[59] G.B.C. 93 - 98

[60] The Testament PP 96-99 and the Dead sea scrolls

[61]Q 25: 77

62 Q.27:59-93

[63] Q.31:20-34

[64]Q.22: 1 – 25

[65]Q.2: 214

[66]Q.87: 1 – 19

[67] Q. 5: 44 – 86

[78]Q.5:109 – 117

[69]Q.2:152

[46] Q.72: 17

[71.] Matt 24:7,8

[72.] Q. 18 Vs 98,99 and S. 21 V.96

[73.] Ms 52:20

[74]. KU.P. 3021

[75.] KU. Vol. 7, P.2157

[47] GB.CH. 51

[48] S. 2:34

[49] 1793

[50] GB.CH. 34

[51] Q. 72: 17

[52] Q. 70: 19

[53] The number of verses containing the word "Shirk", and its derivatives are approximately 165, and there are many other verses of similar meaning in the Holy Qur'an.

[54] Bukhari & Muslim

[55] GB Ch 203

[56] Ibid

[57] GB.Ch. 203 – 204

[58] GB. Ch. 174 P.221

[59] GB.CH.144 P.183

[60] Q 43:36

[61] GB. Ch. 220

[62] GB. Ch. 58

[63] GB.Ch. 72

[64] Gal. 11 – 12

[65] Gal 1:24

[66] Rom 2:16

[67] Page 44 "*Jesus* in India"

[68] Ibid

[69] GB. Ch. 96

[70] GB. Ch. 96

[71] Ps 110:1 -2

[72] GB. Ch. 43

[73] GB. Ch. 44

[74] Page 19 "*Jesus* in India"

[75] GB.Ch 112

[76] GB. Ch 214

[77] GB. Ch. 215

[78] GB. Ch 216

[79] GB. Ch. 217

[80] GB Ch. 218

[81] GB.Ch.219

[82] GB. Ch 220 P 271/272

[83] GB. Ch. 221 P 273

[84] Q 4:157

[85] Q 4: 158

[86] Q 43: 61

[87] Page 19 "*Jesus* in India

[88] Page 53 Ibid

[89] GB. Ch. 220

[90] Page 54 "*Jesus* in India"

[91] Q 19: 83

[92] Q 11: 32

[93] Q 11:33

[94] GB. Ch. 17 P.18

[95] Q 4:48 and 116

[96] Q 31:13

[97] Q 5:75

[98] GB. Ch. 136

[99] GB. Ch. 137

[100] GB. Ch. 82

[101] GB. Ch. 39

[132]A. GB.Ch.41

[102] GB. Ch. 40

[103] The Dead Sea Scriptures, pp 5, 6 and 77 & GB. Ch. 159

[104] GB. Ch. 44

[105] GB. Ch. 43

[106] GB. Ch. 72

[107] GB. Ch 90

[108] GB. Ch. 96

[109] GB. Ch. 96

[110] GB. Ch. 124

[111] GB. Ch. 163 P.212

[112] GB. Ch. 177

[113] Q 2: 138

[114] Q 3: 64 – 120

[115] Q 3: 31

[116] Q 3: 85

[117] S 3: 87

[118] Q 3: 102

[119] Q 4: 80

[120] Q 2:4; Q 35: 20; Q 10: 4

[121] Q. 40: 78; and Q 4: 164

[122] Q 16: 63 – 64

[123] John 16:12 to 13

[124] Q. 5:3

[125] GB Ch. 34

126

[127] Tabrani

[128] Baihagai

[129] Tabrani

[130] Tirmdhi

[131] Friedrich Schiller (1793)

[132] A book on human values British Council Website

[133] A book on human values British Council Website

[134] GB. Ch. 85

166. Lecture series on human values pulished in Britain during the 1990s.

[135] GB. Ch 40

[136] GB. Ch. 19

[137] GB. Ch. 47

[138] GB. 70

[139] GB.Ch 92

[140] GB.Ch. 93

[141] GB. Ch. 94

[142] GB. CH. 95

[143] GB. Ch. 96

[144] GB. Ch. 97

[145] GB, CH. 112

[146] GB. Ch. 118 & 119

[147] GB. Ch. 126

[148] Gb. Ch. 128

[149] GB. Ch. 128

[150] BG. Ch. 133

[151] GB. Ch. 138

[152] GB. Ch. 153

[153] GB. Ch. 154

[154] GB. Ch. 159

[155] GB. Ch. 167

[156] GB. Ch. 182

[157] GB. Ch. 198

[158] GB. Ch. 220

[159] Q. 3:58

[160] Q. 9; 30

[161] Q. 9: 31

[162] Tr. 44: 9 – 11

[163] GB. Ch. 43

[164] GB. Ch. 80

[165] GB. Ch. 109

[166] Q2: 152

[167] Q3: 41

[168] Q7: 180

[169] Q17: 110

[170] Q18: 28

[171] Q19: 2,3

[172] Q20: 42

[173] Q33: 35

[174] Q37: 75

[175] Q33:41, 42

[176] Q39: 22

[177] Q43: 36

[178] Q63:9

[179] Q73: 8

[180] Q87: 14, 15

[181] Muslim & Bukhari

[182] Muslim & bukhari

[183] Muslim

[184] Ibid

[185] Muslim & Bukhari

[186] FAZAIL – E- ZIKR, Virtues of Remembrance of Allah, Chap 2 Pg 30-33. A compilation of Book on teachings of Islam by Maulana Muhammad Zakariya Shaikhulhadith.

[187] Q60: 3

[188] Q 59: 18, 19

[189] GB. Ch. 52

[190] GB. Ch. 53

[191] Q. 18 v.98 – 99

[192] Q.21 V.96

[193] Ms 52:20

[194] Ku. Vol. 7 p. 2157

[195] Ku. p. 3021

[196] Matt 24:7, 8

[197] Q3: 31

[198] The spectacle of Death by Khawaja Muhammad Islam Pages 118 to 119

[199] Muslim & Bukhari

[200] Muslim

[201] GB. Ch. 43

[202] GB. Ch. 44

[203] GB. Ch. 72

[204] Q 3: 85

[205] Q.3: 87

[206] Q3: 102

[207] Muslim

[208] Lecture series

[209] Q 43: 36

[210] Q.76: 28

[211] Q 6: 164

[212] Q 2: 36 – 37

[213] Gb.ch. 53

[214] Q 3: 102

[215] GB. Ch.54

248. GB. CH.55

[216] Gb.CH 56

[217] GB. Ch. 57

[218] Ibid

[219] Q. 56: 11 – 26

[220] Q.56 : 27 – 40

[221] Q. 56 V 41 -56

[222] Muslim

[223] Ibid

[224] GB. Ch. 104

[225] Ms 239:608

[226] Muslim

[227] GB. Ch. 105

[228] Q 18: 107, and Q 23: 11

[229] Q 47:15

[230] Q32:17

[231] B 59:8

[232] RM, Vol. 1 P. 172

[233] Q 76:13

[234] Q2: 25

[235] Q. 3: 132; 57: 21

[236] Rm. Vol. 1 p. 670

[237] Q 57: 13

[238] Q7: 46

[239] Q25:12; 67:7

[240] Q21: 102

[241] Q7: 44 – 50

[242] Q.9: 72

[243] Gb. Ch 59

[244] GB. Ch. 60

[245] GB Ch. 42

[246] GB. Ch.52

[247] GB. Ch. 93

[248] Q 3: 580

[249] Q9: 30

[250] Q 9: 31

[251] Tr. 44: 9 – 11

[252] GB. Ch 220

[253] Q4: 57 – 58

[254] Deut 21: 23.

[255] Gal. 3: 13

[256] GB. Ch. 52 & 53

[257] Imam Muslim no 546

[258] GB. Ch. 214

[259] GB. Ch. 215

[260] GB Ch 216

[261] Deut 21: 22 – 23

[262] GB. Ch. 217

[263] GB. Ch. 218

[264] GB. Ch. 219

[265] GB. Ch 221

[266] GB. Ch. 203

[267] GB. Ch. 204

[268] GB. Ch. 82

[269] GB. Ch. 12

[270] GB. Ch.13

[271] Q. 51: 56

[272] GB.Ch. 112

[273] GB. Ch. 220

[274] Matt 26: 39

[275] Prov. 15:29

[276] Q. 2: 177

[277] Q. 6: 164

[278] Q 2: 36 – 37

[279] Hebrew 7: 3

[280] Josh 10: 12 – 14

[281] 1 Ki; 18: 38 – 39; 18: 41

[282] GB Ch. 94

[283] GB. Ch. 12

[284] GB. CH 13

[285] Matt. 13:17

[286] Q. 2 v 122 – 123

[287] Q 2: 134

ABOUT THE AUTHOR

Dr. M.S. Umoru is a qualified Banker and Accountant, and a product of Harvard University Boston. He has written a number of books on Management including "The Supervisor's Manual" (1972), "The Managers Guide" (1988), "A History of Ayuele" (1991), "So that Tomorrow will be better" (1995), A Co-author of a book titled "Management of the Nigerian Economy under Democratic Administration" (2000), "Effective Management Skills" (2001), Management Concept and Case Studies (2002), "Effective Resources Management" (2003) and "Sorrows of a Nation" (2005).

He was chosen by Biographical Association Cambridge, England as one of the 2000 fascinating Intellectuals of the 21st Century in the year 2002.

He is an Industrialist of International Reputation and has received numerous merit awards for significant contribution to Industrial Development and Management Education in Nigeria including: Gold Mercury of Africa Award for distinguish contribution to Africa Economic development and "Voice of Africa International Award" for distinguished contribution for Economic Development of Africa.

www.ingramcontent.com/pod-product-compliance
Lightning Source LLC
LaVergne TN
LVHW090602110826
845146LV00001B/228